REBECCA ELISE

Where We First Began

Where We First Began
Red Adept Publishing, LLC
104 Bugenfield Court
Garner, NC 27529
http://RedAdeptPublishing.com/

To Patrick, who has given me forever and always, and, TJ who shows me the brightness in my life.

"Blood of heroes hath stained me. Let the stones of the Alamo speak, that their immolation be not forgotten." - Quote from the plaque outside the Alamo main entrance.

In Memory of Those Who Fought and Died at the Alamo

March 6, 1836

Softly call the Muster, let comrade answer "Here"

CHAPTER ONE

*C*ollege Station, Texas
August 2018

With exactly twelve minutes left to make it to my morning lecture, I pull my old Ford into one of the few remaining parking spots on the top floor of Central Campus Garage. On cue, my phone vibrates just as I press down on my parking brake in a routine attempt to make sure the old truck doesn't accidentally roll out of place. *At least Porter is predictable*, I think as my nine-thirty text from him arrives right on schedule.

Text from Porter: *Can you pick up 200 plastic bowls from the store after you are done with class for today?*

I almost forgot about my girlfriend obligations to Phi Gamma's Chilifest preparations. I'm their living, breathing grocery list. I shoot back a quick text letting him know that I'll get them and bring them over after I finish my GRE practice test this afternoon. I grab my bag full of books and slam the truck door a little too hard. The sound could have been heard at the top of the parking garage, but squealing tires against slick concrete drown out the frustration I just took out on my Ford. Even though I met Porter during one of our freshman classes together, we fortunately have different majors, so our schedules have us on opposite sides of campus at the same time. I can only handle his perfection in small doses.

Dashing across the street toward the history building, I try to avoid the never-ending traffic of bicycles and longboards as they cruise down the sidewalk in all directions. My phone vibrates again, and I pull it out of the back pocket of my jeans and check the screen.

Text from Porter: *Bring them before GRE. We need to pack the coolers.*

This time, I don't respond. I'm already running late to class, and after the three years we've been dating, he should know my answer. Graduate school is my priority—Chilifest can wait.

As I push open the doors to the history building, I fight through the groups of students hovering in front of their individual classroom doors. Even though it's already a few weeks into the semester, there are still freshmen wandering around with lost expressions on their faces as they scramble from class to class with their arms full of books. I pull my long brown hair into a high ponytail and unzip the fleece jacket I threw on earlier this morning then shove it into my bag. It's already eighty degrees outside, but there's no telling if the temperature in the classroom today will be frigid or smoldering. It really depends on which professor is in the room at what time—the skinnier, older profs tend to keep the room a comfortable warmth, while the ones with a bit more padding underneath their stiff-collared shirts keep the lecture halls at winter temperatures in order to prevent their constant sweating.

The first class of the morning is just clearing out of the lecture room as I make my way to my usual seat at the back. Porter's response shows up just as I toss my bag on the floor and sit down. I hesitate before I slide my finger across the screen, knots forming in my stomach as I imagine what his response will be.

Text from Porter: *I don't understand why you're already studying—the GRE isn't until next month. Just bring the groceries after class. Love you.*

I roll my eyes as I read the words a second time, imagining him saying what he actually means: *What are you going to do with a master's in literature, Aubrey? You* had *to pick one of those majors that will get you nowhere after college. It's a waste of your money for a pointless degree.*

I can feel my cheeks heating up as my fist clenches, my knuckles quickly turning white. I toss my phone into my bag without a response to Porter, kick it under my chair, cross my legs, and breathe out my frustration in a huff of air. We argued about this at least a dozen times. Academic success is important to Porter, but it's not a trait he cares to acknowledge in his girlfriend.

Is it so terrible to pursue a life learning things that excite me rather than settling for a life chasing the money train with the majority of our graduating class? I've never been one to settle, and after we've spent this much time together, Porter should appreciate that about me.

"Are you all right over there?" a voice asks from a few chairs away.

"Yeah. Fine," I say sarcastically before I turn to look at the speaker. The moment I glare in his direction, I instantly regret it. It's him—the cadet who is head-to-toe heartbreak with a smile that buckles my knees even when I'm sitting.

The people who attend Texas A&M's world-class military program mix with the rest of the student body, so it's not abnormal to see students dressed in their tan ROTC uniforms, but most of the time, the uniforms are wearing the cadets, not the other way around. Tall brown boots stop just below this cadet's knees, and polished silver spurs clink against the classroom floor as he taps his foot anxiously. The sound reminds me of spurs against concrete, a familiar noise that parts the packed sidewalks like the Red Sea as cadets make their way across campus.

My hard stare meets his brown eyes, and I melt, the knots in my stomach undoing themselves as my irritation softens. I don't know his name. In all honesty, I've never been brave enough to ask even though we've shared a few classes over the last three years.

Say something so he doesn't think you're a psycho. The thought flashes through my mind frantically as we look at each other. I shouldn't care what type of person he thinks I am, but for some reason, I do. There's something about the sincerity in his eyes that makes me less angry, and I feel obligated to prove to him that I'm actually the complete opposite of the pretentious, catty person who spoke to him a minute earlier.

"I'm fine. I didn't mean to snap at you. I was just remembering something." I'm suddenly nervous as I smile at him. The tapping of my pen on the side of my chair matches the sporadic movement of my foot against the laminate floor of the classroom.

"Don't worry about snapping at me, but you might want to worry about snapping your poor pen in half." He flashes me a smile, his perfect white teeth showing the slightest bit as dimples form on either side of his mouth.

"I'm Aubrey," I practically spit out before I can even second-guess my hasty introduction. Of all things going through my mind right now, I'm glad that I at least got my name right.

"I'm Ta—"

The room immediately grows silent as Dr. Hubbell walks into the classroom, his loafers squeaking against the scuffed floor as he tries to catch his breath.

What is it then? Tate, Tanner, Talbert? Oh jeez, I hope it's not Talbert. I turn my gaze one last time to the stranger a few chairs down, and I can feel my cheeks flushing as I watch him open his notebook to a fresh sheet of paper—what *I* should be doing instead of gawking at him.

SIX HOURS LATER, I'M finally situated in my normal study nook in the corner behind one of the long, boring sections of medical encyclopedias on the lifeless third floor of West Campus Library. Most of the students fight for tables on one of the lower floors of the building closer to the tiny café and the large section of computers, but fortunately, I found my study sanctuary by accident early in my fresh-man year.

I've been ready for the GRE for weeks, but I'm not the type of person to take preparation time for granted. I'm working on my fifth practice test—my fifth attempt to figure out a rational way to pace myself through each question—with a stomach full of nerves and a bad case of test anxiety. Plenty of people take the Graduate Record Exams multiple times—it's a completely normal thing to do. Most people, though, don't have Porter to deal with if their first score comes out less than stellar. He'd never let me hear the end of it and neither would his parents. Porter hasn't even begun to study for his medical school entrance exams, but I'm betting he'll fly through them with ease after a long night of partying and despite a monu-mental hangover.

I flip through the last few pages of my practice booklet, carefully inspecting my answers one last time before I check the time on my phone. Setting down my pencil, I close my eyes for a long moment and exhale deeply, trying to slow the rapid beat of my heart. If my dreams of graduate school are ever going to happen, then study-ing for the GRE just might be the escape I need to avoid Chilifest completely this year. Unfortunately, even with my GRE excuse, my boyfriend and my best friend are not likely to let me out of a week-end of beer and chili.

Staring at the test booklet, I realize that I've officially run out of excuses for keeping myself in the library all day. Normal people don't willingly hide themselves away among rows of fading covers, stained pages, and the smell of old mothballs, but I guess I only pretend to be normal when it's required of me. I don't even know why I force myself to try to be someone I'm not—someone I'm *expected* to be. The corners of my mouth drop the slightest bit as the thought of this weekend's activities comes spiraling back. This isn't the college expe-rience I expected, and it sure isn't the one I *wanted*.

As I start to pack my study materials neatly into my bag, I hear the flip-flop of sandals turning the corner in my direction. Even though my study spot is hidden from the rest of the library, most of my friends know exactly where to find me when I'm ignoring them.

"I've called you, like, ten times," Paige whispers in her loudest possible quiet voice.

I roll my eyes before standing from my chair and turning to face her. Before my unprepared excuse for ignoring her can leave my lips, she shoves a bright highlighter-yellow T-shirt into my hands.

"What is this?" I think I know exactly what it is, but I really don't want it.

"Just open it and see. I told Heather you were going to *love* the design for our Chilifest shirts this year. I lied of course. You are going to hate them." She giggles, a curious smile crossing her face as she watches me unfold the T-shirt.

The front looks relatively normal—an oversized neon-colored T-shirt with a matching oversized pocket across the left side of the chest. The Greek letters for *Phi Gamma Delta* are written across the pocket in navy blue. *Okay. So far, not so bad,* I think. Then I flip the T-shirt over and gape at the words: "Chilifest 2018. The Only Things Hotter Than Our Peppers Are Our Ladies."

You have got to be kidding me.

I swear, if my eyes could turn a blazing color to match my anger, their normally green shade would be molten red. "Kill me now," I groan, crumpling the T-shirt into a messy ball and shoving it as far down into the corner of my bag as possible.

I turn my stare back to Paige, who looks at me sympathetically. "It gets even better..." Her voice trails off at the end of her sarcastic remark, her hand reaching into the tan bag hanging on her shoulder. "Heather made us bows that match our shirts." Paige closes her eyes.

I open up my palm, and she drops a neon-yellow bow with navy-blue polka dots into it. I pinch the bow between my thumb and pointer finger as if it's the most disgusting piece of garbage I've ever been forced to touch.

"This should be a blast," I mutter as I pick up my bag, link my arm through Paige's, and head back through the maze of oversized bookshelves on the now-empty third floor.

AFTER DROPPING OFF the list of last-minute groceries with the boys, Paige and I start back to our apartment to spend the rest of the evening baking snacks for the weekend and watching Netflix. The Phi Gamma boys went out to the Chilifest grounds a night early to make sure they had their "usual" spot selected ahead of time.

Newly single Paige spends most of the evening gushing about the guy she met at the Dixie Chicken a few weekends before. There's been a long string of guys since her breakup with Porter's best friend, Dillon, but I'm just glad to see she's finding distractions to keep her happy.

"He'll be with a group of friends at Chilifest this weekend." She winks at me as she pulls a sheet of cookies out of the oven.

"Who is?" I ask, keeping my eyes glued to the television.

"Matt. Who else have I been talking about for the last half hour?" She throws the oven mitt at the back of my head, knocking my nose into my glass of wine as I attempt to take a sip.

"Right. Sorry, I zoned out for a few seconds. It's been a long week," I offer by way of explanation, peeking over my shoulder at her and catching the end of her snarky eye roll as she empties the last few sips of the wine bottle into her glass.

"I'm happy for you. Hopefully, Matt will make having to be around Dillon all weekend not so terrible."

Chilifest will be the first time Paige and her ex are forced to spend time in the same area together, and I have a feeling Dillon will be doing his best to rub his single status in her face.

"You don't have to hang out with me the entire weekend, you know." We've had this conversation before. I feel bad asking Paige to stick around the Phi Gams' tent for the weekend, but knowing her, she won't ditch me at an event I don't even want to be at, and I love her even more for that.

"You think I'm going to leave you to deal with the drunken frat boys all by yourself just because Dillon and I are over? You are *crazy*. Or maybe I'm the one who's crazy for doing this, but we made these plans months ago, and I'm not going to bail on you." She takes a seat next to me on the couch, throws her legs across my lap, and takes a long sip from her glass.

"Are you and Porter... you know... *okay*?"

I keep my eyes glued to the screen as she talks, but I can feel her studying my face.

"You don't seem okay, Aubs."

I have the super boyfriend, the one who can balance his fraternal obligations to Phi Gamma Delta, swing As in his biomed classes, and let loose on Friday nights with his friends—all as if getting into medical school isn't even a worry in his mind. Porter is suave, smart, and undoubtedly contagious to be around. He's the type of person who comes off so together that he makes me feel like I'm falling apart every second. But he's safe—at least, that's what I tell myself. I tilt back my wineglass, emptying most of it in a huge gulp. I can feel the alcohol rush through my veins, a flush of color burning lightly beneath my cheeks as I think about her words.

"We're—well, 'okay' sounds like a good word for it." I put the stem of the glass between my knees and let out a deep sigh. *Okay* is not a good word to describe a relationship of three years when everyone around me expects us to be engaged by the end of next semester.

"Really, Aubs?"

"Porter is just different now, I guess. Phi Gamma is keeping him really busy." The excuse sounds even worse than I thought it would. Had Paige asked me the same question last year, my answer would have been much different. Porter's life goals and ambitions once matched my own, and our future seemed brighter—less overly planned and structured. Things began to change when Greek life wormed itself into the center of Porter's world... and into our relationship.

Paige has never been one to pry things out of me, but the slight raising of her eyebrows as she peers at me from over her wineglass lets me know she's not buying it.

"I think we need more wine." I look at her and giggle.

She pulls her legs from their place across my lap, and the moment I stand up from the couch, she lays them back down where I've just been sitting.

"You didn't call seat check." She smirks.

"If you want more wine, your legs will give me back my seat." I practically sing the words as I pull open the refrigerator door and reach for a new bottle.

Within the walls of my apartment, things are much less confusing, and thanks to the wine, the constant noise of my busy mind settles into a distant hum. If every day were this easy, my life with Porter might just become more than okay.

CHAPTER TWO

I'm not sure if it was the two bottles of wine or the restless night of sleep I had after finally turning off Netflix for the night, but pulling myself out of bed at ten the next morning is excruciating. Fortunately, Paige has hot coffee ready and waiting by the time I force myself to pull the neon shirt over my head and tie the matching bow in my long chocolate-brown ponytail.

"Good morning, sunshine," Paige sings as she hands me a metal thermos of coffee. *She must be really into this guy to be this excited at ten in the morning.*

"You are my hero right now." I smile at her as I take a careful sip, testing the temperature of the liquid.

She turns around to face me with a huge pink comb in one hand and a bottle of hairspray in the other. "I'm about to be an even bigger hero for fixing your lifeless ponytail."

"I didn't think I looked that bad..." My words trail off as she pulls me to the floor-length mirror hanging next to the front door.

I force my eyes to glare at the blinding reflection of the neon shirt against my pale complexion. She's right. Between the dark circles under my eyes and my sloppy side ponytail, I definitely need some help. Before I can object, she pulls the bow out of my hair, followed by the stretched-out elastic that has barely been holding up my ponytail.

"Tilt your head back," Paige barks, smoothing my hair as she gathers it into a neater collection at the back of my head. She takes a comb from the back pocket of her torn denim shorts then lifts a section of my ponytail and teases the hair back toward the elastic before she attempts to poof it even higher with her fingers.

Paige looks over my shoulder at my reflection. She scrunches her eyebrows together as she studies me. "Not quite there," she mutters.

She pulls my ponytail tighter against my head then secures the bow back at the top. As she reaches for the hairspray, I close my eyes and hold my breath, waiting for the sickly scent of Big Sexy Hair to fill the entire square footage of our apartment.

"Better," she says matter-of-factly, setting the hairspray back on the countertop. "You can open your eyes now and thank me later."

I open only one eye, scared to see the damage she's done. *Thank her later?*

I give a fake smile as I force my other eye open and take one last look at myself in the mirror. Paige managed to transform me into the closest I will ever be to a sorority girl and just the way I'm sure Porter prefers me to look: big hair, baggy neon fraternity shirt, tiny frayed denim shorts, and my favorite pair of vintage Anderson Bean cowboy boots. At least the neon shirt makes my green eyes pop. I'm not sure that's necessarily a good thing, though.

"You can put makeup on in your truck because we're running late. I'll drive." She hands me her makeup bag and nudges me out the door as she grabs my keys from their hook.

TO THE PEOPLE OF COLLEGE Station, there is only one thing more exciting than football games—chili. In fact, twenty miles outside the city limits sits a small town that dedicates an entire weekend to it each year. And each year, it becomes increasingly obvious that I'm not cut out for Chilifest.

After waiting in the hour-long line to park, Paige and I fight through crowds of people, trying to make our way to the far-left side of the stage, where Team Phi Gamma's purple-and-white tent is situated. Thousands of people with beers in hand crowd into every last standing space within ears' reach of the huge band stage. Faded old couches are set in a circle in front of the chili teams' tents, and coolers packed full of cheap beer are laid out in lines, one after the other. Local radio stations are handing out koozies and free CDs from the different Texas country-music artists headlining the concert, and half-naked drunk girls make fools of themselves as they dance wildly with beers lifted in the air.

"Welcome back to Chilifest," I try to yell to Paige over the screaming guitars pouring out of the speakers nearby. She's standing on her tiptoes, peering over the crowd, already on the lookout for Matt.

Before I can set down one of the containers of snacks at the nearby card table in the center of the tent, Porter's muscular arms wrap around my waist, spinning me to face him.

"Hey, baby," Porter whispers as he fits his hands into the back pockets of my jeans. He knows that I hate when he calls me baby, but by the drunken smile plastered across his face, I know it won't do me any good to mention it right now.

"Hey back." I instinctively hold his neck and kiss him, my lips parting to meet his.

I'm always happy to see him, but everything seems to be easier when we are away from his fraternity brothers—the nights we make time to be alone. He's different when he's around them, always trying to outdo someone in one way or another. Porter Collins is *that* guy, and I'm just *that* guy's boring girlfriend.

I pull myself away from him and set the container on the table just as he hands me a beer. Turning around to look for Paige, I catch her trying not to stare as her ex-boyfriend dances with a busty redhead at one end of the tent.

"Paige!" I yell above the noise in the tent.

As soon as she turns to look at me, I can see the pain written across her face.

"Wanna go walk around?" she mouths, looking as if she's fighting back tears. I knew she shouldn't have come with me.

"One second," I mouth back as I point to the bag hanging on my shoulder. I brought it, figuring that at some point in the day, I would have a few moments to get some studying done. At least, I hoped that would be the case.

I walk out the far side of the tent to where Porter's truck is backed up and toss my bag into the front seat. On my way back to the tent, I look for Porter to let him know where I'm going with Paige. He's standing with two other guys and a group of six scantily clad blondes, all of whom eye me as I kiss him goodbye.

Walk away before you say anything stupid. I try to smile sweetly as I push through the group and head toward where Paige is standing by herself.

"They looked... fun." She smirks, and we both turn to glare at the blondes.

I glance at Porter one last time. "I'm sure Porter is just making sure the Phi Gams maintain their irresistible reputation," I say in a snarky tone, but a part of me always worries about what he does—and who he does it with—when I'm not around.

He always tells me I have nothing to worry about: "Aubs, you're the most stunningly beautiful girl on the planet, and anyone would kill for legs like yours."

I believe him, and I trust him, but I also believe that he's the type of guy who wants to marry a trophy wife—someone who's there to be beautiful and loving, someone who has no dreams and aspirations of her own. Someone not like me.

Paige leads the way through the crowd, her neon shirt standing out against a sea of bikini tops and white T-shirts. Girls sit atop guys' shoulders, watching the concert with beers in both hands, and others stand in groups, checking out the available prospects walking by.

We make our way to the Coors Light booth at the far side of the field then take our place in line behind two dozen other people.

"You know there was free beer back at the tent, right?" I ask, watching as she keeps checking her phone.

"I didn't want to walk to the beer coolers when you-know-who was standing right next to them. Did you see him practically choking her with his tongue? He's disgusting." She shoves her phone back in her pocket and pulls out a crumpled wad of cash. "Better her than me, though. Right?"

I nod, but she doesn't notice. She knows I would have gladly braved walking past Dillon to get her a beer, but I can read between the lines. Paige can't bear being around him at all today, and I'm completely okay with that.

After we finally get our beers, we head back in the direction of the stage but not before Paige spots her handsome stranger from a few yards away. I hear her yell something, and the next thing I know, she takes my hand and drags me at a jog in his direction.

He's standing with a small group of guys near a less-crowded area a few hundred feet from the stage. Paige waves at him, and her face breaks into a truly adorable smile just as she reaches his side and hugs him. I must have been too busy watching her to notice who is standing next to him, because I'm surprised when a familiar voice speaks my name.

"Aubrey?"

I start to panic, slowly looking up at the tall figure in front of me. "Hi." It's the only word I can manage although I really wish I knew his name. The memory of our awkward encounter yesterday will haunt me for at least the rest of the semester.

"You two know each other?" Paige and Matt both ask at the exact same time and start laughing in unison.

"Uh, yeah. We have our nine thirty-five Texas History lecture together with Dr. Hubbell." I smile, trying not to let the butterflies in my stomach turn me into a babbling idiot.

Why am I so nervous around this guy? I look up at him and remember exactly why. He's gorgeous—brown hair, deep hazel eyes, and the most beautifully defined jawline sitting in a face of perfect bone structure.

Bone structure? Who am I? Who even thinks that?

Porter's blond hair and baby blues have always made him a heartbreaker, but this guy is different—completely and refreshingly different. I haven't seen him in anything but his ROTC uniform before, and on one level, I'm glad to see that he looks just as good out of his uniform as he does in it. He's wearing dark denim CINCH jeans with a starched crease line down the front of both pant legs, a black T-shirt that fits over his chest in just the right way, and short sleeves that show just the right amount of muscle in his toned arms. He would even put Maverick to shame if you put him in a flight suit and gave him a motorcycle. *Danger zone.* I play the *Top Gun* tune in my mind then panic a second later, afraid I sang the words out loud.

"You don't look as mad at the world today." His stare catches mine, and I almost forget to reply.

"Today hasn't been such a bad day. So far." I shoot him a smile—a real smile that happens on its own, not one of my premeditated or polite ones. I can feel my entire face break into that smile, and it's such a strange sensation.

Paige must have caught the look as well, because a second later, she pinches the back of my arm, a curious expression pointed in my direction. "What are you doing?" she mouths at me then turns back to the group of guys. "I'm Paige." She sticks out her hand, waiting for someone to either introduce him to her, or for him to do the honors himself.

Crap... I'm such a terrible friend.

"I'm Lee." He takes Paige's hand and shakes it warmly.

Lee? I could have sworn he started to say his name with a *T* in class yesterday. Maybe he goes by his last name. I try to remember the name on his uniform shirt plate, but instead, I only recall dimples and brown eyes.

I turn my attention to the stage in front of us as the music of a new band breaks through the air with a vibrant fiddle and steel guitar. *Maybe Chilifest won't be so terrible this year after all.* I almost laugh at the thought. A part of me knows that the only way to have an uneventful day and actually enjoy myself will be to stay far away from the Phi Gamma Delta tent and the people growing progressively drunker by the hour.

I PICK MY WAY THROUGH the aftermath of Chilifest, trying to avoid the empty, crushed beer cans that litter the yellowed grass. Even though the last concert of the day has ended, the after-party fills the air with its own distinct sound. Different playlists pouring from Bluetooth speakers—or from truck cabs with open doors—create a jumbled mess of music genres that follow me from tent to tent. Little bits of Johnny Cash can still be heard beneath Avicii and the Beastie Boys. It's pure chaos, but it's the sound of college.

I find my way back to the Phi Gamma tent by following Porter's voice, which can be heard from several campsites away. Hopefully, someone is at least sober enough to grill burgers for dinner. The sun is setting against the western side of the field as more and more people leave for the evening, but the parking lots never empty completely. The partying will go on long into the night.

Paige and Matt follow me back to the tent since the rest of Matt's friends, including Lee, have headed over to a party a few rows down. The tent is still packed with people, and by the time we push our way inside, the huge Texas night sky is in full bloom above us. The group of blondes from earlier in the day are still hanging around Porter and a few of the others on couches at the back of the tent. There's a fire burning in a metal pit just outside the corner post, and people are cooking hot dogs skewered on clothes hangers above the orange flames.

Paige and Matt find an empty chair a few feet away from Porter. I smile as she takes a seat on Matt's lap. She leans against his chest as he wraps his arms securely around her. *If Dillon could only see her now.*

A blonde is sitting next to Porter, her Red Solo Cup filled with cheap box wine.

"Hey." I look at him, waiting for him to tell the girl to move.

"Hey, baby. I thought you left a few hours ago." He smiles, motioning for me to take a seat on his lap. The blonde next to him rolls her eyes and shifts over a few inches.

"I told you I was just going to stand closer to the stage with Paige. You knew I would be back." The words sound cold as they leave my mouth, and for some reason, my body tenses and my jaw tightens. One of his friends calls his name from somewhere in the tent, and Porter's attention instantly switches from me to him. *Typical.*

I don't want to be here right now. I don't want to fight for his attention or a seat next to him. If it weren't for the smitten look on both Paige and Matt's faces, I would have headed back to my truck and driven home, but I'm definitely not going to ask her to leave right now. I turn around and head to Porter's truck instead. At least I can try to get some studying done.

After pulling open the passenger-side door of the lifted black truck, I reach for the GRE prep book I made sure to pack inside my bag. After feeling every inch, my hands come up empty. I pull the bag closer to my face, hoping I'm just missing the book in the dark, but other than my keys, the bag *is* empty. *What the hell?*

I snatch it from the car, slam the door, and head back inside the tent to find Porter. He hasn't moved an inch from his place on the couch, and neither has his blonde companion.

"Have you seen my GRE book?" I spit out at him, trying not to make a scene.

He actually smirks at me, his eyes piercing right through me as if he knows some dirty little secret that I don't.

My stomach sinks, and my heart begins to race angrily out of control. "What did you do with my book, Porter?"

He stands up from his comfortable position, hands his cup to the girl next to him, and takes me by the hand toward the fire pit outside. "We needed something to get the fire started, and I figured you wouldn't need that stupid book for one night." He points into the metal pit, remnants of my book and dozens of pages of notes now burnt to tiny black flecks.

I look at him, horrified. There have been times we've fought, times when I've been mad at him for days in a row, but I have never felt hatred toward the person I've convinced myself I've been in love with—until now.

"You did what?" I stammer, my legs feeling as if they can no longer support the dead weight of my body. I stare at him with pure loathing.

Porter's eyes grow wide as he looks at my face, and he takes a step forward, his body swaying just the slightest bit, a sign of the alcohol beginning to take effect. He reaches for my hand, and I pull it back, wanting so badly to slap it across his face as hard as I can.

"I can see now that I probably made a mistake... I thought you would think it was funny. I mean, you've been studying so hard for weeks, I thought burning the books might be a victory moment for you." His face turns a deathly shade of white as he tries to calm the storm he's started.

"You probably made a mistake? Yeah, it might have been a fun thing to do once I *passed* the GRE, but I haven't passed anything yet. In fact, everything you just burned was the only chance I had of passing the freaking test." I reach for the keys in my bag. "Don't call me tonight—I need space," I say to him over my shoulder as I walk away, leaving the always savvy and charming Porter stammering for the first time in his life.

I storm back into the tent and make my way to where Paige and Matt are still sitting close together in one of the oversized chairs. Paige immediately stands from her spot on Matt's lap, rushing over to me as I try to hide the angry tears brimming near the surface.

"Just go. I'll find a way home," she says slowly as I stop in front of her for a single second.

I suck a breath of air into my chest, pull my shoulders back, and walk as fast as I can in the direction of the parking lot. "He *thought* he *probably* made a mistake?" I mutter, fully aware that every person I pass must think I've lost my mind as I converse out loud in the dark.

The parking lot is much less packed than it was this morning, and I find my Ford sitting by itself behind a line of colored flags marking each row. My hands are shaking as I shove the key into the lock on the driver's side door. After a few long seconds, I turn the key, pop the locks, and climb into the familiar comfort of my truck's faded cloth seats. Before I can even start the ignition, the tears start flowing. I pound on the steering wheel as hard as I can, feeling completely defeated—completely *betrayed*.

My phone vibrates, and I quickly silence it and throw it into the empty seat next to me. It vibrates again.

"Damn it, Porter! I told you not to call me!"

This time, I turn the phone off and let it fall onto the floorboard at my feet. I throw my truck in reverse and start back in the direction of the highway. For some reason, I flip my windshield wipers on as though that will make it easier to see through the waterworks pouring from my eyes. As the blades squeak across the bone-dry glass, I realize what an emotional idiot I'm being.

Porter Collins really outdid himself this time.

A single car follows me out of the parking lot and into the pitch-black night of an empty Texas back road, and we turn back in the direction of campus together. I flip on the radio just to kill the silence during the painful twenty-minute drive. After a few miles down the two-lane road, I finally catch up to a car ahead of me that's driving abnormally slow. I tap my brakes the slightest bit, wary that the driver in front of me might have left Chilifest with a little too much alcohol in their system. As we round a long corner, the car speeds up just a bit, staying right between the yellow lines. *Maybe they're not drunk.*

Not even a second after the thought crossed my mind, the car jerks hard to the left, its taillights shining a bright shade of red as the driver hits the brakes. My eyes follow the car across to the other lane, but as soon as the road opens up in front of me, I see what caused the driver to swerve. There's a deer standing in the middle of the road. Its face turns to stare at me, and our eyes connect as I frantically slam on the brakes.

With the driver in front of me now taking up the lane to my left, I have no safe place to swerve my truck. I reflexively pull it hard to the right, toward the ditch. My tires hit the dirt on the side of the road, and I pray that my brakes will bring my truck to a stop. My heart drops. The darkness kept hidden a ten-foot drop that's waiting for me as soon as my tires leave the asphalt. The truck dives downward, the tires losing traction as the right side begins to tilt sideways despite the forward motion of the vehicle.

I instinctively let go of the wheel and close my eyes. For a moment, my body feels weightless as the truck flies through the air, flipping over the ground too many times to count. As it shifts one final time, the weight returns, sending me falling in the direction of the door.

Where my head should have hit glass, it hits solid ground—something that doesn't break. But my body does. Darkness consumes me before everything stops.

CHAPTER THREE

At first it feels like everything is coming back slowly, like a nightmare I can't wake myself from. I think my heart has stopped completely, but maybe I've just blacked out. I try to open my eyes, but my head is ringing loudly, and the more I hear the noise, the harder I squeeze my eyes shut. Bright light shines just on the other side of my eyelids, as if a car's headlights are pointed directly at me.

Maybe someone pulled me from the car. Maybe light is coming from the headlights of my truck.

"Aubrey, open your eyes."

I recognize the voice, I think. Except there's something different. It's more Southern.

"Come on. Just pull them open and let me see that you're all right."

I focus all my strength and energy on making myself blink. *Blink, Aubrey*, I silently coach. *Just open your eyes.*

Time seems to go on forever before I actually manage to lift my eyelids, and as soon as I do, the bright light of day blinds me into pulling them right down again. There's no way it's the middle of the day. It wasn't even nine at night when I left.

I force one eye open again, and this time I catch the gaze of deep hazel staring down at me.

"Lee?" I mutter, the gritty feeling of dirt filling my mouth with earthy flavors as my second eye flutters open. Blinking slowly, I try to pull the image of Lee's face into focus.

"You must've hit your head harder than I thought, miss." He laughs, and I begin to notice the differences in his face. It's definitely

Lee, but his hair is longer, his face stained with the subtle tones of dirt, and his skin tanned from the sun.

I turn my head to the side, trying to figure out where I am, but when I see four hooves standing within a few feet of my face, I quickly close my eyes again. *Nope. This isn't real.*

"I'm dead. I died—I actually died." I start to panic, and sharp breaths stick in my chest. *If I'm dead, then why does my entire body still hurt?*

I try to wiggle my toes but wince when I feel the discomfort running along my spine and up beneath my ribs. "Ow," I mutter, moving my hand to my rib cage as I'm suddenly more aware of the excruciating pain that comes with each breath I take.

"You're not dead." Lee laughs. "I tried to tell you that colt wasn't ready yet, but you had to try him anyway."

Colt? He must be referring to the set of hooves that are far too close to my head.

"How did I even get here?" I try to sit up, setting one arm behind me as the other reaches toward the throbbing coming from the back of my head.

Lee's hands are around my waist a moment later, helping me sit forward as I swallow a mouthful of dirt. "Well, do you want the long version or the short one?"

"Short will do." I straighten my neck and pull my gaze upward, my eyes meeting his.

"You were riding a horse I told you wasn't broke yet, and you fell off and hit your head." He points to the small buckskin horse next to me then looks down at the ground and smiles.

Now that I'm sitting up, I notice his clothes. He's wearing a faded red patterned shirt, tan pants, and old leather chaps that run from his hips down to the heels of his boots.

This isn't real. I'm definitely dead.

As I try to move, another sharp pain rips through my body, and I can't keep from crying out no matter how hard I try not to.

"Hold on, Miss Harrison. I'm going to get you help." Lee takes the horse by the reins and quickly walks in the direction of a large barn a few hundred feet away.

"Miss Harrison?" I say out loud. *Why is he calling me by my last name?*

I lie back down on the dry dirt, looking up into the bright blue sky above me. *This may be life after death, but it sure as hell still hurts.*

I reach for a throbbing section of skin right above my hip, and my fingers suddenly stop when they don't find the neon fabric of my oversized T-shirt. Instead, they find layers of lace clinging to my body. I'm wearing a dress.

I begin laughing uncontrollably. Each giggle feels like a dozen tiny daggers stabbing at my rib cage, yet I can't manage to make myself stop. I'm lying in the dirt, wearing a dress, after falling off a horse and being rescued by a guy who has the same face as Lee but is dressed in an equally ridiculous outfit and has somehow picked up a heavy Texas drawl since I last saw him an hour ago. This is *hilarious*. I wipe the tears from my eyes and recognize my reaction as being hysteria. Suddenly, I'm crying uncontrollably. Real tears, real panic.

Just in time, Lee returns to where I'm sprawled on the ground, and now he's brought an audience with him.

"This really isn't necessary. I get that you guys are playing some sick joke on me, but it can really be over now." I glare up at them through my tears.

"You were right to come and get us, Tapley. She must've hit her head hard." One of the men looks over at Lee then directs his stare down at me.

"Tapley? Who the hell is Tapley?" I try to sit up again, but a firm hand presses me back down.

"What's the last thing you remember, Miss Harrison?" The man studies my face as I stare up at the small crowd that's now gathered above me.

What is the last thing I remember? I could tell them about the deer in the road, how I pulled my truck to the side then felt it flipping through the air until it finally crashed into the ground. I wait for a long moment, not sure what to say. For some reason, I don't think the truth will do me any good right now.

"I remember hitting my head." My words come out slowly. At least they aren't completely a lie.

"Do you know your name?" the man asks.

"Aubrey. Aubrey Harrison." That's the truth—my name *is* Aubrey Harrison. But I don't think I'm the Aubrey Harrison they're looking for.

The man reaches for my hands and gently pulls me upright. For a second, I think I'm okay to walk, but as I move to take my first step, my head starts to spin, and nausea grows in the pit of my stomach. At least six arms are there to catch me as I begin to fall over, but I find myself leaning toward Lee, and he steps closer to hold me steady.

"I think I need to lie down," I whisper as things start to fade into sepia tones—hazy shades of brown and orange—and the dry landscape almost pulses.

Lee picks me up into his arms, and I rest my head on his shoulder as he carries me inside with the small crowd following behind.

Maybe this is really just a dream. When I wake up, I'll be in the hospital or something—that has to be it.

I'm aware that my last thought before I pass out is a rational one. But even as I slip away, my brain won't completely give in to sleep. I can still sense people hovering around me, hear noises, and feel the pain in my body even though my mind is trying to rest. At first, the background is only filled with a constant beeping noise, a steady rhythm to match the beat of my heart. Then I can hear people sobbing and voices I recognize—my family, Paige. I can't hear their words, but I sense their emotions. I can almost feel their pain, and somehow, I know it's for me.

I'm in two places at once—two states of consciousness at the same time—and I'm surrounded by pain in both places. Maybe this is death, or maybe I'm stuck in a place between the two, but whatever it is, I hope it ends soon.

I WAKE, FEELING AS though I've slept for hours. The constant beeping was annoying at first—it kept me from being able to focus on the voices. After a while, though, I was able to tune it out, almost as if it became white noise in the distance of my own mind.

There's still an ache in the back of my head, and my entire body, from my ribs to my toes, feels like it just finished a month's worth of boot-camp workouts in record time. The room is cold, and I can feel wool blankets tucked tightly around me. Somewhere close by, there might be a fire going, but I can't quite tell.

Someone's voice is speaking to me, and I try to focus on the muffled sound. *Why can't I make out what you're saying?* The question is screaming frustratingly through my mind, and if I could stomp my foot, believe me I would. I listen to the voice—the soothing tones mixed with a little bit of sadness—and can almost feel that person holding my hand... I think.

Lee. It's definitely his voice.

Open your eyes, Aubrey! I silently repeat his earlier words at least a dozen times until I feel the weight lifting from my eyes. My lids open, but everything is still out of focus. I blink, and the dim light of the room starts to become clearer. The constant beeping subsides, and instead of a hospital bed, I find myself on a cot in a room I'm guessing is a parlor.

A parlor?

There's a sleeping woman in an intricately carved wooden chair next to me, and as I move my hand, I realize it's wrapped loosely inside hers. When my hand shifts slightly beneath her grasp, her eyes shoot open and turn downward to where I'm lying on the cot.

"*Aubrey.* You're awake!" Her voice is tired, and her glassy red eyes match her look of exhaustion.

"Yes." It's the only word I can say to the woman who I'm obviously supposed to recognize though I have no idea who she is.

"How are you feeling? How's your head?" She pushes a fallen piece of hair away from my eyes, and I catch a glimpse of it.

I have never had curly hair in my entire life. The thought suddenly makes me shiver, and my mouth feels as dry as Texas soil during a summer of drought. My name is still Aubrey, but I now have curly hair, and I'm in a dress. *What if my face is different? What if I'm no longer the slender five-foot-ten Aubrey Harrison who has stared back at me in the mirror for twenty-three years?*

I quickly try to sit up, but my entire body protests as the blood rushes to my head and forces me back down. "How long have I been asleep?" I ask the woman, touching my temple.

"A little over a day. It's just past nightfall now." She reaches behind my shoulders and helps me upright.

I can see her better as the glow from the fire at the back of the room lights up the parlor just enough for me to make out my surroundings. She appears to be in her mid-forties, her dark chocolate-brown hair just beginning to show strands of gray throughout the curls that have fallen loose from the braid that stops in the middle of her back. Her eyes are a rare shade of dark-green jade—the same color as mine, at least the last time I checked. She looks so familiar, so much like me, much more so than my mother—the mother I've had for twenty-three years.

Footsteps creak against the faded wood floor, and I recognize the man as soon as he comes into view. He's one of the men who hovered over me as I lay sprawled on the dirt yesterday.

"Charlotte, why didn't you tell me she woke up?" He's wearing a long wool coat, dirty tan pants, and a dark-brown hat. It's not a cowboy hat, but it holds the same shape, only smaller. His beard is salt-and-pepper and his eyes a pale shade of blue-gray. He looks eerily similar to my dad, only more worn—more rugged.

He takes off his hat, tosses it on an empty chair in the far corner of the room, and sits next to me on the edge of my cot. "You gave us a scare yesterday. Your mother and I were worried you'd finally cracked that thick skull of yours." A smile sneaks across his face as he squeezes my arm.

Your mother and I? I play his words back, a lump forming in my throat. *You can wake up anytime now, Aubrey.* I swallow hard. Oddly enough, I find myself holding back tears. These people sitting next to me, worried about me, are strangers. To them, I'm their daughter, but to me... well, to me, they are nobody at all.

"You know, when we named you after Uncle Aubrey, we weren't quite prepared for you to have the same stubborn disposition. Your uncle would have liked to believe he was a grand horseman. I assure you, it was quite the opposite." He chuckles then helps me to a sitting position next to him on the cot.

Angry noises come from my stomach, saving me from remarking on Uncle Aubrey and my lack of apparent horsemanship skills.

"You must be starving," the woman says through a smile. "I'll go get supper started." She stands and makes her way to another room adjacent to the one I'm sitting in. Fortunately, the man next to me doesn't hover but quickly follows his wife out the door.

I pull my legs from their stretched-out position on the cot and place them on the cold wood floor below me. Faint shades of purple and black make their way up my legs in scattered patches of bruises, and I can feel every one of them as I pull myself stiffly to my feet.

The room is bigger than I imagined. Large pieces of handmade furniture are against the wall, and a long wooden table sits at the center. There are bookshelves from floor to ceiling in one corner, and a large cowhide rug lies between two plush chairs in front of the fireplace.

I catch movement at one end of the room, and as I turn toward it, I find my reflection in a circular metal-rimmed mirror hanging on the wall. The floor makes terrible protesting noises as I step quietly in the direction of the mirror. I don't know why I feel like I need to be sneaky in a house that I apparently live in, but I'm trying as hard as I can to tiptoe across the room.

As I face the mirror in front of me, I inspect the person staring back. I'm not sure what I expected given the circumstances—maybe green skin, a pointy nose, and a face full of moles, though the Wicked Witch of the West would have made more sense if I'd ended up in this place by way of a tornado rather than a car accident. Either way, I definitely wasn't expecting it to be me.

It is me. This is me. I trace my jawline, then run my fingers up to my forehead and down the slope of my nose. It's definitely my face. The only difference between this Aubrey Harrison and the one I have been for twenty-three years is the long, curly, brown hair. Well, that and the white nightgown that nearly matches the pale shade of my fair skin.

I don't realize how cold it is until I see the thin fabric of the gown I'm wearing. I look for a blanket or a jacket nearby—something to cover me up—because I feel as if I'm wearing nothing at all. There's a colorful blanket resting on the back of a leather chair behind a desk a few steps away. It's intricate, and the vibrant shades of its threads stand out against the dark wood and stone of the room.

It reminds me of the beautiful Mexican ponchos people would wear during downtown San Antonio's yearly Fiesta Festival.

I reach for the blanket and pull it tightly around my body, but before I can head in the direction of the warm fireplace, my eyes fall upon an open book at the center of the large desk. There are two full pages of names, dates, and dollar amounts written in fancy script—a ledger, I'm guessing. I quickly scan the pages and come to the last entry at the bottom:

2 February 1836.

My jaw drops, and my hand flies to mouth. It's 1836.

CHAPTER FOUR

The Settlement of San Antonio, Texas
February 1836

After sitting through a very quiet and extremely awkward dinner, I make my way to a bedroom on the second floor of the large stone house and crawl into a bed that belonged to the person I'm now supposed to be—a person I have no idea how to be. I don't know this version of me.

I shut my eyes at least a dozen times, trying to force myself to go back to sleep, hoping I'll wake up from this nightmare. I dread the thought that sleep might only bring back the constant beeps and muffled voices I heard the last time I gave in to its call. Neither here nor there is a place I'd prefer to be, but at least staying awake under the blankets of a stranger's bed brings me silence rather than pain.

I've spent a few torturous hours tossing and turning and have shed a bucket of tears by the time the glow of the sun begins to break through the darkness. It's the dawn of the first real day I'm forced to become someone else. I crawl out from under the thick layer of blankets, grab one from the top, and wrap it over my shoulders as I make my way to the large window at the edge of the room. There's enough light in the sky for me to see a few miles into the distance, and I recognize the rock-and-cedar landscape spanning out in every direction.

It's definitely still Texas. At least I have a familiar place to call home.

My room must be facing the back of the house because the window looks out into a large pasture of dry coastal grass where a few hundred plump beef cattle move around in small groups as they graze together. I spot the back of a large barn near the far corner of the house, and sitting to one side is the wood plank corral layered with the red dirt I woke up on not two days before. A few horses are standing quietly in the corral, and as soon as I spot the small buckskin colt at the center of the group, I instinctively reach to the back of my head, where a fair-sized knot still painfully exists.

"Thanks, dude," I mutter, glaring out the window at the colt.

He perks his ears forward and turns his long face in my direction as though trying to find my location behind the glass on the second floor. A quick knock at the door startles me, and I pull the blanket tighter around my body, feeling more inappropriately dressed than I would have in just my bra and panties. I try to clear the groggy tone out of my throat before I speak.

"It's open," I call to the person on the other side.

"Aubrey, can I come in?" Charlotte's voice rings from the hallway.

Isn't that what "It's open" means?

I pause, trying to think of what the real Aubrey Harrison from 1836 might say, and I finally decide that opening the door is better than saying something odd.

"Hi, uh, Mother?" The words come out as more of a question than a greeting.

Charlotte eyes me quizzically. "Robert just arrived to check in on you." She smiles as she pushes her way into the room.

Just when things couldn't get more complicated.

"Um, tell him I'm feeling much better and thank you for checking on me." The words leave my mouth in a scrambled mess of *ums*.

Charlotte tilts her head, her brows pushing together in a tight line as she studies my face. "He means to see you, Aubrey. He rode all the way from town." She walks over to a chunky wooden wardrobe taking up most of the wall, reaches inside, and returns with a long deep-purple cotton dress. After laying it across the bed, she takes the blanket from around my shoulders and starts lifting the white night-gown over my head.

Well, this just got real personal real quick. My legs feel like lead, and my entire body is frozen as I stand naked in the middle of the room like it's the most normal thing in the world.

She hands me a different bundle of white cotton fabric that I'm guessing I need to put on immediately. I unfold the layers and hold the strange knee-length chemise out in front of me. I bring the fabric down over my head quickly. Before I can inspect myself in the mirror, Charlotte is already behind me, pulling and straightening the thin fabric into the right position. She then holds open the dress at the level of my knees, and her eyes motion for me to step inside the dark-purple shell. Even though the fabric is plain, it's more extravagant than most women wore—*wear*—in this day and age. I wonder who Robert is.

After Charlotte fastens the long chain of buttons, she promptly turns me toward the mirror on the front of the wardrobe. I take a long look at myself, inspecting the outfit. It fits my body perfectly as if I've worn it a hundred times.

"Hold still." Charlotte's voice is calm and quiet, but I can hear the seriousness hiding in her words. Robert must be important to the family.

She gathers my long curls at the back of my head and gently pulls the tangled ends through the soft bristles of a bush.

"Do you have a ribbon?" I ask, trying not to release what little air I have in my lungs as I speak.

She looks at me with a curious expression and opens the lid of a small metal box on a table by the bed. After searching for a moment, she removes a length of silver ribbon and hands it to me as she steps back, watching as she waits for me to do something with it.

"Brush?" I ask again, holding out my hand.

She quickly places its brown handle in my palm. I tilt my head back and brush the hair closest to my face back into line with the rest of my long locks then gather it in a ponytail and wrap the sections of fabric around my fingers into a long loose bow. The ends of the ribbon fall into place on either side of my ponytail. Straightening my shoulders, I look at myself in the mirror, and despite the strangely foreign way I feel wearing the dress, the familiarity of my ponytail makes everything much less daunting.

"You look like a child with your hair in ribbons." Charlotte twirls the ends of my hair around her fingers, her eyes glancing over the silk bow. "You should pin it up."

"No." The tone of my voice stays steady, and I turn to face her with a forced smile across my face. If I'm to wear dresses and petticoats, I will wear my hair as I please.

"I'm sure your fiancé will have *something* to say of your ribbons." She huffs as she takes me by the hand and leads me in the direction of the stairs.

ROBERT ALLCORT IS NOT what I expected at all. The moment I turn the corner to the downstairs parlor, my eyes meet with the hard dark-green eyes of a thicker young man standing no more than six feet tall. He has a strange rosy tint to his cheeks that appears more permanent than blush, and although he's fairly average looking, his clothes are elegant, made of rich fabrics in deep earthy tones. I can tell he flaunts his money to compensate for what he lacks in looks.

"Aubrey, darling, what have I told you about riding those horses of yours—especially the ones broken by that farm help your father refuses to get rid of? Really, George, we need to find you some better help." Robert's eyes glance over every inch of me, inspecting me like I'm a cow he's prepared to buy for whatever price he names.

"I know you're not fond of Tapley, Robert, but he's been loyal to this family for years—something that's hard to come by these days." George throws a defensive glance in my direction and takes his place by Charlotte on the sofa.

I'm engaged to this jerk? I stare at him, half glaring and half giving a fake smile as if someone is forcefully pinching my cheeks. All of the sudden, the stunt Porter pulled at Chilifest doesn't seem so terrible. Even he isn't this much of a tool.

Aubrey Allcort. Just the idea of having that name leaves me cold all over.

Everyone in the room is now staring at me, waiting for me to respond—waiting for me to say something instead of just offering a fake smile.

"I didn't mean to get in an accident," I blurt, suddenly wanting to kick myself for my choice of words. "I mean on the horse, that is." I sound like an idiot. Maybe the real Aubrey Harrison *is* an idiot. She'd have to be to want to marry this guy.

Robert is still looking at me, piercing me with his judgmental eyes as if trying to see into my mind, as if I'm completely transparent. Then he starts laughing. It's a terrible laugh, like nails against a dry chalkboard—the kind of laugh an entire room notices and cringes to hear. The only thing that flashes through my mind is the thought of slapping him across his face so hard that he stops laughing or, better yet, just stops talking completely.

"You are so strange sometimes, darling. I'm so thankful that you frequently enamor people with your beautiful face so that the things you say may go ignored completely."

My face must be turning an angry shade of red because Charlotte is looking at me. Before a rebuttal to Robert can leave my mouth, she breaks the uncomfortable silence that's taken over the room. "Aubrey, why don't you come join me on the sofa." She clears her throat, signaling George to hand over his seat to me.

"Thank you, Mother," I reply, shooting her a gracious look.

Robert takes a seat in an empty chair across from the sofa, and George leans against the mantel above the fireplace. In the torturous fifteen minutes that follow, Robert requires all attention on him as he boasts about the latest and greatest business acquisition he and his father have smooth-talked their way into now controlling.

Keeping my eyes open quickly becomes a challenge. Fortunately, I catch movement outside the large windows on the wall across from me. A group of cows and calves are crossing the field in the direction of a large corral at one corner.

Two men are driving the herd on horseback. Their arms and hands barely shift, yet the horses respond to their subtle commands and change directions with the movement of the livestock. One of the men is older, close to the same age as George and with similar salt-and-pepper hair. I turn my focus to the second rider, a man in his early twenties with a full head of dusty-brown hair. Until a few days ago, I had only ever seen Lee in a military-regulation hairstyle, but even now, with longer hair and the faint hint of stubble on his face, he's instantly recognizable and undeniably handsome. I can't peel my gaze away from him as he and his steel-gray horse navigate the cattle flawlessly.

"*Aubrey*," a voice snaps.

I turn my attention back to the room. Once again, everyone is staring at me, waiting for me to say something. Robert turns to the window behind him, finding exactly what—*who*—I'd been staring at.

He turns back to glare at me, his eyes a sickly jealous shade as he huffs out an angry breath. "Well—" His eye twitches, and the edges of his pig-like nose flare.

"Oh. I'm sorry. I guess I'm still really tired. I'm finding it hard to stay awake." I smile, hoping my subtle jab at Robert's boring bragging session doesn't go unnoticed.

Robert frowns, the already red tint of his cheeks flaring one shade brighter. "I asked if you would be accompanying me to the Settlers outing two evenings from now." He picks at the cuff on one of his sleeves nervously.

"I'm afraid that will depend on how I'm feeling after my terrible... fall." I fake smile again, folding my hands across my lap and hoping my eyes look sweet enough to sound sincere.

"Of course, darling. I need you to be fully recovered as quickly as possible." He stands up, makes his way over to the couch, and holds out his hand for me to take.

Of course. It's all about what he needs.

I try to ignore that sarcastic thought as I oblige him and put my hand lightly into his. He walks me over to the front door, Charlotte and George following a few steps behind.

"I will check on you again tomorrow, then." He places an eager kiss on the top of my hand, his lips too wet as they leave their mark sloppily behind.

As soon as he lets go of my hand, I bring it to my side, trying to discreetly wipe off the wetness on the fabric of my dress. Without another word, not even a goodbye, Robert heads out the front door to where his horse is waiting. He struts away, his head bobbing obnoxiously with each quick step. I want to kick a rock at the back of it.

"Has he always been so appalling?" Before I can stop, the question leaves my mouth in a huff of air.

George's eyes are suspicious as he studies my face. "Robert has always been a difficult person to be around, but you haven't seemed to object the match until today."

Backtrack, Aubrey. Backtrack quickly.

"What I mean is... today he just seemed more difficult." I know that response isn't any better.

I quickly head up the stairs before their questioning eyes stare a hole through my chest. Shutting the door behind me, I'm happy to be back within the quiet and solitary walls of the bedroom. I pull on one end of the bow in my hair and untie the ribbon so that my curls are released to their normal position draping my shoulders.

Making my way to the window on the back wall, I look far into the few hundred acres of property behind the house. My eyes scan the area for a certain young man on his dark-gray horse, and I find him a few hundred yards outside the corral near the barn. I lean against the edge of the window, watching as Lee works the cattle effortlessly, and I once again find myself unable to take my eyes off him.

CHAPTER FIVE

An entire day after my first encounter with Robert, I'm finally brave enough to venture outside the safety of the house's stone walls. Maybe I will find a way back home or at least a hint of how I got here.

The day I woke up on the hard ground of the corral outside, the weather was almost the perfect temperature, with the sun kissing my skin gently as opposed to the fierceness of its rays in summer and early autumn. Today, however, the air is much colder. The chill seeps into every small crevice of the house as the dimly lit fire downstairs tries to fight it off in an earth-shattering feud.

In the back corner of the old wardrobe, I find a pair of long tan pants made with fabric the soothing texture of soft cotton, which my body appreciates after a few excruciating hours in a dress. I move to the trunk at the foot of the bed, dig out a pair of stiff leather boots, pull them onto my feet, and lace them over the cuffed pant legs. I peek into the wardrobe one last time, searching for an alternative to my long-sleeved blue blouse. I manage to find a red patterned shirt and a knee-length black wool coat. After undoing the long line of buttons down the center, I pull it on and head in the direction of the front door.

Charlotte is knitting a dark-green granny square at her usual place in front of the fire.

"I'm going outside for a bit," I call as I reach for the old metal handle on the front door.

She turns around quickly, a smile crossing her face as her hands automatically continue their knitting movements. The moment she sees me, though, her smile fades, and her eyes grow misty. "Aubrey, why on earth are you wearing Thomas's old clothes?" she stammers, dropping the square piece of knitted yarn onto her lap.

Thomas? Who the hell is Thomas? Play it cool, Aubrey... say something. Knots begin to form in my stomach as I stare dumbly back at her and blink rapidly.

"I, uh, didn't want to dirty a perfectly good dress. I don't think he'll mind if I borrow them for a few hours." My words stumble, my face flushing hot and no doubt turning a bright shade of red to match the shirt that I now know isn't mine.

Something about the look on her face after my response makes me think that Thomas isn't around to care about his clothes.

"I'll be back shortly." I promptly pull open the door and step into the chilly temperature of the Texas afternoon.

It's the first time I've seen the outside of the stone house I've been stuck in for the last few days, and it looks oddly close to the way I envisioned it from inside its walls. Medium-sized gray stones make up the entire surface of the house's two-story structure. Three large first-story windows face outward from the front of the house, the overhang of the porch's wood roof shading the inside from the blinding Texas sun.

The grass covering most of the property is still brown and dry from the last few months of winter. My boots crunch across its surface, the weight of my body leaving small footprints in a straight path from the porch to the barn. There are a few men moving around the property, some replacing wood boards on a long side of fencing and others stacking bales of hay underneath a tall covered building a few steps away.

"Mornin', Miss Harrison," one of the men calls as I walk past.

I recognize him as the other man who was riding with Lee yesterday. I nod back, shooting him a small smile.

Ask him if he's seen Lee. The thought is annoyingly overbearing as I continue in the same direction, but for some reason, I ignore the urge to ask him.

I can hear the chirping of the birds hiding in the barn's rafters as I cross under the threshold. The earthy smell of sawdust and fresh manure tickles my nose, making it hard not to sneeze—I haven't smelled the scent of horses in what feels like ages. Small wooden stalls line either side of the dirt aisle, and a huge dark-bay draft horse picks up his head with a mouthful of hay and nickers at me as I pass by. The horse walks to the front of his stall and pokes his head into the aisle, looking for attention.

Backing up a few steps, I walk over to him and reach my hand right below his nose. He sniffs me carefully, the long whiskers around his nostrils brushing the top of my hand.

"Well, hi there, handsome." I slowly bring my hand to his face and scratch the space underneath his forelock as he buries his head into my chest.

"The colt's still not ready yet," Lee says, his voice breaking through the air.

I turn around too fast, startling the horse. He flings his head in the air and nearly knocks me over.

"You haven't even been here five minutes, and you're already scaring my horses." He frowns at me and sets down the leather saddle he's been holding on a wooden rack against the wall.

"I'm sorry... I didn't mean to scare him. You—you just startled me a bit."

He's staring at me with an odd expression written across his face. "Miss Harrison, what are you wearing?" He motions toward all of me and crosses his arms.

"I found them in my wardrobe... I needed something to wear." I shrug and pull at the sleeve of the wool coat.

He waits a few moments, his brows pulled together as he scowls. "Well, I guess Tommy's ghost doesn't need a fresh set of clothes." He reaches for a bundle of leather straps tossed in a heap on the floor.

Tommy's ghost. I repeat the words a few times to myself, trying to wrap my mind around them. This explains a lot.

"You're acting a bit off since your fall, Miss Harrison." He brings his hazel stare to my eyes. A keyhole in the roof allows a beam of sunlight to rest on his head of dark-brown hair like a subtle halo.

"Aubrey," I blurt with sudden urgency, making Tapley recoil. "My name is Aubrey."

"You of all people should know why I don't call you Aubrey anymore." His stare turns cold, and I can see the tension set in his jaw as he clamps his teeth together.

He couldn't be any more wrong—I don't know why at all. Right now, I don't know a lot of things about the person I'm supposed to be pretending to be, and within the span of a few short days, I seem to have done a pretty fair job of messing up her life.

How can I tell him that I don't know why he is calling me Miss Harrison? My name is Aubrey. I want to hear him say my name. I suddenly feel like the sound of my name from his lips will somehow make this entire situation feel real. My name in this place means that I'm here—that I'm not dreaming.

"Lee, please just call me Aubrey." My words are pleading, desperate, as I take a step toward him.

"The last time I called you that, I believe your exact words were 'It should've been you, not Tommy—I'll never be able to forgive you for this.'" He throws the bundle of leather hard into a wooden box in front of one of the stalls and slams the lid shut before he turns his back on me. "And my name is Tapley, not Lee," he adds as he's walking away.

"Wait, L—Tapley," I yell after him and take a few rushed steps when he doesn't turn around.

I reach for his arm, and as soon as my hand touches his skin, my hairs stand on end, and my heart begins beating rapidly beneath the layers of my clothes. "Tapley, please wait," I whisper.

He stops with his back to me. The tense muscles in his shoulders relax before he turns to face me. This time, his eyes are no longer hard and cold—they're sad.

"The way I feel about you now..." He shakes his head, and I'm afraid he's not going to continue. I need to know what we were, or are, so I know what he's expecting from me. "You forced me to turn off everything I felt for you in the past," he says finally.

I cautiously nod, hoping a show of painful admission will keep him talking.

"You kicked me under the rug like I was dust. Like the feelings you had for me were a layer of dirt you were trying to wipe off so no one could see me at all. Do you know how hard it was for me to stop loving you after everything I've been through—with that fire?" His words tremble as they leave his lips, and he takes a step closer to me.

"I'm sorry... for the things I've done... said... to hurt you. Hurting you is the biggest regret I've ever had." I look up at him, and suddenly, the urge to touch his face becomes overwhelming. My eyes trace the line of his jaw to the tip of his chin as I try to memorize the image of him.

It's true—I'm overwhelmed with regret as I listen to his words, but I know that the regret I feel isn't from something I did to him—or rather, that the person I am now did to him. The pain the other Aubrey caused shows clearly in his eyes as he seems to wait for my next move. I take another step forward, and now our bodies are within inches of each other. I can feel the heat from his breath as it hovers in a cloud in the cold air.

"Aub—" He stops.

I can sense someone walking into the barn. "Aubrey?" This time, it's Robert's voice that says my name.

I roll my eyes, hoping that if I don't turn around, he won't really be there.

"Aubrey!" he says again, and I can almost feel him breathing behind my neck as he taps his boots impatiently on the dirt floor.

"Yes, Robert?" I try to ask sweetly as I spin on my toes to face him.

"Your mother said I would find you out here." He glares at Tapley with sharp green eyes.

"And you indeed found me." I tear myself away from the closeness of Tapley and place myself between the two men.

"I'm going to take your adventurous attitude as a confirmation that you are feeling well enough to attend the Settlers Day activities tomorrow?"

I can tell by the way he pulls his shoulders back and the flushing red of defiance across his cheeks that this time, Robert's invitation is more of a demand.

"I'm not really sure that—"

"Nonsense, Aubrey. You are going with me tomorrow. My parents are expecting you." His lips start to rise at the corners as a smirk crosses his face, but a shadow crosses the floor, and I realize his smile is not directed at me. "Tapley, I've been meaning to mention that I might have an acquaintance coming to tomorrow evening's events that I think would be a good match for you. I've already told her so much about you, and she seems eager to meet you for herself. Can I tell her to expect you at the Settlers party?" Robert asks with a sickly, amused tone.

"I wasn't planning on going tomorrow, but since you went to all this work on my behalf, I guess I can change my evening plans," Tapley replies.

I can feel his eyes linger on me as if he's hoping I'll stay, but then he's gone, out the back door of the barn, leaving me alone with Mr. Rhinestone Cowboy.

"I look forward to seeing you tomorrow, then," Robert yells after him. As soon as Tapley is out of hearing range, Robert lets out one of his hideous chuckles as he places his hand around my waist and turns me back in the direction of the house. "I'm especially looking forward to tomorrow." He peeks over at me and looks startled. "What in heaven's name are you wearing, Aubrey?" His eyes study me with an unsatisfied edge.

That seems to be the big question today, doesn't it?

As we make our way back through the grass and to the front porch of the house, I steal a glance behind me, hoping to see the image of Tapley one last time. My heart begins to race, sputtering to life as if it was all but deathly still until that exact moment—the moment I find him in the corral. He's working the buckskin colt, his voice quietly calling out commands as the animal trots in a circle around him. I try to tear my eyes away before Robert notices, but I find myself clinging to the familiarity of the sight of him. He's the only thing I find real in this strange reality—other than myself, and I'm still not sure even I can call myself real.

I wish I could tell him about the car accident and the confusion I was tossed into the moment I woke up in 1836. The burden of my secret is almost unbearable as the pressure to be someone I'm not becomes more excruciating by the minute. I'm saying, doing, and even wearing the wrong things, and I have no idea how to navigate the situation differently.

I need to talk to someone to take the weight off my shoulders. Then again, am I ready to be that delusional girl who thinks she's time traveled from the future? I've completely lost my mind.

CHAPTER SIX

Within the last two days, I've learned to fake smile—a lot. If I were still at College Station, my fake smile would be turning me into one of those emotionless Barbie Dolls hanging around with Porter at Chilifest, but now I find myself curtsying with perfect fake-high-society etiquette as if I've been pulled straight out of a Southern debutante class. For the first time in my life, I find myself missing the perfectly carved shallow layer that makes up the emotional capacity of the Deltas and Thetas. I would gladly send myself two centuries forward into the decade of fluorescent shirts, themed frat parties, and Texas-sized bows if it were to mean that I never had to wear a dress ever again.

Dinners in 1836 are painfully long, with food that shouldn't take two hours to finish. Even if I ate my meal quickly, I would still be stuck sitting around a table with my parents, listening to Robert as he controls all aspects of the conversation.

I sneak a peek at him from his place across from me, and I instantly regret it. He stabs at the meat on his plate, and the juices seep into a pool beneath it as he slices off a piece. His fingers are chubby, and wet lines of perspiration gather around the neck of his dark-brown shirt. Just imagining how ripe and pungent he must smell is enough to chase away what little appetite I have. Nothing about him is redeemable or attractive in any way. I was used to Porter flaunting his family's money, but at least he had moments where his charm and his intelligence made him bearable to be around. Certain qualities made him easy to love despite his arrogance, but I have trouble finding anything good about Robert.

Is the Aubrey they all know so much different from me? Just go along with it. Don't mess up the life of the person you're stuck in.

I move my food around my plate, hoping to make my loss of appetite less noticeable. Fortunately, everyone's attention is focused on Robert and whatever story he's using to keep us stuck at the table with him. I look over at Charlotte, her glassy stare matching the bored yawn that breaks across her face. She tries to hide it behind her hand. George is at least managing to keep his eyes open, but I can feel his leg tapping from underneath the table.

There's a loud knock at the front door.

"I'll get it," Charlotte and I both say at the same time.

She looks over at me, and her expression turns sympathetic.

"It seems you need more than just help around the farm, George," Robert says, his displeased gaze directed my way.

"You know what help we can afford is used on the farm. There is no extra for help around the house," George responds calmly. I don't understand how he can be so passive with a man so utterly vain. A second knock interrupts the awkward tension in the room.

"Will someone please answer the door?" Robert barks in what I've come to recognize as his typical bossy fashion and shoves another piece of meat into his mouth. Even away from his own home, Robert expects an attendant to wait on his every need. Soon he will expect that from me.

"Go ahead, Aubrey," Charlotte mouths to me, and I shoot her a thankful look as I push my chair away from the table, quickly excusing myself.

I reach for the metal lantern sitting on one of the bottom steps of the stairs and pull open the front door.

A faint smile crosses my face when I see the tall muscular figure of Tapley standing on the porch. The temperature dropped into the low thirties the moment the sun set earlier in the evening, but looking at the way Tapley is dressed, I almost forget about the chill in the air. The sleeves of his white cotton shirt are rolled up above his el-bows, and the top few buttons down the center of his shirt are left undone. I find myself staring at the dips and curves of his toned chest revealed in the small open section of his shirt.

"Can I come in?" he asks, his voice sheltering a strangely amused tone as he watches me stand speechless in the doorway.

"Yes—I'm so sorry. Please come in." I move out of the way so he can enter the house.

As he passes in front of me, his hand brushes the edge of my dress, and his eyes drop to meet mine for a fragment of a second. If I could only hold his gaze longer, I could put my finger on the look he is giving me. But it is gone almost as quickly as it came, leaving me breathless for what feels like an eternity.

His attention shifts to the table of people to his right, and I feel the eyes of all three of them staring at us.

"I apologize for interrupting your meal, but one of the mares is foaling early, and I need some extra cloths and warm water if you have any to spare." He walks right up to the edge of the room but never crosses its threshold.

Charlotte quickly rises from her place at the table and makes her way to the kitchen. Behind Robert's cheeks, the familiar flash of red surfaces—a reaction I've come to expect when Tapley is in his pres-ence. Everyone for a hundred miles can see how much Robert hates Tapley, and I have a feeling it has something to do with me. A few minutes later, Charlotte returns with a basket of clean white cloths and an iron kettle full of water. She places the basket in my arms and carefully hands Tapley the container of hot liquid, a trail of steam filling the air.

"Wait here." She trots back to the kitchen and promptly returns with a full plate. "It sounds like you have a long night ahead of you, and I made extra food." She hands it to him and opens the front door. "Aubrey will help you carry everything back to the barn."

Charlotte places her hand on the small of my back and steers me out the door right behind him. I should object or at least feel bad about leaving my fiancé alone as I follow a handsome figure into the dark, but I don't. I feel not even a single fragment of remorse.

The night sky above us is filled with billions of stars, their light shining brighter than the dull flame dancing from the metal lantern in my hand. This sky is a Texas sky, and it feels like home—even though I've never been farther away from home than now. Tapley and I are silent as we make our way to the closest end of the barn, and for the first time since dinner started, I actually feel awake—alive—even though Tapley acts like I'm nonexistent. I'm just a pair of legs following closely behind him as he keeps his eyes forward, never saying a word or slowing his step to match mine. He's keeping his distance, but it's an effort so obviously forced that it looks painful.

As we enter the barn, I can already hear labored breathing coming from inside one of the stalls. Other than the flames from a few hanging lanterns spaced at equal distances down the center aisle, the barn is almost completely dark. Tapley unties the ropes secured in front of the stall opening and takes a knee next to the big chestnut mare, who's lying on her heavily swollen belly.

"Can I stay?" I ask, placing the basket of clothing next to him.

He turns to look at me over his shoulder, his hazel eyes a deep shade of grayish green in the dim light. "You don't have a jacket, and I don't think your fiancé will approve of you catching a cold." He pulls himself back to his feet and steps closer to me.

"I'm not that cold, and I don't care about what my fiancé approves of or doesn't. He doesn't own me," I stammer, my words coming out in a jumbled mess as I try to ignore how little space is between us.

"He doesn't yet, but he might as well." He sucks in a breath.

I feel myself shivering, but I'm not sure if it's from the cold that has gotten under my skin or the truth in Tapley's words.

"Not cold, Miss Harrison?" He gives me a skeptical look and takes a step closer. "Your skin would say otherwise."

His fingers touch my arm, and the edges of his lips curl in a small smile. I didn't notice the goose bumps scattered over my skin. In fact, I didn't feel a chill in my body until he touched me.

"It's Aubrey. Just Aubrey."

"Well, then, Aubrey, if you're set on staying here, you'll need something warmer than that dress." He slides past me.

I stand motionless, unable to move or breathe, as I watch him walk away. The sound of him saying my name attaches to my memory as if it's been wandering, lost in my mind, for ages.

Tapley opens a wooden door across from the horse's stall, and the glowing flames inside a small stone fireplace light up the room just enough for me to see inside. There's a cot against one wall of the tiny room and a faded tan-and-white cowhide lying at the center of the floor.

So this is where he stays. I knew Tapley lived somewhere on the property, but I didn't realize he'd be living in a tiny room so close to the house... so close to *me*.

He returns a few seconds later with a plain gray wool blanket and drapes it over my shoulders. The blanket smells like tanned leather and grass, and the scent of it fills me as I pull it snuggly around my body. It smells like Tapley, a scent I find strangely familiar. There's a bale of hay in front of one of the stalls down the aisle, and before I can thank him for the blanket, he's already lifted the bale effortlessly and brought it over to the corner of the stall for me to sit on.

"Do you remember the last time you camped out with me during foaling season?" He takes a seat next to me.

"Actually, no." My words flow naturally without giving me a moment to stop them.

"I see." His head drops the slightest bit as he picks apart a piece of hay.

I didn't mean for the words to be as harsh as they came out, but the truth is... that wasn't me. But with the way I feel now, sitting next to him in the quiet of the barn, I know that if I'd been the one making those memories with him, they'd be ones I would never allow myself to forget.

The mare stirs a few feet from where we're sitting, and Tapley slowly gets up and moves behind her back. "Easy, girl," he whispers, placing his hand gently on her angry belly as she pushes. A few seconds later, she relaxes a bit and lets out the deep breath she's been holding in through the last group of contractions. "It's going to be a long night." He looks up at me and tries to smile, but I can see a hint of sadness in his eyes.

"What I said earlier—I didn't mean to make it sound like I don't remember. I wish I did." I study his face against the dancing light from the lamp resting closest to him.

The Lee I know from my history class possesses a certain confidence—something that forces a person to notice even the slightest movement he makes. That Lee is different from the young man in front of me. Tapley's demeanor is quiet, reserved, as if he's trying to disappear unnoticed into the space around me. I still feel myself drawn to him, and I long to know everything about him—what makes him happy, what things he loves most in this world. Despite the familiarity of his face and the smoothness of his voice, he's a complete stranger to me.

"Look, Aubrey, I know it's been quite a while since we've spent time together like this. So I understand why you don't remember—I just hoped you did." His attention turns back to the mare as her breathing picks back up.

"After my accident the other day, I've just had trouble remembering things." My words are hollow, and the truth of the actual accident I'm referring to is trapped on my tongue.

He says nothing, but I can almost see the wheels turning in his head.

"Thank you. For the other day." I take a deep breath, another subtle wave of leather filling my nose.

"It's my fault you fell off that colt." He reaches for the basket of cloths.

"I don't understand..." Standing from the hay bale, I grab the iron kettle and sit beside him.

"I knew that colt wasn't ready for you yet, but you insisted on saddling him up and sitting on his back. I should've said no, but I've never been able to tell you no. Refusing you anything is just something I don't know how to do." He turns his hazel eyes to meet mine, his lips parting the slightest bit as the sweet scent of his breath fills the air.

I find myself staring at his mouth, studying the way his lips curve perfectly at the top. When I force my gaze back to his, he is still staring at me in the same strange way—a way that no one has ever looked at me before.

"I'm sorry that I ever hurt you," I whisper, my eyes dropping. The truth is, I am sorry. I'm sorry that anyone could ever break the heart of a man so beautiful, so kind.

I feel him watching me as I become more aware of every movement he makes—every blink of his eyes—as all his attention is focused on me. He slowly brings his finger to the base of my chin and lifts my head back up until my eyes meet his, and he stares into them deeply, intently, as if he's trying to see right into the center of my soul and uncover something he's looking for. *Something I must be missing.*

"Aubrey!" someone yells in the distance, but I'm lost in this moment with Tapley, and the voice sounds miles away.

Tapley doesn't break his stare, and I can almost feel his heart beating in the same steady rhythm as my own.

"Aubrey!" the voice yells again. This time, the mare lifts her head, and we force ourselves to look down at her.

"You should probably go before your fiancé comes looking for you. I don't want him causing the mare any more unrest." He pats the sweaty neck of the horse, and just like that, he's back to being distant.

I lay the blanket across the bale of hay, and the scent of him immediately goes away as the cold air nips at my skin. I sneak one last look at him, half hoping he will acknowledge me before I start down the barn aisle, and my heart drops when he doesn't lift his eyes from the horse. Two minutes ago, I had made a connection with someone in this foreign world I've been thrust into, but now the connection is gone—like a frayed end to a bad break—and a subtle look of pain is once again behind Tapley's otherwise blank expression. I hear footsteps crunching on the grass on their way toward the barn, and I jog down the aisle, hoping to intercept Robert before he makes things worse.

"There you are. I was worried he'd done something terrible to you." Robert wastes no time in opening his mouth right as I walk straight into his chest.

"What the hell—" I blurt as I nearly fall backward at the impact.

"What did you say?" He looks at me with a peculiar stare, his eyebrows pulling together fiercely.

"Nothing. It was nothing." I lift my shoulders back and cross my arms in front of my chest.

If I could say the things that are actually flowing through my mind... if only he knew that he's the one doing terrible things to me just by being here. I roll my eyes and silently walk beside him as he talks the entire way back to the house.

CHAPTER SEVEN

Enduring Robert's endless talking for four hours in a single night is on my list of terrible things never to do—right alongside long-distance running, trying to be a vegetarian, and wearing jumpers even if they're trendy. Just one hour with him would make that list. The idea of having to endure him for an entire lifetime is something I find absolutely horrifying.

After he finally leaves for the night, I peel myself out of the itchy dress I've been stuck in all day and tuck myself sloppily into bed, wearing one of the horrible white nightgowns. I miss the simplicity of falling asleep in nothing but my underwear, but being caught in only my bra and panties in the year 1836 is something I'm pretty sure would get me sent to the stocks or forced to walk around with a scarlet letter stuck on my chest—although, I'm not sure if Texans use stocks in a town square for public humiliation. Hanging might be more their style.

Sleep comes more easily tonight than last night, but the fear of hearing the constant beeping in the darkness of my dreams is a small detail I forgot about. The moment my eyelids become too heavy to open again, the faint trail of beeps comes creeping back up. Tonight, there's something different about the constant mechanical music. In the background, I can make out faint voices so subtle that, at first, I'm not sure they're really there. I focus on them, pulling them forward as if trying to hear a person on the other end of a telephone call while standing in a stadium full of a million cheering people.

"Aubrey—I don't know if you can hear me, but please try." The voice is muffled, but it's definitely male. At first, I think it might be Porter, but he's never sounded so soft-spoken and broken.

"Whatever you do, don't die on me. I can't lose you again—not this time. Whatever happens, know that I will find you." The voice speaks again, and I can almost feel him reaching for my hand, the sensation of touch like a static current in the air.

"I'm not dead. I can hear you," I try to call out to the voice, wishing I knew its owner.

The beeping changes, its consistency interrupted as it shifts into a faster pattern.

There's no way... it can't be.

I force myself to take a deep breath as if trying to slow my heart rate after adrenaline has kicked in. The beeping slows immediately, the pattern returning to a steady beat. It's a heart monitor—I can hear the beeping of my heart monitor from the other side.

"Aubrey?" The voice is clearer now, and this time, I know who it belongs to—Tapley.

My heart begins to race again, and the beeping quickens. *Look at my monitor, Tapley! I can hear you—just look at it.*

This time, though, my heart doesn't slow. Its beat keeps increasing until its sound grows hazy, and my mind is suddenly jolted into a whirlwind of oblivion. I'm being pulled backward out of one reality, and a second later, my eyes open into another. I'm back in the room I fell asleep in—back to the white nightgown and oversized wardrobe, the reality of a world I don't belong in.

"So much for a good night's sleep." I pull back the covers and set my feet on the cold wood floor of the bedroom.

Making my way to the window, I see a faint trail of smoke coming from the barn's fireplace and hints of dim candlelight still shining at one end of the building. Tapley must still be waiting on the mare to foal. With everyone in the house now asleep, I could sneak down to the barn unnoticed, but a strange feeling in the back of my mind stops me.

Earlier in the barn, time slowed to the speed of a waltz, and the slowness and closeness between us erased all my worry and fear. When our eyes were locked into each other's stare, the weight of the secret I was carrying dissipated into nothing—like I was able to share it with him without a single word. It was the best feeling in the world, but something about the intensity of that moment was enough for one night.

There's a chance I might wake up from all this at any time, but there's also a chance I won't. The year 1836 might be my new state of permanence. I try not to think about all the people I left behind—my parents, Paige, Porter. My entire life was gone in a single flip of my truck, and now I'm stuck in a time when trucks don't exist, and the only person who I may have once called a friend only feels the pain of a broken heart when he looks at me. A heart I didn't break. One I would never break.

"What a mess." I exhale a warm breath into the cold room as I gaze out into the dark countryside.

I grab my long wool coat from its place in the wardrobe and slide it on as I quietly make my way downstairs. The embers from the evening's fire are barely glowing in the stone cradle of the fireplace at the center of the room, and the creaking of the floorboards is reminiscent of every child's worst haunted-house nightmare. I reach for one of the metal lanterns, its candle extinguished and the white wax hardened. Walking to the fireplace, I tilt the candle into the faintly burning embers and pray that there's still enough heat to light the wick. It lights after a few seconds. I place it back inside the safety of its metal container and make my way to the large desk in the corner of the room.

George's personal ledger is still lying across the center of the desk, along with numerous piles of other handwritten pieces of parchment. He's a cattle broker, buying and selling livestock to people in the area. George and Charlotte live a good life in a time when good lives are hard to establish and even harder to hold onto. They've built their family a solid place in this town, and if I had been born into their family, instead of thrust into someone else's life, I'm sure I would have grown up loving them.

As much as I try to be their daughter, I can't let go of the fact that I'm someone else's daughter—I'm someone else entirely. I put on the dresses hanging in the wardrobe, and I try to stay inside the exact footprints that Aubrey Harrison left behind, but I can't help but feel like I've already stepped outside the lines a few too many times. *If she came back to her life tomorrow, would she even recognize it?* She's not me, or I'm not her—I'm truly not sure which, but as long as I'm living her life and breathing air into her lungs, it has become my life... and it might be the only life I have left to live.

My fingers brush over the slick surface of the desk as I try to memorize every little detail I come across. The room smells like cedar and smoked meats, but there's also a hint of sweetness in the air. I can smell lavender amid the earthiness, which I attribute to Charlotte and her bags of herbs hanging in the kitchen. As much as I feel like a stranger in this house, the smell of lavender is familiar. It reminds me of the lavender iced tea my grandmother used to serve when the Texas heat soared above one hundred degrees. Pieces of the life I had in the future have somehow followed me here—or maybe they started here in the first place. I'm a living, breathing personification of the chicken-or-egg conundrum.

I turn to the shelf behind the desk and scan the dull-colored spines of the old books. I don't know if I'm looking for anything in particular, but my gaze stops when it finds a dark-gray book tucked away on the top row. "Harrison Family" is written across the spine in faint gold print.

I reach out and gently tug it away from the rest of the tightly packed books. Before I can lay it on the desk, something tips over from where it had been carefully tucked away next to the book. A small wood-framed portrait now rests facedown. I place the book down on the desk and pick up the frame, hoping I didn't break it. There's a young man with brown curls and striking dark eyes who looks to be around the same age as I am. He's wearing simple clothes—a dark coat and collared shirt against a pale background.

I turn the portrait over, careful not to leave my fingerprints on the front.

Thomas B. Harrison, 1813–1834.

"Tommy," I whisper, trying to remember what Tapley said about the young man.

He mentioned something about me blaming him for Tommy's death—telling him that he should have died instead of Tommy. Everything is beginning to make sense, and the mystery of this life I've stepped into is becoming more and more tragic each day I wake up as the 1836 Aubrey Harrison. There's faint writing below the dates on the back of the picture, and I try to make out the small cursive handwriting.

"Died in the San Antonio River on October 5, 1834." I read the words out loud, trying to picture the San Antonio River. There is a river running through the center of present-day San Antonio, but I've never seen the water move fast enough to be of any danger. The San Antonio River I know has cement, restaurants, bars, and hotels lining either side. The River Walk is a tourist attraction, not a rushing river of tumultuous speed or danger. *What could've happened there that killed Tommy, and why did Tapley take the blame?*

I carefully stick the painting back on the shelf and turn my attention back to the book on the desk. As I begin flipping through its pages, I find decades of family history—details from the year George and Charlotte settled in San Antonio. The Harrisons were one of the "Old Three Hundred"—the first three hundred families in Texas—and their family history in Texas dates all the way back to 1822.

Turning the page, I find names and ages of the Harrison family members in 1817, when they still lived in Virginia. I form a family portrait in my mind, imagining a much younger George standing with his hand resting on the shoulder of beautiful Charlotte. Sitting in her lap is a curly-haired little girl who can't be more than two, and standing to Charlotte's right is a brown-haired boy only a few years older. This page in their family history was written just a few years before they settled in San Antonio.

Flipping through a few more pages, I find a section about the very first Settlers Day celebration in February of 1825. In February of each year, the small group of immigrant settlers in Mexican San Antonio put on the celebration. If this event is happening tomorrow, that means I'm in February 1836.

I swallow hard, a lump forming in my throat as I'm suddenly overwhelmed with tears. Even though I'm no longer living as a college student in the twentieth century, I remember seeing the date on the ledger the very first night I woke up in the house, but I must have been too overwhelmed to put the pieces together. Now that being stuck in the 1800s is something I've had a few days to wrap my mind around, I can see things clearly—I can see how close I am to unavoidable danger.

"March 6, 1836," I whisper, my voice barely audible as the mere sound of my words sets my hair on end. I know what happens to this town—to these people—and it's not good. In fact, it's one of the most tragic events in the history of our country.

"All those people," I choke, not because my heart is breaking for them but because soon my heart will be breaking *with* them. I'm about to face the same fate.

The Battle of the Alamo is right around the corner, and I have absolutely no way to stop it. I have to get out of here—back home to my own time.

Taking the lantern in my hand, I find where I left my leather shoes near the bottom of the stairs and push them quickly onto my feet. I try to pull open the front door quietly, and I freeze at the slightest squeak of the wooden frame. Holding my breath, I squeeze through the tiny opening in the door then quietly shut it behind me.

I head in the direction where everything started—where dirt, hooves, and a pair of unforgettable hazel eyes greeted me a few days ago. *There must be a way back,* I repeat over and over again in my mind, wishing the words would lead me to the answers I am searching for. I find my way to the empty, quiet round pen outside of the barn.

Shouldn't there be a ripple in the air or a tingle in my skin? I know there is something here that will take me home. I jump a few times, testing the ground. If I jump hard enough, I *could* fall back through. But the ground doesn't give way to a dark hidden hole. The only hole I see is the one created in the dirt from my frantic, hopeful jumping.

"There has to be," I whisper into the silent night air around me, but nothing responds—no feeling of electricity or even a rush of air from my distant future. *What if there is no way home?*

I stomp my boot against the cold, hard dirt, remembering how solid it felt when I hit my head. Maybe a sharp crack against the dirt would wake me from this nightmare. As the thought circles in my mind, I can feel the sharp ache of pain return in the back of my head. *Ouch.* I rub the base of my neck. I don't think I'm quite recovered from the last time I hit the dirt, or maybe I'm still feeling the ache of concrete and glass from when I flew from my old truck—the truck I will never drive again.

That cruel realization sends a sharp feeling through my chest. If my breath weren't visible in the cold air around me, I would have thought I'd stopped breathing entirely. Shivering, I pull my wool coat closer around my body and leave behind any hope I had of finding a way home in the round pen as I walk away.

I have to tell them. I need to warn them about what's coming. But the idea falters as every cliché time-travel rule tries to change my mind. *Altering the past means changing the future. What if those changes directly impact my reality? How much would history change if I stopped the coming war?*

I just need a few days to think this through. I head in the direction of the barn. There's no longer smoke coming from the fireplace, and I can barely see a faint trace of light.

Maybe Tapley has finally gone to bed for the night.

My shoes crunch against the frosted grass, and my warm breath breaks through the chill as I leave a light trail of fog behind me. I slide open the barn door and hold my lantern in front of me as I take a step into the darkness. Most of the horses are quietly standing with droopy heads and closed eyes as they sleep.

As I come upon the stall where the mare was in foal a few hours earlier, I nearly trip over a dark bundle lying across the ground. Shining my light at the dirt floor below me, I find Tapley sleeping on the cold dirt as he stays close to the mare and her newborn foal. It's dark in the stall, but I see the tiny foal curled up in a pile of hay below its mother's feet.

The combined cuteness of dozing foal and sleeping Tapley is just about killing me. I try not to giggle as I glance back down at his head resting on his arm and the peaceful look on his face. He shivers, and I take a step back, afraid that I woke him. A moment later, he settles back into his quiet slumber. I find myself unable to take my eyes off him.

Something about him settles me. Even asleep, he somehow has a magical way about him. The worry that took over my mind not a few minutes before is turned off—almost as if he's the white noise I needed to calm myself.

He has to be freezing. The only thing keeping him warm is the wool blanket that he wrapped around me earlier. "I guess it's my time to return the favor," I whisper and shimmy out of my warm gray coat. I gently lay it over the top half of his body, and a few seconds later, his shivering settles.

I turn around to leave, but the barely lit fire in his small room catches my eye. I quietly walk around him and head in the direction of the fireplace. There's a small stack of logs piled on one side of the stone structure, and I toss a few of them on the dying embers. I wait a few minutes, hoping the logs catch, and I feel rather proud of my handiwork when new flames eagerly warm the room. I push the metal grate in front of the opening to guard the room from any sparks that might stray from the safety of the fireplace.

As I make my way out of the room, I see a small stack of old yellowing paper sitting on a corner table by the empty cot. I walk over to it, and my heart begins racing in its small crevice in my chest when I find my own image on the pages. Tapley has etched the details of my face, the subtle shape of my long curls, and the gentle slope of my jaw as it meets my neck in exquisitely perfect detail. The shading is remarkable. I've never felt more beautiful than the way he's drawn me on the pages I'm holding in my hand.

A part of me wonders if I've intruded on something he never wanted me to see, but another part of me now wants to understand everything about this man. *How can someone who feels pain every time he looks at me draw me so beautifully as if my words have never hurt him and my selfish ambitions have never led me to toss away his love? How can he create these images of someone he thinks he'll never have again?*

I glance back at where he's sleeping, and I begin to see him differently. I begin to see the purity of his soul as if it's the only bright burst of color in my pale and dismal gray world. People like him don't exist in real life, yet the person who drew these pictures is completely and undeniably real to me... more real than I am to myself.

CHAPTER EIGHT

I've been to plenty of parties in my life—fraternity formals, college mixers, history club events, family reunions, and even a prom or two—but never in my wildest dreams would I have imagined myself wearing Western-style dresses, lace-up boots, and ribbons. To top it all off, there will be a wagon pulled by the handsome bay draft horse I met a few days ago. If I've had any firsts that top my list of unusual life events, Settlers Day is now number one.

I've apparently overslept on that monumental morning because Charlotte is already knocking at my door just a few hours after sunrise. "Why are you still in bed? There's so much to do this morning, and we still need to make it to the square before noon," she sings, pulling the covers back and tossing a deep-green bundle of fabric in my lap.

"I thought the events started at four o'clock." I yawn, suddenly remembering how little I actually slept last night.

"Yes, but the other women are expecting us to help them finish the last-minute preparations the same way we help them every year." She reaches into the trunk at the foot of the bed and pulls out a pair of white lace shoes with a slight heel on the bottom. "Besides, this year, Settlers Day will represent a new era in this town. Today, we will celebrate the Texans' victory at the Battle of Bexar."

"I'm getting dressed... *now*?" I look at her and try to hide another yawn.

"Of course, Aubrey." She lifts her eyebrows and crosses her slim arms across her chest. "Sometimes you act so peculiar."

Charlotte is already dressed for the evening, her pale-blue outfit standing out against her dark hair and fair skin. The color makes her look younger, more like the woman I saw in the portrait. I pull myself out of bed, pick up the green dress she gave me, and shuffle in her direction.

"Aubrey, your *hair*. There's hay in your hair." She pinches a single piece of hay from my hair with her thumb and pointer finger then drops it onto the wood floor.

I can tell she's looking for an explanation, but she probably knows that I don't have one. She doesn't respond to my silence on the matter. Instead, she bustles around the room, pulling various items from drawers and dressers that I haven't even explored yet.

My knowledge of mid-1800s attire has greatly improved over the last three days. Now that I'm up, I'm able to quickly dress myself without standing naked in the center of the room like a lost sheep that's just been shorn. I try not to fumble as I pull on each layer of clothing: awful white corset thing, white lace stockings, starched petticoats, and finally, the long-sleeved green dress.

Charlotte wastes no time as she begins the arduous task of closing me in, button by button, and I watch my already thin silhouette change from small to tiny. There's quite a noticeable difference between today's dress and the simple cotton ones I've been enduring. The fabric is thicker, with hand-stitched rickrack forming small patterned leaves in a shade subtly lighter than the delicate sleeves and the bottom of the hem. It's still very simple, but it possesses a graceful elegance that my usual minimalistic fashion tastes can appreciate. It's totally me—meaning that I can completely pull this dress off and feel absolutely myself in it.

"We must do something with your hair." Handing me the brush, she forces an optimistic smile across her face and turns her attention to a small wooden box beside the mirrored table.

My hair is undeniably a mess, but it's not an entirely lost cause. I look down at the brush then back up at my reflection in the mirror.

"I really need you to burst in and save the day, Paige," I mumble.

"What was that?" Charlotte looks up from tinkering with the hair combs in the box.

"Nothing," I respond.

But my mind is still on Paige. She would know exactly what to do in a situation like this. The best I can do right now is try to think like her. My progress with the brush goes better than I expect, and soon enough, the knots have been tamed, revealing loose brown curls.

"Better!" Charlotte smiles as she hands me a silver hair comb with delicate floral detailing along the top. "My brother gave me this hair comb on the morning I married your father." She starts to move her hands through my long hair, organizing it at the back of my neck. "I wish you could have known him. You are more like him than you know. His name suits you well." She pauses and looks at me for a few long seconds in the mirror.

"But why did you name *me* after him? Shouldn't his name have been for my brother?" I ask, unsure if my question crossed a line.

"Your uncle died after Thomas was born. It was George's idea to pass his name to our next child. When you were born, your father kept his promise. You were given the name Aubrey even as a girl." She pulls the last few stray curls back into line.

I can feel a lump growing in my throat though I'm unsure of why her words are of any impact. I hardly know George and Charlotte, but each day I'm held in the past takes me further into their world—into *their* lives.

"I see. I hope I carry his name well," I reply, letting a smile cross my face to hide my uncertainty about who I am and where I've come from as my two lives start to blur together.

"Please hand me the comb." She rests her open palm on my shoulder as I hand her the silver hairpiece she once wore in her own brown curls. Carefully sliding the comb into my hair, Charlotte releases a contented sigh. "Much better... I will see you downstairs. I need to finish preparing a few things before your father brings us to town."

Alone in my room, I turn to the side and admire Charlotte's handiwork in the mirror. "If I had curls this perfect in college, I would've gotten at least an extra half hour of sleep every morning." A satisfied smile crosses my face, and for the first time, I notice the vibrant jade color of my eyes against the deep green of the dress. Charlotte sure knows how to pick a gown for a party.

Let's just hope I don't have to dance.

THE SETTLEMENT OF SAN Antonio is nothing like I ever imagined. I can't even remember the number of times growing up that I walked through the huge downtown of that modern Texas city. As I sit quietly on the wagon, I can almost envision the high-rise buildings and the faint sound of laughing tourists and mariachi music coming from the River Walk.

There are small buildings—some of stone and some of stucco—lining either side of the dirt road, which is busy with passing riders on their sweaty horses and stray lines of loud-mouthed livestock as they're driven in herds into town. It's like every old Western movie I watched growing up but more rustic—more Hispanic in its architecture.

George steers the horse and wagon around a gentle corner in the road, and as he pulls it to a stop near the center of town, I can see a small gray stone fortress sitting quietly in the distance. The Alamo. She's beautiful in her untouched form, before the turmoil and death that will soon poison her sweet soil. A week ago, I would have given anything to go back in time for a single moment to see pieces of history like this, but a lot has changed in a week. Now I would give anything to go home—to just go back to a few days before the madness began.

George steps down from the front of the wagon and offers his hand to both Charlotte and me as we awkwardly try to step onto the ground in our dresses.

"I'll be back with Tapley in a few hours." He smiles and kisses his wife's cheek sweetly.

With my arms full of baskets containing an assortment of fresh breads and cooked vegetables, I follow Charlotte in the direction of a stone building situated behind a towering oak tree with branches so heavy they've begun to grow toward the ground in a tangled web of ancient wood. I try to keep my white shoes from catching in the hem of my dress as I carefully make my way up a few steps leading to a pair of large double doors surrounded by open windows on either side. As soon as we walk in the room, at least a dozen other women in their best dresses come flooding right to us and take the baskets from our hands. I stand stunned for a moment, trying to take in how quickly everyone is moving.

"Aubrey, there you are," a blonde chimes from across the room. I try to look away from her, but I'm not quite fast enough.

Oh crap... she's coming over here. Normally, I wouldn't try to run away from people at a party, but she clearly knows who I am, and I have no clue who she is.

"Where have you been? I missed you at Mass the other day. I have so much to tell you. Wait... didn't you fall off your horse or something?" She says all of this in a single breath.

Oh great. Another person in my life who doesn't stop talking.

"Good afternoon, Mrs. Harrison." She smiles sweetly and curt-sies even faster than she speaks.

"Good evening, Ella. It's nice to see you again," Charlotte says be-fore she heads in the direction of a group of older women who are busily laying out food on top of large wooden tables with matching lace tablecloths.

"So... what happened?" Ella is still looking at me.

"Um, well, I'm doing okay, and yes, I fell off my horse, but I'm fine... I think. Is that what you wanted to know?"

I look at her, worried, but she returns my look with a big smile, links her arm through mine, and pulls me in the direction of an empty table in front of one of the open windows. She glances at me peculiarly but resumes talking the moment we sit down. I try to keep up with her gossip, but I find my attention turning to the busy street outside.

"Do you think there are more of them this week?" she asks, a nervous tone suddenly clouding her bubbly demeanor.

"More of who?" I shift my eyes to hers.

"Mexican soldiers, of course. That's what you were looking at just now, right?"

I didn't actually notice the Mexican soldiers until she brought them up—I guess the entire scene of 1836 San Antonio has been enough of a distraction for me to miss them completely. I turn my attention back to the busy streets, and I easily find the dark-red-and-navy uniform of the Mexican militia. I know that the Texas settlers were granted permission to live here by the Mexican government, but something about the presence of those soldiers on soil I've grown up knowing to be American sends a sick feeling of dread crawling up my spine.

"They're everywhere," I mutter as I watch a small group of them traveling down the street on horseback.

There's a handsome dark-haired man at the front of the group, the crisp navy uniform tunic accented with gold buttons and tasseled epaulets. His white pants and black boots are so polished that they actually catch the sunlight and reflect it in a metallic glare. There's a large red section of fabric across his chest and a broad-brimmed felt hat on top of his dark hair. He turns his head in my direction as if he feels my eyes burning a hole into him from the safety of the stone building. His face is set in a tense and angry line, and his bold, sinister eyes are so dark that they're almost black.

I turn away quickly, but I can feel his eyes lingering in my direction.

"You heard the rumor that James Bowie arrived in town a few weeks ago, right? I wonder if he'll be here tonight?" Ella asks.

If James Bowie is already here, then the siege of the Alamo is nearly upon us.

Fortunately, Ella changes the subject. "So... will Robert be your escort tonight?" She almost shakes with excitement as she folds her hands across her peach-colored dress.

"Yes, Robert will be here." The words feel painful as the reality of this evening's company begins to settle in my mind.

"Don't sound so joyful," Ella says, lifting her eyebrows and pulling her full lips together into a tight line. "You are going to marry into the wealthiest family in this town, and you find the thought of him worse than curdled milk. Any girl here would take your place in a heartbeat, just so you know." Her scowl lightens up into the fakest smile I've ever seen.

It's good to know that females had the ability to be catty a long time before Greek life hit college.

"You're right. I'm more than lucky to be engaged to such a rich and eligible man," I lie. Something about my deception makes me feel one step closer to becoming the person they all see when they look at me.

Ella certainly seems to buy it. "Oh, Aubrey, he's such a great dancer. I wish half the fellows in this town were as good as him." She eyes the large empty space at the center of the room, and I suddenly realize exactly what the point of Settlers Day is.

It's a bloody town dance. I have to dance. Tonight.

Another group of girls my age walks through the double doors, and Ella is immediately on her feet and headed in their direction. Sitting alone at the table, I try not to hyperventilate. There are a lot of things I will tolerate out of pure courtesy, but dancing is something I just don't do. When Porter and I would go out dancing with friends, the floor was always so packed with people that I could get away with being less than mediocre. Then again, I also had Porter to lead me, and I trusted him not to let me fall.

Robert's arms around me might be the worst thing I'll have to endure—ever. I can't believe I'm engaged to that man. One day soon, he'll be expecting me to do more than just dance with him. I try not to imagine him grunting on top of me, but once the thought crosses my mind, I can't remove it, no matter how painstakingly miserable it is.

There'd better be alcohol at this shindig—lots of alcohol.

"Aubrey, we need your help over here!" Ella yells from the corner of the room, surrounded by a large group of young women.

"I don't know how much help I'm going to be," I mutter and pull myself to my feet. As I walk across the room, I scan every table for signs of alcohol and say a silent thankful prayer when my eyes come across a tower of aged wooden barrels sitting against the wall in the corner.

I just hope they contain something strong.

CHAPTER NINE

The transformation that a group of women can create in just a few hours is quite impressive. With streams of colorful hanging flowers and perfectly placed metal lanterns on each table, the simple stone building has been transformed into an elegantly rustic space. There's a huge iron chandelier hanging from the ceiling with at least a hundred burning candles sending a warm and inviting glow into every corner of the room.

Though everything around me is beautiful, the thing I appreciate most is the feeling of friendship and familiarity that fills me when I'm among the people of this settlement. San Antonio isn't just a settlement built to thrive and grow on this land. It's also a community of people who look out for one another—a family. By the time the last candle is lit and people begin filling the room, I start to welcome Settlers Day.

I watch as the sun drops lower over the curved front of the Alamo in the distance. The view is breathtaking, yet the sight of the mission is also heartbreaking.

"Ah-hem," I hear from a few feet behind me, and I close my eyes as I turn around, fully expecting to see red-cheeked Robert staring at me condescendingly.

"Why are your eyes shut, Aubrey?" Tapley asks.

I quickly open my eyes, and I catch my cheeks warming as my gaze finds his. I've never seen a man so stunningly handsome, yet he appears simple and approachable at the same time. The way his hazel eyes shine with flecks of deep green while he looks at my dress makes him almost painfully desirable. His brown hair is neatly combed, and it seems a shade lighter against the charcoal gray of his pants and jacket. A bold black shirt shows beneath the gray. Something about seeing him in black reminds me of the time I saw him at Chilifest. The color suits him impeccably well.

"You look beautiful." His voice shakes a bit as the subtle hint of nerves surfaces—nerves he feels because he's looking at me.

"Thank you. You don't look so bad yourself." I smile at him but then suddenly realize that the modern compliment I just gave him might not be well received in this century. I clear my throat and try again. "What I meant to say is that you look irresistibly dapper."

Oh crap… that's not any better.

I stare at him, petrified, my cheeks growing hot. I fully expect him to turn around and walk in the other direction. Instead, his eyes sparkle as he studies my expression, and then his face breaks into a perfect smile.

He laughs. "I think I know what you're trying to say." He pauses, studying me. "Thank you, by the way—I mean thank you for the coat last night." As soon as the words leave his mouth, he turns and heads away from me.

Wait! I almost call after him, but I'm not sure what I would even say if he turned back toward me. As I watch him walk away, I exhale, praying that my skin is beginning to return to its normal shade, but then I catch his sweet scent as he moves past me. My cheeks now burn for a different reason.

"Aubrey. There you are." From the corner of my eye, I see Robert beelining in my direction. I plaster my newly perfected fake smile across my face just in time.

"My parents are waiting, darling." He holds out his arm, and I grudgingly take it.

He acknowledges almost every single person as he leads me across the room. My lips already hurt from smiling too much. I dread a reality as Porter's trophy wife. I'd be beautiful, silent, smiling—his very own hollow porcelain doll to smash at will. We stop just in front of a larger gray-haired man and a skinny, sour-faced woman whose blond hair has flecks of gray to match her husband's.

"Aubrey, dear, you look the picture of health. You had us quite worried after that fall of yours." The man's eyes linger a little too long on my chest as he places a wet kiss on my hand.

My stomach churns.

"The room looks exquisite, doesn't it, Mother?" Robert's eyes span the length of the room, checking over each and every detail as if he expected the complete opposite.

"It's quite lovely," the woman says in a curt tone, squinting.

Well, they're as pleasant as I imagined. I lock eyes with Robert's mother by mistake, and I can feel her judging my every move. Her petty smirk curves almost into a snarl as her nose twitches.

I turn my attention back to the room and try to ignore Robert as he starts on about one of the stories I've had to listen to a dozen times already. When he's not looking, I mouth his exact gloating words, pleased at myself for getting them perfectly right. He's at least as predictable as he is pretentious, though I'm sure he'd have a fit if he saw me silently mimicking him.

The room is buzzing as people gather beneath the romantic lighting of the chandelier. A small group of violinists sits next to a single harp player at the front of the room, playing methodic classical notes. Their stringed instruments have probably traveled here with the original families that settled here, and each of them is played with its own sense of cultured expression, yet the notes join together to create perfect harmony. This is what Settlers Day is about—the combination of people living and adapting in a new and exciting place.

Most of the men have cups full of bitter red wine, and a few lucky tables have glass bottles of whiskey resting in between plates of food. It's definitely a party, and except for Robert and his family, I find myself easily enjoying the festivities as if it's a completely natural place for me to be. Fortunately, Robert has yet to ask me to dance, but I have a feeling it will be an unavoidable event of the evening. He's currently standing with a handful of young men his age while they laugh and converse loudly on one side of the room.

I look around for Tapley, scanning the bodies for gray and black. The room is crowded, but I'm able to spot him sitting alone at a table on the other end of the room. His head is down as if he's intently studying something, but there's nothing in front of him but a lacy white tablecloth and a whiskey bottle. He's holding a glass half filled with brown liquid, and there's not a single person sitting with him. In fact, no one else even seems to notice that he's in the room.

Am I the only one who sees how handsome he is? I force my stare away from him before someone notices. At least a dozen single young women are just waiting to find their forever in one of the eligible men in the room, and as far as I know, Tapley is one of those men.

It's time to do some discreet Tapley-information digging with the gossip queen herself. Ella is standing at the edge of the dance floor a few yards away from me. As I make my way in her direction, I see her eyeing a light-haired man at a table nearby.

"See something you like?" I ask, nudging her playfully.

"I wish." She lets out a heavy sigh, watching as the man leads a brunette to the line of dancers.

"Come on. Someone here has to be worthy of your affection," I say.

She scans the room quickly, a slight frown interrupting her usual smiling face. "You know my family isn't as well off as yours, Aubrey. I need a man who can give me more than my parents ever gave me. They expect me to marry up, and that type of man is hard to come by in this town. It seems you snatched up the last one." She clamps her jaw closed, clearly holding some grudge against me and my unwelcome engagement.

Suddenly, I feel bad for being so disgusted by the thought of marrying Robert. I no longer live in a time period where I have the luxury of being picky about who I spend the rest of my life with. The roles could be reversed, and I could be looking at a life similar to Ella's—one with an uncertain future and the possibility of being alone forever.

"What about Tapley?" I point across the room to where he hasn't moved an inch.

She turns her head, her jaw almost hitting the floor as she gasps. "Of all people—I never thought the day would come when you actually tried to pass Tapley Holland on to one of your friends. The entire town knows he's cursed."

"Holland," I whisper as I watch Ella storm off in the opposite direction. She was clearly offended that I suggested someone she finds so intolerable.

Cursed. The word burns in my mind.

Another line of dancers is forming at the center of the room, and I can feel Robert walking up behind me before he even attempts to speak.

"Shall we?" He holds out his chubby hand, and I force myself to take it.

Let's get this over with. I have absolutely no idea what I'm doing, but I take my spot in line behind the rest of the women on the right side of the dance floor as they stand directly across from their partners.

Just do what they do, and try not to fall down.

The music starts, and luckily, it's an extremely slow song. The older woman next to me curtsies to her partner, and I do the same. In the horrible five minutes that follow, I turn circles with Robert at least twenty times, change direction another ten, change partners twice, and end right back up with Robert for the final turn. It's over almost as soon as it starts, yet the time moves slower than mud. I did it—it wasn't pretty by any means, but I managed to fake my way through my first dance in 1836 without making a fool of myself.

Robert takes my hand and leads me to the front of the room. At first, I think he is going to give his compliments to the small group of musicians, but then he turns to face the crowd and claps his hands to get their attention. People stop what they're doing, set down their drinks, and focus their attention on us.

Robert clears his throat and straightens his brown jacket before he speaks, his face turning a bit redder than usual. "I want to thank all of you for coming to this year's Settlers Day celebration. The small town of San Antonio has taken tremendous steps together in order for this city to grow. We've doubled our buildings, our crops, and the numbers of our livestock. We have families bringing more and more people into this town, and I can only dream of where we will be in ten years. Despite waves of conflicts with the Mexican Army, we still continue to thrive here, and I can only hope each year will bring peace within this diverse community." He hesitates, and a small smirk starts to grow at the corners of his mouth. It's the smirk he wore when he spoke to Tapley about coming to the Settlers event.

The hair on my arms begins to stand on end as a sick feeling boils in the pit of my stomach. Robert is about to do something bad, and I have no idea how to intercept it. All eyes in the room are still glued to him, and I hear a few people laughing from the far corner—the same group of men Robert was just standing with.

He clears his throat again. "I would also like to take a moment to introduce a special guest tonight. This particular guest came specifically for one of our own eligible young men. Tapley Holland, I would like to introduce you to the special lady I told you about." He eyes Tapley from across the room and motions to a man in front of the closed wooden doors.

The doors swing open, and a squealing pink piglet wearing a bonnet and tiny skirt runs into the room. Everyone scatters away from it.

"She's all yours for the night." He points to the animal as the high-pitched noise of its squeals fill the room. "If you can catch her, that is." People begin laughing at the joke, watching as the piglet weaves between the tables and underneath the women's long dresses.

My eyes find Tapley, and I watch him throw back the remaining whiskey in his glass, stand, and head in the direction of Robert and his friends. I can feel my blood boiling and my heart racing as Robert continues to laugh hysterically—the piercing hyena-like laugh that I've grown to hate in less than a week.

"What were you thinking?" I yell at Robert, taking a step closer.

At first, his glance bounces from person to person as if he's waiting for someone to scold me. When no one comes to his aid, he lets loose an arrogant rebuttal. "I was thinking that he should keep his eyes off you and focus on finding the type of female he deserves—the ones he can find in that barn he sleeps in."

I can't hold back my anger, and I can feel my hand pulling into a tight fist.

Don't punch him. You'll only hurt yourself.

I have a better idea. I release my balled fingers and slap his face as hard as I can, the impact sending needlelike pricks into my skin the instant the sound cracks through the room. There's now a bright-red handprint to match his angry red cheeks, and everyone is standing frozen, staring at me then moving their eyes back to Robert. Tapley stops in his tracks a few feet away from us with wide eyes and a confused expression.

For a split second, I'm sure Robert is going to slap me right back, but instead of taking his anger out on me, he lunges at Tapley and throws a hard fist into the side of his face. I watch as Tapley takes a step toward Robert, blood beginning to drip from his nose. *He's going to hit him back.* I start to panic, but just as I think things are about to get much worse, Tapley turns around and walks out of the room and into the darkness of the Texas night.

An awkward tension hangs over the room for a few seconds. Then the band begins playing again, forcing people to go about their business. Robert turns to me, about to unleash his flood of angry words right in my face.

"Don't—" I hold my finger up at him, turn my back, and walk away.

"Aubrey, wait," Charlotte calls.

I know she's following close behind me, but I don't stop. Heading straight for the door, I grab the half-full bottle of whiskey still sitting on Tapley's table and start into the darkness after him.

CHAPTER TEN

Tapley can't be too far ahead of me, but I have no idea where I'm going other than heading away from the soft music of the dance. Except for the faint glow coming from the stone building, the sleepy town is covered in a dreary shade of darkness.

"Aubrey, you mustn't rush off like that in the dark. Come back inside, and I'll send your father after Tapley." Charlotte catches me by the arm in the middle of the street.

"I have to find him. Robert did this to him, and I need to make it right. George... I mean, Father can't do that."

"You realize what everyone will think. You've rushed into the night after Tapley, leaving your fiancé inside. The Allcorts won't easily forgive this."

"And I won't ever forgive Robert for what he's done to Tapley," I respond desperately.

Charlotte studies my face, her brows tense, before her expression softens. "Something in you has changed, Aubrey. I don't see the anger in you that you had after Tommy's death. If Tapley is causing that change, then you should go after him. I will wait for you by the wagon so the rest of the town doesn't assume you've gone after him alone." She releases my arm and begins to walk away.

And a moment later, I'm alone in the middle of the dirt road. *She just left me to find Tapley—just like that?* The sound of footsteps against wood brings my thoughts back to the person I'm desperate to find.

"Tapley, please wait," I call down the empty road, hoping he can hear me.

Whiskey bottle still in hand, I start toward the center of town. The clicking of my white heels echoes against the stone buildings on either side of me. There are horses tied to wooden hitching posts and empty wagons resting in a long line as if the Wild West has stopped to rest.

"Tapley," I call again. I hear someone a few steps behind.

"Mother, I thought you were going to wait by the..." I spin on my heels and right into the hard chest of a person who definitely isn't Charlotte.

"Ouch," I mutter, reaching up to my throbbing forehead.

"Young women shouldn't be walking alone in the dark unaccompanied," the man says, chuckling as he helps steady me without asking my permission.

"I'm not alone. My mother is waiting at the wagon," I reply, my words getting lost somewhere in the cold air between the tall stranger and me.

I try to look up at him, but my eyes stop when I see the gold tassels on the shoulders of a deep-blue jacket with matching polished gold buttons and a pair of bright-white pants. *Mexican Army.* I force my eyes to his, surprised when I find the same dark stare and black hair of the man I saw riding through town earlier in the day. Standing only a few inches taller than me, he's much fitter than the majority of the soldiers he's been riding with. His face is clean-shaven, and his hair is tied back in a small ponytail at the base of his head. There's no doubt in my mind that he's exquisitely handsome, but something about him unnerves me.

"I'm looking for someone who just left the party." My words are nervous as I become more aware of the empty town around me.

The man's dark eyes shine as he studies me, a smirk steadily holding its ground across his face. "I find it odd that foreigners are allowed to have such an event in a Mexican settlement." His accent is strong, but he speaks English well enough.

Foreigners. In less than a month, you'll be the foreigner here. I hold back my remark through gritted teeth. "This event is for the people who've been allowed to settle here by your government—the people who've helped build this settlement. Mexican or not." I try to push past him, but he blocks my step.

I should remind him about who recently won the Battle of Bexar, but I'm not sure how legitimate the Texans' control of this town is. History is written by the victors, after all. If the Mexican Army still has a presence in the city, then I don't think the settlers ever stabilized their claim after they won in Bexar. Or maybe the Mexican Army only gave up control in order to regroup and prepare for something bigger—something like the Alamo.

"You have many ideas for a woman your age, yet you're still so pleasing to look at."

Had he made that comment in 2018, I'd be firing back all the feminist remarks I kept hidden from Porter. Once again, I find myself forcing my mouth to stay shut. I have no idea what kind of man I'm dealing with or what kind of things can happen when a woman speaks up against someone like him. I find myself offering a fake smile for the millionth time tonight, but now it hides the fear I'm feeling as I stand across from him. I could break the whiskey bottle over his head and make a run for it, but I don't think I can run fast enough in this dress.

"Aubrey, are you all right?" Tapley calls from somewhere in the darkness nearby.

"Excuse me—I need to go." I quickly turn around and find Tapley standing a few yards away, between two buildings.

Without waiting for the stranger's reply, I jog straight to Tapley, my scared eyes instantly finding his. The closer I get to him, the more I can see the look on his face—an angry, almost defensive glare clouding his hazel eyes as his mouth is pulled into a tense line. He wraps his arm around me and pulls me close as we head in the direction of the pitch-black alleyway he appeared from. I don't look back.

"Where are we going?" I try not to trip as we weave around piles of empty wooden crates.

"Do you trust me?" he whispers.

"Yes." My reply is instantaneous. If I trust *anyone* in this crazy life I'm stuck in, it's him.

We turn a sharp corner behind the back of one of the buildings, and Tapley pulls open a side door leading into a long one-story wooden building. I can already smell the sweet scent of hay and horses before I step into the large open space of the livery stable.

At least fifteen horses stand quietly in small stalls lining both sides of the large room. Bales of hay are stacked from floor to ceiling on one entire wall, and bags of oats make up another pile in the corner.

"Are we allowed to be in here?" I whisper, though I'm not exactly sure why I'm whispering.

"The horses won't tell if we won't tell." A sly smile crosses his face, and he winks at me. But then all the teasing fades away. "You have a bad habit of attracting terrible men, you know." Tapley sits down on the straw-covered floor and leans against the wall of hay bales behind him.

"Robert is one thing. However, the other man outside... he just appeared in the street when I was looking for you." I sit down beside him, still clutching the glass bottle.

He sighs heavily and takes the bottle from my hand. "May I? Unless you were planning on drinking alone..."

"Actually, I was bringing this for you. I was about to crack it across that soldier's skull if he didn't walk away from me." I giggle, rather proud of my backup plan.

"It's a good thing I got there before you had to waste perfectly good whiskey, then." Tapley takes a quick swig and sits quietly for a few minutes. I can hear the gentle sound of violins still playing a few buildings down. The Settlers party has picked right back up even after the stunt Robert pulled.

"It's hard to admit this out loud, especially when my nose is still burning from Robert's hand, but Colonel Amat is far worse than that monster fiancé of yours." He takes another swig. "For your own safety, Aubrey, promise me you'll stay away from that man."

I reach for the bottle, and this time, I take a hard drink of the sour whiskey. Then I take another. "I'm sorry about what Robert did to you. I wish I could've hit him harder. He deserves worse than I gave him." I pull my knees up to my face and rest my chin on top of them.

"I think you did a pretty good job of wounding his pride in front of a room full of people even if your hand didn't do much damage."

I can sense him smirking as he speaks, and I turn my head to look at him. "He's really quite awful. I don't know how I ended up—" The words get caught in my throat as I try to hide a quiet sob.

He reaches his arm around me and pulls me closer until my head is resting on his shoulder as I hold onto my knees.

"You don't owe me an explanation, Aubrey. I understand why things worked out the way they did." His voice is soft and soothing as he holds me, but he's wrong—he doesn't understand at all.

"Tapley, you don't get it." I try to find the right words as I pull my shoulders back and swivel to look at him.

He's staring at me, his eyes trying to read my every thought, studying each small movement I make. I gaze back at him. My heart is beating so quickly that I'm sure he can hear it.

"What don't I get, Aubrey?"

There's something magical about his voice when he says my name. It's so simple, yet him saying that one word is the most magnificent, beautiful sound I've ever heard.

"I wish I could just go back to when things were simpler—to when I didn't have to be this person everyone sees when they look at me."

If I'd said these words yesterday, they would have meant something else entirely. I would have been wishing to go back home to college and friends—to the life I lost the night of the accident. But as the words leave my mouth right this second, I'm wishing for something altogether different. I'm wishing to go back to the time Tapley was in love with me, the years before Tommy died and my engagement to Robert was even a possibility. I just want a chance to understand the feelings I have for Tapley rather than pretending I'm oblivious to their existence. If I'm destined to live this life, in 1836, I need to explore these feelings.

He doesn't say anything—he just looks at me silently—but I can see the wheels turning in his head.

Just speak! I need to know what you're thinking. The tension between us is overwhelming. I don't know what to say to him, but I long for him to say something—*anything*.

I take another long sip from the bottle, hand it back to him, and scramble to my feet. Tapley watches as I pace in a small circle a few feet away from him. Everything would seem so much simpler if I didn't have to carry around the weight of my true reality—the reality of where I really come from. But if I were back in my old life—my real life—would things really be that different? I'd be in another place where a version of Tapley exists, but I'd be tied to Porter.

I almost trip over my own feet as the truth comes crashing down around me. I wish to go back to a time before things between Tapley and me took a turn for the worse. In college, he was there in the background, but I never chose to see him because the blinding image of Porter was always in the way. If I'd met Tapley first, would Porter even be in the picture?

I've spent all this time hating the Aubrey Harrison whose life I've taken over, but she's really not so different from the Aubrey Harrison who was selfish enough to stay in a relationship with Porter because it was simple. *Easy.*

Statistically, I'm easy. Even in my mind, the words sound terrible. *What is wrong with me? I get to a fork in the road, where I have to make a decision, and I always decide wrong. But what if there isn't just one fork?* Maybe I've come to 1836 to do something different this time—something I should have already done before.

I look down at Tapley, who's still watching me with a strange look on his face.

"Dance with me." The words flow out effortlessly as if they've been waiting on the edge of my tongue for days.

"Here?" One of his eyebrows lifts the slightest bit, and I can see a smile lurking somewhere in his expression.

"Yes. Here." I stop pacing and wait for his next move.

He places the bottle on the ground, takes off his jacket, and takes slow, even steps in my direction. "Only if you put this on." He shakes the jacket at me. "It's getting cold in here."

Nothing about me feels cold right now. In fact, I feel just the opposite. I place one arm in each sleeve as he holds it open for me and pulls it over my shoulders. The familiar scent of him sends my heart racing again. It's a feeling I'm growing rather fond of. His hands linger on my shoulders for the smallest moment, and I can sense him thinking carefully about each and every move he makes, meticulously deciding when to touch me and when to linger.

I turn to face him, and he wraps one hand around the small of my back while the other reaches for my waiting hand. I can feel a subtle roughness to his skin as my fingers wrap around his, but the sensation is pleasantly comforting. He's not breakable. I place my free hand around his shoulder, and he begins leading me in a slow and steady waltz, our steps carrying their own tune against the music coming from down the street.

I'm conscious of each and every one of his ragged breaths. His chest comes closer to mine as he takes air into his lungs. I lean my head against it in the most natural move, my mind automatically telling me to move closer to him as if I've done it a thousand times before. We move to each other magnetically, my heart almost pausing for a single second just so it can synchronize with his. Nothing has ever felt like this before. It's the right kind of easy—not the kind you hide behind because it's safe, but the kind you run to as fast as you can before it dissipates entirely.

His grip around me tightens, and even though we're still lost in a dance together, it feels like we're one person, one body. We stay like this through the entire song, moving yet growing closer, and when the music no longer seeps into the room around us, he still doesn't let me go. I can feel his hands trembling as he holds my waist, and his breathing grows shallow.

"Are you all right?" I keep my head where it is, listening to his heartbeat.

"I don't know," he whispers, his lips close enough to my ear that I can feel their vibration as he speaks.

"Don't hold everything in so much, Tapley. You're so careful with what you say, but I promise you that I'm not as fragile as you think I am." This time, I force my head away from his chest and look straight into his eyes, my arms still wrapped around him.

"Aubrey, you've always been the strong one—it's me that I'm worried about. I'm worried that the moment I let you go, I'll break into a million pieces all over again." His eyes pull away from mine, and he lets out a jagged breath.

"Then don't let go." Four words—it's all I can say with a stomach full of butterflies.

"There's something else..." His eyes turn back to mine, and this time, there's something bolder about them.

I wait for him to speak, though I'm afraid to hear his confession. I feel like this is the moment when the bomb will be dropped—when he'll say, *I want you, but it's better if I walk away now.*

"I'm waiting to come up with a reason why I shouldn't kiss you right now." He loosens his hold on me ever so slightly, but I can feel his fingers gripping the fabric of my dress harder.

"Any luck?" I force the question out of my mouth as I feel a warm flash surfacing in my cheeks.

"No."

The word explodes inside me like fireworks. "How long are you planning on waiting—for a reason, that is?" I mutter, and this time my fingers are gripping his black shirt tighter.

"Until you tell me to stop waiting for a reason." The intensity of his gaze spreads a fire through my body.

"Stop waiting." I can't get the words out fast enough. I've just given him every reason to do exactly what we both want him to do.

Tapley doesn't hesitate. He runs his fingers along the base of my neck and up to my chin then tilts my face up to his. His fingers linger on my jaw before his lips urgently find mine. For a single second, his kiss is hard, tense—but then he relaxes, and I can feel him giving in to the feelings he's been fighting. Somehow, we've finally made it to the emotions we should have never forgotten.

The single touch of our lips is enough to ease the longing of the last few minutes, but as his lips part and his eyes open to mine, I find myself wanting more—needing more. My fingers tangle into his hair. I breathlessly pull him toward me, and he doesn't stop me. This time, his lips are sweet, but his mouth is even sweeter, the taste of him unlike anything I've ever experienced. He runs his hands down my back, and even with a layer of fabric separating his skin from mine, I melt, and he's there to catch me as my knees weaken. I feel him lift

me off my feet, holding my body to his as our lips remain unbreak-
ably connected. I wrap my arms around his neck as he supports me
effortlessly. Kissing him with my feet off the ground is the closest I'll
ever come to the blissful sensation of flying—it's the closest I'll ever
be to heaven as I'm stuck between my two worlds. I never want to
leave. This is the world in which I get to love him.

CHAPTER ELEVEN

The wagon ride home tonight is a blur. My emotions try to pour outward like a beautifully unstoppable fountain for the entire world to see, but I can tell by the stone-faced expressions of Charlotte and George that my feelings are better left inside the safety of my own mind. Charlotte sits next to George as he guides the horse and wagon in the direction of the house a few miles outside of town. Neither of them speaks about what happened during the Settlers dance, but I know my actions will have consequences for me and possibly even for them as well.

Tapley is sitting close enough next to me that he doesn't feel far away, but he's not too close. What happened back in the livery stable is between us, but our lips did a good job of telling each other exactly where our feelings have brought us: together. George has blankets for each of us for the cold ride home, and underneath the safety of the dark-blue quilt, Tapley's hand wraps around mine. Every so often, I turn to look at him ever so subtly, a slow and blissful feeling coming over me. As I look at him right now, his eyes are closed, and he looks more at peace than when I saw him sleeping in the barn last night. It's as if all his pain and worry is finally gone—he looks more breathtaking in his moment of uninterrupted happiness than I've ever seen him. He's my own Adonis, the foundation of everything in my world, making me want to remain here in this strange place—a place that's now as much mine as it is his.

His eyes open slowly, shining in the darkness as they mirror the millions of stars in the Texas sky above us. He smiles at me and wraps his fingers tighter around mine. I don't want this night to end and force me into a place where I have to be away from him for a single second, and as George turns the wagon down the long driveway to the house, I wish I could freeze time to this exact moment.

The horse brings the wagon to an abrupt stop outside of the barn doors, and George quickly stands. Tapley's fingers loosen around mine, and my heart nearly stops as he moves away from me. He jumps out of the wagon and holds his hand out to help me to the ground next to him. George is already removing the leather harness from the horse, and Charlotte is nearing the front porch of the house, her arms filled with empty baskets. I reach my hand out to Tapley and jump to the ground. As he faces me, he places his hands on either side of my waist, his lips grazing my forehead in the only sentiment of goodbye he can express. Before I can turn away from him, he leans his face next to my ear and whispers words that I feel like I've been waiting on forever.

"I never stopped loving you, Aubrey." He pauses for only a second and then releases me, leaving both of us breathless.

I almost call after him—the words I'm holding back are fighting to be released from the tip of my tongue. I don't know how or when these emotions happened to me, but I know without a doubt that I love him more than I can even comprehend. It's a strange feeling, yet it isn't new or unexpected. I've said the words *I love you* before—but they've never been this powerful, this real.

My feet drag as dead weight as I force them to move away from where I'm standing. I need to make it to the house before I fall apart completely—before George begins to suspect something that I feel like the whole world can already see. Maybe it's still just Tapley and I who know, but the way I love him isn't something I want to hide for the rest of my life, especially when I know the fate of this town—*our fate.*

With shaking hands, I find the front-door handle and push into the warmth of the house. I can hear Charlotte in the kitchen, but I don't want to give her the chance to ruin this night by bringing up the *slap heard around the room*. I pull off my white heels and leave them at the bottom of the stairs so I can tiptoe up them.

As I walk into my room, I find its silence and privacy a relief. I shut the door and make my way to the window looking out over the barn. The wagon is now empty and resting to the side of the corral, and George is nowhere to be seen. I find Tapley brushing the big bay draft as it stands quietly in front of the barn doors. I watch him for a few minutes as he tends to the animal attentively, smoothing out the areas underneath where the harness was attached. Just as he's about to put the horse away for the night, he pauses and turns in the direction of my window. With his free hand, he brings his fingers to his lips then touches the space on his chest just above where his heart is resting. I look back at him and mimic his gestures, my hands moving from my lips to my heart as if they already know the motions.

It's dangerous for us to be in love during a time like this—it's unexpected. But I want this more than anything I've ever wanted before, and I can barely breathe just thinking about it. We'd be like fire and gasoline—igniting and burning until there was nothing left in our world but blackened ashes beneath a cover of smoke.

I WAKE UP EARLY THIS morning, not really knowing what to expect or how to act. Last night, when I was only thinking about Tapley and me, things were much simpler, and I felt like I could finally think clearly. I still have to face the reality of Robert and both of our actions at the Settlers party yesterday. I expect him to have an endless flow of angry words and red cheeks for me at some point, but I have just as many things to say to him, as well. When all of this blows up, I plan on telling him how petty, jealous, and immature he is for pulling that prank, and then I plan on breaking off our engagement. Even if I weren't in love with Tapley, I would rather spend the rest of my life alone as a wrinkled old maid than grow sour and hateful, like Robert's mother, because I'm forced to marry a monster.

I dress quickly and head downstairs to a quiet house. I can smell barley and peppered beef cooking in the kitchen, but there's no sound of Charlotte or George yet. Sneaking out the front door and toward the barn, I have to keep my feet from running, which can be quite dangerous in these inconveniently long dresses. There's still a thick layer of fog in the air, and the sun hasn't quite broken over the hill-country backdrop. I can hear the horses stirring from inside the barn, and I'm hoping Tapley is awake.

I pull the heavy cedar door open, I slide inside, and pause to let my eyes adjust to the dim light. The familiar bay sticks his head out of his stall and bobs it in the air a few times as if to get my attention.

"Oh, good morning to you, too, handsome." I walk over to him and scratch his neck.

"I hope you're talking about me." Tapley's voice comes from somewhere behind me, startling me.

I take a deep breath before turning around, hoping to calm the racing speed of my heart. Before I can move, I feel his hands around my waist as he places the smallest, gentlest kiss on the side of my neck. If his arms weren't around me, I would have crumbled to the ground beneath his touch.

"Good morning." I turn to look at him over my shoulder, and his face breaks into a smile. I turn to face him and wrap my fingers around his. We exhale at the same time, and puffs of air hover in the chill around us.

"You're up early." His eyes are intently set on mine.

"I couldn't sleep any longer." It's the truth. There's a proverbial clock hanging over my head, counting down the seconds with an annoying loud click, a constant reminder of what little time I have left—time I don't want to waste sleeping.

"Neither could I. I didn't get much sleep at all."

"Would that be my fault?" I smirk, bringing my hand to the side of his face, my thumb tracing his jaw.

"Yes and no. Even if I wanted to close my eyes and stop thinking about you for just an hour, I was afraid that I'd wake up to you telling me that I have to forget about last night. I'm so worried that your feelings for me will pass as quickly as they returned. When I saw you standing here just now, I'd already prepared myself that you were here to say goodbye." His eyes break from mine as they turn to stare down at the floor.

"Tapley, I'm not here to say goodbye." I wrap my arms around his neck, and he pulls me to his chest, the warmth of his body instantly igniting my own skin. "I'm here to say good morning."

"Good morning, Aubrey," he whispers, and I rest my head on his shoulder.

I know I'm here for another reason, too, but I'm almost afraid to say the words out loud, because once I do, I can never go back to my old life. Once I say them, I become 1836 Aubrey Harrison forever. No one before him, not even Porter, has ever taken my mind off who I used to be or made me want to forget everything I've left behind.

"There's something else," I stammer, my heart beating so loudly that I almost can't think above its deep bass line—as if it's gasping for air. I'm ready to show him that my heart is real, to share my secret for a chance to get lost in these feelings with him.

I keep my head resting against his shoulder, afraid that his deep eyes will calm my nerves and make giving myself up to this obscure reality that much easier. He doesn't push the words out of me. He just waits until I'm ready.

You might not get another chance at this, Aubrey.

"I can't say that I never stopped loving you because I don't know if that's true or not. But what I do know is that I love you now, and I love you more than I ever loved you before."

"Say it again." His voice is barely above a whisper this time.

I pull my head off his shoulder and gaze up at him. His face is hard to read, almost as if he's lost in his thoughts.

"I love you, Tapley." My words are confident this time. I don't need to embellish how I feel with anything extra because the fact of the matter is that I love him—it's that simple.

His eyes brighten, almost glowing as he brings his forehead to mine, and we stand toe to toe, face to face with each other. "Again." He smirks, almost swaying me back and forth in the barn aisle.

I shoot him one of my sly *Oh, really?* glances, biting my bottom lip as I try to keep a serious face. "Are you forcing me to make up for all the time I've ignored you?"

"Possibly." He takes in a sharp breath and begins pushing me back to the stall wall behind us.

One hand grips the small of my back while he tangles the fingers of his other hand in my long hair. As soon as I feel the wall pressed hard against my back, he brings his lips to mine, the sweet scent of his breath making me dizzy as I part my lips and try to remind myself to keep breathing. The way he kisses me today is different—less desperate and unsure. He knows how I feel about him. He knows that last night isn't something I'm going to ask him to forget about. With each brush of our lips and touch of our tongues, our breathing grows more rapid and our bodies press harder into each other. I know the familiar feeling growing in the pit of my stomach, and I know the path it usually leads to.

How far had Tapley and Aubrey taken their love? The way he kisses me makes me think the feeling of me isn't brand-new to him. He knows every move my lips are going to make, and he responds to each one as if he's done it a thousand times. His hand traces my side, and his touch is familiar as I break into a thousand tiny pieces against him.

He stops suddenly, pulling his lips from mine, and places his hand against the wall to the side of my head. I look up at him, completely and utterly dazzled, feeling as though my legs have turned to wax and melted completely.

I stare into his burning eyes, hazel with small flecks of gold, as he stands against the sunrise breaking through gaps in the boards of the barn. "Don't stop."

"Someone's coming." He steps back from me and straightens his shoulders as he tries to slow his breathing.

"How can you hear them?" I run my fingers through my now tangled hair and peel myself off the wall.

"The horses can hear someone before we can, and I've gotten pretty good at reading their body language since I share a roof with them." He laughs as he reaches down to an unbound bale of dry yellow hay.

"Hold out your arms and pass these around to each horse." He places a bundle of hay in my open arms.

At the first mention of hay, all the horses peer out of their stalls. Some paw the ground impatiently, while others nicker at Tapley as he pulls out another bale. Just as I'm tossing a handful of hay to the bay closest to me, the barn door swings open, and George walks in.

He shoots me a strange look the second he sees me. "You're at the barn before sunrise, passing out hay?" He puts his hand on his hips and moves his suspicious stare from me to Tapley.

"I couldn't sleep." It's the only excuse I can come up with, and I can see he's not buying it.

"So you decide to do barn chores. Because you can't sleep."

I turn my back on him and walk a few steps to the next stall, tossing Tapley a wide-eyed glance. "Yes." The word leaves my lips sounding more like a question than a definite answer. I can feel George's gaze resting heavily on my back as he walks past me in Tapley's direction.

"I need help bringing a small group of cattle into town today. Mr. Allcort thinks the increase in Mexican militia is a good sign that the butcher's business is about to pick up. As much as their presence worries me, I also know that Colonel Amat needs to feed his soldiers." George grabs the last remaining pile of hay and tosses it into the stall with the mare and her foal.

"You're going into town today?" I call to them as I head down the long barn aisle.

"Yes," Tapley and George say at the same time.

Tapley clears his throat and quickly looks down at the ground, trying to escape George's eyes.

"I'm going with you." I cross my arms in front of me. I have a feeling George would absolutely not let me go had I asked for permission rather than stating my intention. When the words leave my lips, Tapley nearly falls over.

"Aubrey, you haven't ridden into town with me since your brother..." George doesn't finish his sentence. He doesn't need to. I can see the pained look across his face at the mere mention of Thomas.

"Well, I think today is a good day to change that." I've started to understand the person they believe I turned into after Thomas's death, but that person isn't me. I don't have her emotional pain at all, and even if I did, I wouldn't have pushed away the people I love the most. I don't want to be away from Tapley for an entire day, and I don't know what the future holds for me in this lifetime. I don't want George and Charlotte to continue believing I'm someone I'm not.

"Fine. But you're not riding that buckskin colt of yours." George points at the horse pacing restlessly in his stall.

"She can ride Quinto." Tapley grabs a bridle from a nail on the wall and hands it to me. "I'll use one of the other horses."

"Quinto?" I mouth to him so George doesn't hear me.

Tapley rolls his eyes at me and points to the stall where the stunning steel-gray horse I'd seen him riding a few days ago stands with a mouthful of hay.

Right... Quinto. I take a few steps and look into the horse's dark-brown eyes. "Please don't kill me today," I say to him softly, brushing his long gray forelock to the side of his face.

"I'll get Quinto ready. You need to go change into something other than that dress. Your mother can pull out your old riding clothes, or you can just help yourself to your brother's things again." For the first time, stone-faced George smirks, giving me something other than a polite smile—he actually looks happy that I'm going with him. Even though I'm worried about falling off a horse for the second time this week, I'm happy too.

CHAPTER TWELVE

The last time I straddled the back of a horse was when my parents forced me to go to camp the summer before high school started. Once freshman year and boys caught my attention, horses took a back seat in my life even though we always had two or three turned out to pasture on our property.

After quickly braiding my hair, changing out of my dress, and pulling myself into a faded brown split skirt and a light-yellow button-up shirt, I look as ready to ride a horse as I've ever looked in my life. I'm thankful for the simplicity of being away from long dresses and etiquette for the day. Tapley has the gray gelding saddled and waiting for me by the time I make it back to the barn. There are four of us in total making the ride into town today, and I'm hoping the three men aren't expecting me to be much help.

"Come on, Aubrey," George yells from the back of his horse as he waits by the pasture gate.

"Here goes nothing." I pet Quinto on the neck before gathering the long leather reins in my left hand and grabbing the horn of the saddle. With my free hand, I reach for the back of the saddle, put my foot in the stirrup, and pull myself up as gracefully as I can manage. I try to center myself on the horse's back, moving my weight from side to side to make sure the cinch is tight enough.

Breathe, I remind myself. I exhale and look for Tapley somewhere in the field. When my eyes find him, I can feel myself instantly calming down, the nerves in the pit of my stomach subsiding into the background. Gently pushing my heels into the horse's side, I steer him through the open gate and trot into the huge space. I relax, a smile fighting its way across my lips at the familiar feeling of having a horse beneath me and the sound of hooves against the ground. I push my heels against Quinto one more time, loosen my death grip on the reins, and feel him move from trot to gallop in a single seamless motion.

Just like riding a bike.

I nearly gallop right past Tapley, but as soon as I see him smiling at me, I softly tug on the reins and stop the horse right next to him.

"You look good up there." He almost blushes as his eyes inspect me from the saddle.

"We'll see if you still think that by the end of the day." I laugh and point Quinto in the direction of where George and the other man are already breaking away a small group of cattle.

The vast property this family owns is nothing compared to the view it sits on. Gently sloping Texas hills line the distance for miles, their sandstone peaks bright against the brown grass covering the ground. It's more than just the view of the hills that makes me fall in love with Texas all over again, though—it's the way the bright-blue sky covers the space above us and the white blanketing clouds are uninterrupted by buildings, planes, or smog. Texas in 1836 is the purest I've ever seen her, the most beautiful she's ever been.

Tapley rides up next to me, smiling playfully before he spurs his horse into a gallop. *A challenge?* I do the same to Quinto, the gray horse matching the other horse's stride almost exactly as their hooves break through air in a constant rumble of thunder. Just as we're nearing the group, a herd of deer jump the fences and run across the pasture in front of us. I pull on Quinto's reins hard, and he skids to a stop. The vision of the deer in the road right before my accident is all I can see as my vision darkens and my heartbeat sputters in an unnatural rhythm. There are no cars here, no two-lane asphalt roads for me to crash on, but I still can't get the image out of my mind.

"Aubrey. Aubrey!" I hear Tapley calling my name, but my eyes are closed, and my body feels paralyzed. "Aubrey... are you unwell?"

Tapley pulls his horse up beside me and reaches for my hands. "Aubrey. You're all right. Look at me... come back to me."

I pull my eyes open, trying to ignore the sick feeling in my stomach as I take a few deep breaths. My eyes find his, and I know I'm okay. "Yes, sorry. I'm better now." *Come back to me.* His words were perfect. I never knew that I needed to hear them, but now I can't live without them.

"Do you need to return to the barn? I can send Louis back with you."

"No, no. I am feeling better." I take a deep breath, hoping Tapley is unable to feel the rapid beat of my heart through my hands.

His brows are still tense as if he doesn't believe me, but he loosens his grip. I'm not going to make him send me right back to the barn because he thinks I can't handle this. I can totally handle this. Tapley nods and trots his horse in George's direction. I follow closely behind.

"Open the gate by the road," George yells to me over the protesting noises of the cattle.

I trot to the gate and manage to get it open while remaining in the saddle. I'm thankful that Tapley has loaned me his horse for the day because Quinto knows more about this cattle drive than I do.

The three men on horseback guide the cattle through the gate and onto the open dirt road leading into town. I manage to shut the gate quicker than I opened it and pick up my pace to catch up with the group.

"You've got my back, right, bud?" I pat Quinto on the neck. Even if the day goes completely downhill from here, I'm at least confident that I can stay in the saddle.

TO MOVE EVEN A SMALL group of cattle requires a significant amount of time. It takes more than an hour to go a mile—in fact, double or maybe even triple that. Town is just under two miles away, but by the time we finally pass the first building on the main stretch, it's nearly noon. We ride doubled up on either side of the small group of cattle, trying not to spread the entire width of the road as we weave around other riders and wagons driving in either direction. People eye the livestock as they pass by, and George smiles proudly at the attention his cattle receives. He has the best stock in the area, and it definitely shows when compared to the small groups of bony beef cattle already waiting inside the huge corral at the center of town.

A man opens the gate, and we steer them one last time through the wide opening at one end. There's a chill in the air, but Quinto's neck is already slick with sweat, and a thin layer of foam rests underneath his heavy leather tack. I follow Tapley to a large stone watering pit a few feet away and slide off the saddle as we let our horses take a much-needed water break.

George hands his horse to Louis then heads into a smaller wooden building between a bank and what I think is a bar.

"How do you feel?" Tapley walks in front of his brown-and-white-spotted horse and stands next to me.

"I feel good." I shoot him a smile, trying to contain the urge to run my fingers through his messy brown hair. My body is already a little sore from sitting in the saddle for a few hours, but it's nothing I can't ignore.

Tapley begins to take a step toward me, reaching for my arm, but then he suddenly freezes. "Uh... we have company." He clears his throat and gestures to his left.

I turn my head to look over my shoulder and see Robert making his way in our direction.

"I'll just be over there." Tapley nods in the direction of the bar and leads his horse to the nearest hitching post. We haven't discussed my relationship status with Robert after last night's events, but I've been dreading our inevitable meeting since the moment my palm met his cheek in an angry fury. As I watch him waddling over to me now, the mere sight of him makes me want to slap him all over again, but another part of me is screaming at the top of its lungs that I should be the bigger person. By the time Robert reaches me, he's already out of breath from walking forty feet. His face is even flushed.

"Your father said you'd come with him into town. I'm hoping your intentions are to make amends for your behavior last night."

He wants me to apologize for my *behavior? He's got to be out of his mind.*

Robert places one of his fat hands on the horse's rump, leaning into poor Quinto and expecting him to support his weight. To my dismay, the horse doesn't bat an eye, just stands quietly.

You can totally kick him, Quinto. Please just kick him for me and save me the trouble. As I sort through all the awful things I want to say to him right now, I keep hearing an annoying voice telling me to be subtle with my words.

"I actually rode with my father today because I wanted to. But you are right. I think last night does need to be addressed." I try to make my expression as polite as possible, but my eyes keep wanting to send *F-you* darts right at his face.

He clears his throat the same way he did right before his speech at the Settlers dance.

Oh great... here we go again.

"We are soon to be married, and with this marriage, you will have to learn what is and is not acceptable behavior. Last night your behavior was unacceptable."

"*My* behavior was unacceptable?" I burst out. Blood pours into my face, my anger brewing right beneath the surface. If he can't sense the fury in my tone, I'll be more than happy to elaborate.

Robert pauses. He must not have expected me to have any opinion on this. "Aubrey, I understand that my behavior was *also* not appropriate to someone in my position. But how can I expect people in this town to respect me if my future wife doesn't even respect me?" He reaches for my hand as if his explanation should be sufficient to end the discussion.

I don't want to marry this man. I *can't* marry this man. "Then maybe I'm not the best choice of wife for you." I don't take his hand. After my words leave my mouth, I reach for the reins on my horse and leave him behind completely, his hand still outstretched.

I tie Quinto next to where Tapley is waiting, and we step up a set of small wooden stairs and onto a porch underneath the overhang of the bar. Robert storms up a set of stairs the next section over and walks into the same building that George is in. I steal a peek over at Tapley, and I can tell by the grin on his face that he overheard the blowup loud and clear.

"I'll give you a few minutes to yourself. I'll be just inside if you need me." He squeezes my hand and walks me over to an empty bench outside.

I take a seat on a wooden bench, hoping to relax for a while before I have to swing my legs back into the saddle for the ride home. There's yelling coming from the small wooden building, and I can only assume Robert is having another temper tantrum. I think I just broke off our engagement, but I'm not really sure how that works in this time period. I'm sure George and Charlotte will have some things to say about it, but I'm also pretty sure they find him just as appalling as I do.

A few minutes later, George walks out of the building with tense lines written across his face. He stands in the road for a few minutes, staring at his cattle in the corral, then speaks to a man standing by the gate. As he turns around to where our horses are standing, he spots where I'm sitting alone on the bench and makes his way to me.

I haven't spent much time alone with George since I've been here, and even though I know he's my father, I don't feel like we're close. Death has a peculiar way of dividing families—of turning happy hearts against each other under the pressure of grief.

George sits down next to me, takes off his hat from his head, and lays it on one of his knees. "I hope you and Tapley know what you're doing, Aubrey." He runs his fingers through his salt-and-pepper hair and sighs.

"I don't quite know what you mean," I lie, not sure if he knows just how apt his comment is.

"James Allcort is refusing to buy our cattle." He doesn't turn to look at me, yet I can almost feel his eyes staring at me even though they're fixed in the direction of the corral.

"He's refusing to buy them because of what I did yesterday?" I choke on my words.

"You of all people know how emotion can drive a family's decisions. I don't disagree with your actions last night—in fact, it's quite the opposite. Robert brought your reaction upon himself because of his own carelessness. James Allcort sees it differently. He only sees the humiliation of his family—his loved ones. But, Aubrey, you were protecting the ones you love from humiliation." He finally turns his blue-gray eyes to mine. "I'm proud of you."

I fight back angry tears. "I do love him."

"I know you do, and I would much rather you love Tapley than be miserable for the rest of your life." He moves his hand around my shoulders and pulls me close as the tears break through my eyes.

"Father, we should leave—all of us, even Tapley. We can go to another settlement and start over. Someplace without Robert or the Mexican Army. Somewhere *safe*." I whisper the last two words, but when George looks at me, I can tell he heard my plea. Yet he doesn't fully understand the fear behind my words. I fear for the people I've grown to love, and I now know that I can't leave them alone to die in this town.

"I won't leave behind what we've built here, Aubrey. The land, the cattle. All of it belongs to this family. I won't leave behind the ground where I buried your brother. Even if the Allcorts try to run us out of town, I won't let them take away what this family has bled for—died for."

We sit in silence for a few minutes. His fears are different from mine, yet we're equally plagued by worries for the future. George worries about the future he's built for this family, and I worry about my future with Tapley. When I found myself in 1836, I wanted nothing more than to return home to my own time. But now things have changed. My roots have grown in the same soil my father is determined to protect, and my heart is bound to Tapley, who I refuse to leave behind.

"I think I need a drink." He squeezes my shoulder and stands.

I watch him walk through the double doors of the bar, and once again, I'm left alone to face this unfamiliar town. I stare blankly at the busy streets, my eyes following people from one end of the road to the other until they disappear into buildings or turn a corner. As I watch them, I can feel my old life disappearing just as effortlessly.

"Look who I find all by herself again," interrupts a deep voice, breaking me from my mindless distraction and startling me as his body blocks my view of the street. I don't even need to look at his face to know who it is—the gold buttons give him away.

"Colonel Amat." I turn my attention to the Mexican officer.

"Ah, it seems you know my name, but I've yet to learn yours." He gives me a devious smirk.

"Aubrey Harrison."

Should I offer to shake his hand? Salute him?

"Well, Miss Harrison, may I sit next to you?" His eyes drop to the empty space to my right.

"You may." I try to move over as far as I can to the edge of the bench, hoping to put space between us.

"I almost didn't recognize you in clothes other than your dress." He motions to my riding attire.

"I helped drive the cattle into town this morning. It's not an activity a dress is really suited for." I try not to meet his dark-brown stare.

"Did you come to sell your cattle to Mr. Allcort?"

"That was the intention, but it seems the status of my engagement to his son, Robert, has complicated my father's business relationship with the Allcorts."

Colonel Amat chuckles, and his eyes move from the cattle in the corral back to me. "Well, Miss Harrison, it seems as though fate joined us together today." He moves his hand to my knee, his tan fingers squeezing it ever so slightly.

"I don't quite follow you," I say through gritted teeth, his touch making me progressively more uncomfortable by the second.

"Mr. Allcort purchases cattle by my orders, and if I were to decide to purchase my cattle elsewhere..." His words hang in the air as he waits for me to respond.

Tapley warned me to stay away from this man, but maybe there's a chance he can help undo the messy situation I've put George in. If I can find an alternate buyer for our cattle, then maybe my broken engagement with Robert won't impact George financially.

I try to put on my most serious face, my eyebrows pulling together and my lips resting in a straight line. "If you happen to be interested in purchasing cattle from my father directly, without having to pay a percentage of your money to Mr. Allcort, then I'm sure my father will be willing to discuss this proposition with you further."

All right, Aubrey! I silently muse. *You sounded completely adult through that entire spew of sentences.*

"If you'll give me a moment, I'll just go retrieve my father for you." I look in the direction of the doors a few feet away from me, but I notice Colonel Amat laughing before I can stand to my feet.

"Your father is in a bar. It's better that I go find him than have you walk through those doors and cause a scene." Without hesitation, he makes his way to the doors and disappears.

After a few long minutes, Tapley, George, and Colonel Amat walk out of the building. My stare meets Tapley's as he comes to take a seat next to me.

"I don't know what you did or how you did it, but you somehow managed to just sell your family's cattle without getting the Allcorts involved." He leans back against the bench, removing his hat and resting it on his knee.

I turn my eyes to George and watch as he shakes hands with Colonel Amat. A moment later, both of them turn to look at me, but the colonel's gaze lingers like a smoldering ember. His eyes finally break away from me once George begins heading in our direction.

"Whatever you did, Aubrey, was a miracle. It's a miracle the Allcorts aren't going to be happy with, but it's a miracle all the same." He reaches for my hands and pulls me into his embrace.

Tapley still looks stunned as we walk down the steps and to our horses, but as he pulls himself into the saddle, he sends me the most brilliant smile. I take a deep breath, put my foot in the stirrup, and ignore the soreness in my legs as I sit back down in the saddle.

As I turn Quinto back down the road, I can feel a pair of eyes on me. The sensation follows me as I make my way outside the city. It's a bone-chilling, haunting feeling that stays with me the rest of the ride home.

CHAPTER THIRTEEN

I t's nearly dark by the time we finally make it back to the house, and every muscle in my body is aching to get out of the saddle. Smoke from the chimney is rising into the air in a steady stream, and even the spectacular smell of Charlotte's cooking has made its way to the barn. I'm not sure if Charlotte knows about Tapley and me yet, but now that George is well aware, I'm sure the news will quickly spread.

By the time I bring Quinto to a stop outside the barn doors, the three men have already dismounted and have begun to pull heavy saddles off their tired horses. I look at the precious ground below me. I'm dying to set my aching feet down on its soil.

Attempting to swing my leg over one side, I find myself falling back to the saddle in a heap. All three men are watching me with sickly amusement, but at least Tapley looks somewhat sympathetic.

"I can't move." I groan a little too dramatically.

George looks over at Tapley and begins laughing. "Your problem, not mine." With the reins of his horse in his left hand, he takes the reins of Tapley's horse in the other and leads them both inside the dark stable.

"Don't leave me up here," I beg and lean all the way back until my head rests on the horse's rump.

"If you spent more than one time in the saddle per year, you wouldn't feel so bad right now." Tapley walks over to me and slaps the side of my thigh.

"Ouch! That was unnecessary." I quickly sit up and glare down at him.

"Well, how does the rest of your body feel now?" He smirks.

"I don't know. All I can feel is your handprint burning on my leg."

"Then get off the horse while you aren't thinking about how bad the rest of you hurts." He holds his arms out and waits to catch me.

Pain diversion... nicely played.

I step with all my weight on the foot of my one throbbing leg, letting my heel sink into the stirrup, then heave my other leg over the saddle. Tapley puts his hands around my waist and guides me safely to the ground. The discomfort of sitting in the saddle for another minute has nothing on the pain of trying to walk once I'm finally out of it. I feel Tapley reach for my hand and wrap his fingers around mine as he steadies me.

We walk through the grass the short distance to the front porch, neither of us worrying about who sees us together. It's a nice change from the two days we spent trying to hide our feelings from the rest of the world. Charlotte is already standing on the porch with a lantern in her hand, the gentle glow from the candle making the trek up the steps less difficult. Her lips pull into a slow smile when she sees us together, her eyes expectant rather than surprised.

Tapley pauses and lets go of my hand right before I walk through the door. "Good night, Mrs. Harrison, Aubrey." He nods to each of us and turns to walk back down the steps.

"Tapley, why don't you join us for supper tonight? You deserve a hot meal after your hard work today." She doesn't wait for him to respond before she turns back into the house.

Tapley abruptly stops, pauses for a few seconds, then turns back to face the door, where I'm waiting. I'm aware of the huge smile plastered across my face as I hold my hand out for him to take, ready to lead him into the house as my guest and not my father's hired help.

The last time I saw Tapley in the house, he was awkward and closed off. I never want him to feel like that again. I lead him over to the couch closest to the fireplace.

"You can be yourself here." I watch as he cautiously sits down. "I'm going to see if Charlotte needs any help in the kitchen—I'll be right back." I squeeze his hand before I unwrap my fingers from his and head to the kitchen.

Charlotte's back is turned away from me. She's busy stirring the contents inside a huge iron pot.

"Can I help you with anything?"

She jumps, startled, and turns to face me, a plain white apron tied around her neck and covering her dark-blue dress. "It's a nice change to see you in the kitchen, wanting to help. Actually, it's just a nice change to see you with a smile on your face again. I can't remember the last time I—" She stops short as I throw my arms around her neck and hug her.

"I'm sorry if I haven't been myself for a while, but I'm trying to change that. I hope you'll give me a chance." I let go of her, take a step back, and smile.

She stares at me with wide eyes, a shimmer of tears showing ever so slightly before she regains control of her emotions and pushes the tears away. "When you stood up for Tapley in front of the entire town, I saw something different in you, Aubrey. You were no longer angry at the world for what happened to Thomas—you perfectly balanced the feelings of compassion and anger instead of sheltering emotions behind grief. It was like you just woke up one day and wanted to pick right back up on life. You started living. Loving." This time, the tears break through her eyes, and I struggle to fight back tears myself.

The Aubrey Harrison she just described is the person I've always believed that I am. Instead of becoming someone else in this unfamiliar life, I made that person become me. I am now Aubrey Harrison, and I don't have to hide it.

At the sound of George's voice coming from the parlor, Charlotte quickly reaches for a basket filled with fresh bread and sticks it in my hands. "Why don't you start bringing things to the table? If we make your father wait too much longer for his supper, he'll turn into an angry ol' bear."

I send her an understanding grin and take the basket into the dining room. I can hear George and Tapley deep in conversation in the next room, and I try to set the table quietly so I can hear what they're saying.

"But why would Amat want to keep his purchases away from Allcort's ledger book?" Tapley asks.

"There are rumors that Santa Anna has a few thousand men camping out not thirty miles east of town." George's voice is almost angry, and I hear him digging around on one of the shelves.

"So Amat is purchasing cattle off the records for the rest of the army?"

My breath catches in my chest, and my fingers begin to tremble. I practically arranged a deal between my family and the Mexican Army that's camped out and waiting to attack the city. *I'm aiding the enemy...* The handful of silverware I'm holding drops to the floor.

"Aubrey?" George yells.

My feet feel like lead as I force myself to walk on trembling legs. "I made you sell your cattle to the army that's about to attack the city?" I stammer. In an instant, Tapley is by my side, keeping me from crumbling to the ground as he leads me to the couch.

George looks at me with kind, understanding eyes as if he's trying to wash away the guilt I'm feeling. "If I hadn't agreed to Amat's terms, he would've found another seller in the city—a seller who isn't as honest as this family is."

"After James Allcort tried to end our business relationship because you damaged his pride last night, he left the window too far open. Amat knew what he was doing when he approached you, Aubrey. He already knew we needed a buyer. What he doesn't know is that I've already informed the Alamo's garrison of the business transaction, and as long as Amat keeps buying cattle from me direct-ly, we have a good idea of how many Mexican soldiers are nearby. Had I refused to sell the cattle to Amat today, our town might have been caught off guard and left vulnerable for the Mexicans to take back. Allcort's loyalty can be bought, but this family's loyalty will al-ways be to this town and its Texian settlers." George shakes his head. "Besides, we don't actually *know* that they're planning to attack."

If I didn't have a filter, I'd be warning them about what Santa Anna is planning. I could tell them about the future. The fall of the Alamo inevitably leads these people to independence from Mexico. If I were to try to change that right now, I might be changing history. They die for independence—they fight and win a victory against an army that has threatened them since the moment they made Texas their home. I'm from 2015. I've seen movies, and I know that mess-ing with history is never the right answer. But maybe I can still pro-tect the people I love under this roof.

Charlotte calls everyone to the dining room, and we silently make our way to the table and take our seats. For the first few min-utes, she tries to make small talk, but everyone seems too preoccu-pied for conversation. George's hard expression has returned, and Tapley seems too concerned about me to even eat his food. I'm dis-tracted by the truth of the future as it rests on my shoulders, the weight so heavy that it's hard to speak at all. Tonight I hoped to have my first normal evening since I've been here—an evening with George, Charlotte, and Tapley. An evening with no secrets. Yet I still have to hide the biggest one of them all.

After the painfully uncomfortable dinner, I walk with Tapley back to his room in the barn. I don't want to leave him, especially not after today. A part of me wishes I could fast-forward with him back to the twentieth century—a time when lying in someone's arms for an entire night is socially acceptable. Despite what is appropriate in 1836, I know the way I feel about him—it's one thing I am completely certain of. What I fear most right now isn't the red-and-navy uniforms of Santa Anna's army or the raven-like stare of Colonel Amat. My biggest fear is that the clock hanging over my head will one day reach midnight, and my twisted fairy tale will end—my time with Tapley will be over.

He pulls me into his arms outside of his small room and holds me for a long time in the darkness. It's the first warm day we've had all week, and the crickets are out in full force, their constant song bellowing through the night air.

"Don't let go," I whisper as my head rests on his shoulder. I breathe him in as he holds me close. His hair smells like cedar and lavender—bold yet soft.

"If I don't let you go, I'm going to keep you here all night." He kisses the top of my head but keeps his arms secured around my waist.

"I don't mind if you keep me here." I tilt my head upward to look into his eyes, and my lips move to his with a magnetic pull. I tangle my fingers in his messy brown hair, and his grip on my yellow blouse tightens. His breathing grows ragged and desperate.

"If I don't let you go, George will kill me. In fact, he'll probably kill me with that pitchfork right over there," he whispers through each movement, his teeth finding my bottom lip as I try to stop his excuse.

"If you are going to force me back inside that house, I'm going to at least make you regret it." This time I push him up against the wall, leaning into him as he braces himself.

I feel him struggling to rein in his emotions as a quiet moan escapes his lips. His hands slide down my back and find their way under my shirt, his fingers brushing up the line of ribs along my sides. He spreads his legs just enough to where he can pull me closer to him, and I can feel the heat pouring from his body as his touch grows more urgent. I mimic his movements, my hands moving underneath his shirt and tracing his sides. He shivers at my touch and pulls his lips away from mine, keeping his eyes closed as the back of his head rests against the wall.

I watch as what he wants fights with what he knows he should do, and I suddenly feel bad for pushing him to walk the line he's clearly trying to resist.

"I should go." I take a step back and pull him away from the wall.

"You should definitely go before I let you try to change my mind again." He laughs as he brushes his fingers back through his hair. "I love you, Aubrey Harrison. Even though you're tempting me to show you just how much." He kisses my forehead one last time and sends me back in the direction of the house.

This time, as I walk up the front porch steps, my legs are unsteady for another reason. The effect Tapley Holland has on me is unlike anything I've ever felt, and the intensity of it threatens to rip me apart. It's all so inexplicably real and beautiful that I can't get the thought of him out of my mind. I've felt that new-love infatuation before, but the way I love him doesn't feel new at all—it feels ancient and substantial. He almost holds me up as if he's my own foundation. I take off my dirty old boots at the foot of the stairs just as a huge yawn breaks its way across my face.

Charlotte turns the corner as I reach for the banister and tosses me a large white towel. "I have the bath ready for you. I figured it might help relieve some of the soreness. And it wouldn't hurt to get a few layers of dirt off your skin." She smirks and points to a door down the hall.

Bath is practically the greatest word I've heard all day. Towel in hand, I head down the hall to where warm water and soap are hopefully waiting for me.

THE NEXT MORNING, I pull myself out of bed a few hours after the sun has already filled the sky. Every part of my body aches. Even muscles I didn't know existed somehow feel like they've been twisted and torn from my body and then stuck back in their rightful places. The warm bath last night was helpful, and fortunately, I was so exhausted that I didn't dream of anything at all—not even the distant beeping. Perhaps now that I've given my heart fully to Tapley, there's no longer a part of it to share with the future. My fate is now fully entwined with his.

I can hear voices coming from downstairs, and I quickly dress myself, hoping Tapley is waiting for me in the parlor. With no plans for riding today, I'm forced to shrug myself back into a linen dress and stiff leather shoes. I run a brush through my damp curls and braid them to the side.

I pull open the door and carefully step down the stairs on my still-wobbly legs. I can smell eggs cooking in the kitchen, but Charlotte and George's voices aren't coming from the dining room. With a silly smile still plastered on my face, I turn toward the parlor, and as soon as I see who is sitting in the chair, my heart stops faster than my feet.

"Colonel Amat," I blurt.

I turn to look at George and Charlotte. Their expressions are hard to read, but Charlotte's eyes meet mine with a hidden sadness.

"Ah, Aubrey. Please join us." George stands up and offers me his place on the sofa. He walks a few steps to the empty chair nearest to Amat and sits down.

Colonel Amat's eyes are on me like a branding iron, the heat searing through every pore in my body. He clears his throat, the noise breaking through the awkward tension that began the moment I walked into the room.

"Aubrey," George begins then suddenly pauses as if he's searching for the right words. He clears his throat again. "Aubrey, Colonel Amat has come by this morning to speak with us about the status of your... hand." He looks at me, waiting for my reaction.

My hand? Well, I have two hands, so I'm not sure if Amat is talking about my right hand or my—I almost gasp. My *hand.*

I try to breathe, but the room feels like it's shrinking around me. I suddenly feel like Alice after she's grown too big for the space around her. I'm suffocating. Unfortunately, this doesn't have a simple *eat me* or *drink me* type of fix, either.

"Miss Harrison, I've come to settle the terms of our engagement. My intentions are to make you my wife," Amat says in a sickly-sweet voice, making my hair stand on end.

I try to focus on finding something to say in response—something appropriate and not profane. A thick gray cloud of pain slowly begins to encircle my future, plaguing its momentary brightness until it's an eternal shade of black—as black as the eyes staring back at me.

CHAPTER FOURTEEN

For the last hour, I've felt completely lost in my own skin. Inside the safety of my own mind, I'm crying and screaming all at once. I don't let even the hint of a single tear show as I sit watching, expressionless, as the rest of my life crumbles into pieces—pieces that will blow in whatever direction Colonel Amat commands the wind to move.

Why me? Was I not blunt enough the first time we met in the road? Can he not see that I hate everything about him and what he stands for?

Looking back on our conversation yesterday, I feel like it wasn't the cattle he was interested in purchasing from George. It was me. I'd unknowingly sold myself right alongside the livestock.

I force myself to stand up and walk with Charlotte and George to the door as Amat prepares to return to town. It's one of those strange out-of-body experiences, and I'm practically watching the whole thing play out in front of me as if I'm hiding in the corner of the room. *Invisible.* But as everyone's eyes are now on me, I feel the pressure resting heavily on my shoulders, pushing the weight so hard that I can feel my legs begin to bow and break.

"Thank you for stopping by, Colonel." George shakes his hand and passes me a sad glance.

Amat then turns to me, reaches for my hand and looks into my eyes. "As we will soon be family, you can call me Augustine." He places a kiss on the top of my hand. His lips are smooth and drier than Robert's, but even at the mere brush of his lips, my fingers tremble in his, and I cringe as he grips them harder before releasing my hand.

He smooths the front of his blue jacket and quickly exits out the front door, his black leather boots clicking on each step as he descends the stairs. As soon as George shuts the door, he places his hands on my shoulders and looks down at me. I didn't realize my body was swaying unsteadily until he balances me, but the entire morning, from when I woke up to right now, seems so far off in the distance that I'm having trouble remembering it at all.

"George, she looks faint. We need to sit her down." I hear Charlotte's voice from somewhere behind me.

Two people move me to the edge of the stairs, and I realize that I'm sitting. I don't remember actually telling my body to do so. My heart pulses to the soft, steady beeping somewhere in my clouded thoughts, and I press the balls of my hands against my eyelids to stop all the confusion.

"I'll go find Tapley. Stay here with her." George begins to walk to the door but not before the mention of Tapley jolts me back to reality.

"No!" I scream at him, frantic as I fly to my feet.

"Aubrey, honey, sit down. I'll bring him to you." This time, I'm not sure whose voice it is, but I don't listen.

I have the door open, and I'm running down the porch steps before they can react—before I can stop *myself*. I almost trip over the long hem of my dress but manage to grab enough of it in my shaking hands to keep it out of the way as I head to the barn. I have no idea where Tapley is or if he's even near the barn. If I have to wait inside the safety of the barn until I find him, I will.

The big bay horse at the end of the aisle spooks as I race through the double doors. Quinto will be put away in his stall if Tapley is working around the barn. I quickly make my way to the gray gelding. The stall is completely empty. Tapley is gone.

He's out in the pasture somewhere. I head through the doors on the other side. Rushing outside, I find him watching the mare and her new foal at the back of the large pasture closest to the barn.

"Tapley!" I yell as I make it to the metal gate.

He quickly looks in my direction with a smile on his face, but then his smile falters. I try to get the gate open as fast as I can, but I can't undo the mess of long metal chain with my hands shaking so severely. Frustrated tears begin pouring from my eyes, and I can hear Quinto's hooves pounding through grass as he gallops toward me.

"Aubrey?"

I hear him calling my name, and the only thing I can do is look up at him with tears running down my face.

"Aubrey, what's wrong?" Tapley reins Quinto to a skidding stop inches before they collide with the gate, and he is instantly on his feet. I feel his hands move to mine, helping me with the chain, and we pull the gate open together.

I can't even speak. I throw myself into the comfort of his arms instead and bury my face against his shirt. Even the familiarity of his scent can't calm the storm of emotions hanging over me. The sweet smell of hay mixed with rich Texas soil almost makes things worse, reminding me of all I'm going to lose if Amat gets his way. *Home. Tapley.* His name rushes through my thoughts faster than I catch it, faster than I can hold it before it's gone completely.

Tapley's hand gently brushes the side of my cheek, clearing away the wetness. He doesn't push me to tell him what's wrong. He doesn't force me to choke on the words as I struggle to catch my breath between sobs. I can feel him staring down at me. Had this been any other occasion, I would have tried to hide myself away from anyone until the tears stopped. I am definitely an ugly crier, but the chance to hide that fact from Tapley has already come and gone.

Quinto's hot breath steams against my shoulder as he tries to nibble at the ends of my hair, and his efforts are enough of a distraction to help me calm down. I try to take a few deep breaths, but the air burns like a thousand tiny daggers pressing against my lungs as my chest rises and falls rapidly. After a few minutes, my breathing slows, and I'm able to pull my shoulders back and bring my eyes to Tapley's. Pain has etched its way across his face. His hazel eyes are sad, and I can see the remnants of his own tears from the clean trail they've left behind on his dusty skin.

I bring my hand to his face, and this time, I wipe away his tears. "I love you, Tapley Holland. Don't ever forget that. Promise me you won't forget." I feel my throat tightening again as my emotions try to fight their way back through.

"I promise I won't forget." Tapley pulls my face to his, and his lips press against mine, rendering me breathless. "Now, please tell me what's going on. Not knowing what's causing you pain is unbearable."

"Colonel Amat." I choke, struggling to form a complete sentence. I don't actually know what to say—what words I should use to tell him that I've been coerced into an engagement with a man who is an enemy of every person in this town.

"Yes? I saw him ride up earlier this morning. But what does this have to do with why you're crying, Aubrey? I'd assumed he was here to discuss the terms of his purchases with your father."

"He was here to discuss his terms—of a sort." I take a deep breath, trying to sort through my next words carefully. "He was here to discuss his terms regarding me. He came to state his intentions of engagement."

Tapley's face falls as fast as my heart is breaking. Then the hint of sadness leaves his eyes, and he begins to flush, his jaw tightening as rage surfaces in its place. His breathing is suddenly short and ragged. His hands drop from my face to his sides, where his fingers curl into angry fists.

"I want you to take Quinto inside the barn. Get him settled in his stall, then wait for me inside my room." He hands me the braided leather reins and looks into my eyes with a cold stare.

"Where are you going?" I reach for his hand, trying to calm him down. He can't ignore the frantic tone in my voice. "Please don't go after Amat—he'll kill you, Tapley. I can't lose you." I'm holding onto his arm as hard as I can, and he'll have to drag me with him if he's going after Amat.

His expression softens. "Aubrey, if I were planning on going after Amat, I wouldn't have handed you my horse. It's an awfully long walk into town. Though the walk would give me plenty of time to find ways of killing him. Slowly." He squeezes my arm, and I relax my grip on his as well. Without another word, he walks through the open gate and in the direction of the house.

I lead Quinto into the empty barn, the only noise around us coming from the sparrows jumping from beam to beam in the rafters above our heads. Quinto stands quietly in his stall as I pull off his bridle and hang it on an empty peg along the aisle. I forgot how heavy old Western saddles can be. After sliding it from Quinto's back, I raise it awkwardly to the rack before I drop it on my toes. When I'm done fighting with the saddle, I head back to the stall and tie the ropes securely in front. Quinto is already busy munching on the leftover hay from his breakfast, and I reach over to give him one last pat on the neck before I leave him alone to his afternoon snack.

I turn the metal knob of Tapley's door and push my way inside. The fire from last night is still glowing, and I toss another log on top, hoping to ease the chill in the room. I take a seat on the single chair at the center of the room and watch mindlessly as the flames dance higher with each second that passes. I know Tapley wants me to stay here for a reason, but I'd rather be a fly on the wall in the house right now. Whatever he has to say to George and Charlotte, he obviously doesn't want me to hear. Maybe he's only trying to spare me from feeling any more pain than I've already endured.

A while later, I wake up, not realizing I had dozed off. I blink my eyes open. The room around me is much darker as the sun has already set for the day. I begin to panic when I think I'm still alone in the barn and quickly sit forward in the chair as my eyes try to adjust to the dim light. One of the logs in the fireplace has fallen from the metal holder.

"I'm here, Aubrey." Tapley's voice comes from the cot behind me in the corner of the room.

I pull myself to my feet, turning to where his voice came from. He's on the edge of the cot, his legs parted slightly and his head in his hands. I go to him quietly and sit next to him on the cot. I brush my hand through his hair, and he leans into my touch.

"Why don't we just pack our things and leave San Antonio together? We can leave tonight—before Amat realizes we're gone." My voice is quiet, and I can almost make out the dull thud of my heartbeat against the stillness of the room.

Tapley finally pulls his face from his hands, his eyes red and wet from his own angry tears. "If we leave tonight, your family will lose everything—the farm, their house, the cattle... you," he whispers.

"How? That doesn't make sense." I try to hide the frustration in my voice.

"Aubrey, this land was given to your family by the Mexican government. This land belongs to them, but your family is allowed to be here as long as they have a grant. If you refuse this engagement, Colonel Amat will see to it that he takes back this land, and he will marry you anyway."

"So I have no other choice. I have to marry this man just because he says so?"

"Yes, unless you prefer the second option." His eyes find mine, and I see the anger beginning to grow inside the unusually dark shade of his irises. "You'd have to marry Robert instead." He struggles to even say Robert's name, balling his fists so tightly that the tan skin over his knuckles loses all its color.

"But I want to marry you. Tapley, you are the only person I want to marry," I blurt, awkwardly realizing that the thought has been quietly brewing in my mind for days.

Tapley quickly shifts to his feet, pacing the small room in front of me from wall to wall until I'm almost sure he's going to throw his fist right into one of them. "Do you not think I've already thought of every possible option to get you out of this? I pleaded with George for hours, trying to convince him that I'm a viable alternative for your hand—that marrying you would solve all his problems. But, Aubrey, the truth is that marrying me won't solve your problems at all. I'm no one to this town. I'm just a body they see fit for work—no better than the cattle bought and sold in the town square. I'm disposable. And if I married you, Amat would just have me killed, and then he'd still take you as his wife. Out here, no one misses a farmhand. The Allcort family has the support of this town, and if you married Robert, Amat would have the entire town to go through before he got to you. Your family would have a benefactor—a way to survive financially and fight Amat if he tried to take the farm away." He throws his words at me as if he's rehearsed them a hundred times—as if he's trying to sell me on the idea.

"We could leave. Just us. We could start over somewhere else."

"I have nothing to give you, Aubrey. No land, no home, no fortune." He falls to his knees in front of me, his hands reaching for mine as he stares into my eyes.

"Aubrey, I would marry you a thousand times if it meant I could save you from the monster we all know Colonel Amat is. I would marry you knowing I would die the very same day, but I can't marry you and die knowing you'll still end up with that man. But if I don't marry you, and that choice saves you from him but puts you in the arms of another, I would make that choice a thousand times as well because I love you. I will always love you, and a little piece of me will die each day I'm not with you—but, Aubrey, you will live." Tears begin to fall down his cheeks, but he never takes his eyes from mine. I can feel his love turning to ash with each second that passes as he waits for my response.

"When?" It's the only word I can think to ask as my heart is ripped into a thousand ragged pieces, my only source of happiness in this world stripped away from me forever.

"Tomorrow. Your father rode into town before sunset to speak with the Allcorts." Tapley reaches to my face and tucks a wet strand of hair behind my ear.

I sit still for a long moment, my hand wrapped around Tapley's, and our eyes never pull away from one another. "I understand if you want me to go back to the house," I say. "I'm sure you need some time to think." Each word feels like a punch to my chest as it leaves my lips.

"No, Aubrey. You're staying here with me tonight. I'm not going to let you go until the very last second before you leave me tomorrow. Your father has to at least give me that." He pulls himself back to the empty space next to me on the cot, scooping me up into his arms as if I weigh nothing at all.

For the very first—and the very last—time, we lie down together. We've been forcing ourselves not to do it, because society has rules when it comes to being in love in 1836. That set of rules may not apply to an officer in the Mexican Army.

CHAPTER FIFTEEN

I've been numb for hours—too tired to cry, too broken to feel. Neither of us slept last night. We lay together on the small cot underneath the thick wool blankets as the cold front blew in like a hurricane just outside. The room was completely silent except for the sound of wind and freezing rain against the roof. Tapley held me close to his chest, our bodies fitting together seamlessly. As the sun finally peeks, unwanted, over the horizon, he still clings to me.

I finally turn over to face him, my eyes sore and inflamed from yesterday's emotions. He runs his fingers through my tangled curls as he stares into my eyes without saying a single word. I bring my lips to his, a sharp anguished breath leaving my lungs as I kiss him for the last time before I pull away from him. Tapley touches my face, his thumb brushing over my lips, and his eyes seem to be trying to memorize mine before I fade away—drifting into his past like distant smoke.

"I'll go with you anywhere, no matter what it costs me. Just say the words, Tapley," I beg.

"It would cost you your livelihood, Aubrey. What good will running away do you if you can't live?" He pulls away from me and moves to the edge of the cot. The moment he takes his eyes from mine, I feel him leaving me even though his body is still here. His heart is gone, and I can see the pain that my mere existence used to cause him already beginning to take over.

I bring my feet to the edge of the bed, stand up, and rest my hand on his shoulder. "Please say something." My body begins to tremble. I feel him slipping away.

He stands next to me and pulls me into his arms but still says nothing. Tapley holds me tight a few more minutes, kissing the top of my forehead, then steps away from me. I try to reach for his hand, but he opens the door to his room and walks into the cold, empty barn. I'm alone. No final goodbye or last breathless *I love you*. He's gone, and the life we almost had together disappears as quickly as the wind outside moves the dry Texas dirt.

I push my shoes onto my feet without even bothering to tie the laces. Without Tapley here, the walls of the barn feel like they're closing in around me—as if I'm not welcome here any longer. I find the wool coat I left a few days ago hanging on a hook in the corner, but instead of taking it with me, I leave it for him. I can't bear the thought of him forgetting me.

I find myself racing to the house, worried that if I stay a second longer in the barn, I'll fall apart completely. Charlotte and George are already waiting in the parlor when I walk into the house, their faces a dismal pale shade that likely matches my own.

George motions to the chair next to him. "Come sit down, Aubrey."

I can only imagine that I look even more horrifying than I feel, but there's no willingness left in my body to act like a proper lady this morning. I sit down in the chair and lean my head against the plush burgundy cushions. Neither of them says a single word about me staying the night in Tapley's room—they don't mention Tapley at all. My life with him ended the moment he kissed me on the forehead for the last time this morning.

"Your father returned late last night from his meeting with the Allcorts, and everything is arranged," Charlotte says quietly.

"We will be heading into town around midday, but nothing about this will be elaborate, Aubrey." From George's choice of words, it sounds like he's expecting me to have aspirations for some perfectly beautiful wedding day. I'm marrying Robert Allcort, for heaven's sake. Nothing about this marriage falls anywhere close to my dreams.

"I just want to get this over with." My voice is harsher than I expect, and they both flinch.

"We will ride into town. The wagon will draw too much attention to you today. No one must know of this wedding if it's to pass beneath the watchful eyes of Colonel Amat's men. They'll see you ride into town today, but I'm hoping we'll have enough time to do what's needed."

"You mean enough time for me to marry Robert before Amat steps in and marries me first?" My words aren't exactly a question—they're more like a confirmation of my fate.

"Yes," George says in resignation.

"So if one marriage doesn't happen, I'll have a backup to step right in. Well, for whichever one I end up marrying today, I should probably at least make myself look presentable. We wouldn't want either eager suitor running off, would we?" I stand and rush to my room.

At this point, I just want to get this over with. I can't stand another second of seeing George and Charlotte tormented by my pain. There's a pale dress laid out across the top of my bed, and I can hear Charlotte's footsteps approaching from the stairs.

"I had it made after your engagement a few months ago. I know it isn't much, but I hope you at least have something to remember today—even if it's not the day you want." She turns me around to face her, a glisten of tears forming at the corners of her eyes. "You will be okay, Aubrey. Sometimes these things don't work out how we expect, but it doesn't mean that it won't work at all. I think you will make an exceptional bride to Robert, and I hope that your strong will and even stronger heart will help make him the best man he can be—a better man. Lord knows he has a long way to go to be that kind of man." She hugs me tightly, and I know she's letting me go.

The embrace is over as quickly as it started, and she immediately reaches for the dress on the bed. I turn to look at myself in the mirror, and I can no longer find anything recognizable. My face hasn't changed, but the life that used to shine vibrantly behind bright-green eyes has been extinguished into darkness. I'm now just a shell—a body that will walk, talk, and be Aubrey Harrison. The old Aubrey Harrison is long gone, lost in a place where she can wake up each and every morning to hazel eyes and dusty-brown hair—a place where she can live, love, and grow old with someone who she fearlessly loves no matter what stands in their way.

Charlotte pulls off yesterday's dress, and I find myself standing naked in the middle of my room for the second time. Unlike last time, though, I have no emotions to hide—no shame or embarrassment to shield me. I just stand motionless, my broken heart beating steadily as my lungs pull in air as they always do.

She hands me a pair of white cotton bloomers, and I pull them on over my legs without question. I place my arms through the tight corset top, and Charlotte tugs the laces in place as I take shallow breaths. She adds petticoats where the corset meets the bloomers then pulls the thick white fabric of the dress over my arms. Though I've never been fitted for this wedding gown, it perfectly matches every curve and dip of my entire body. I don't know the common fabrics of this century, but the dress is undeniably beautiful. As she fastens the buttons running along my back, I sneak a glance at myself in the mirror. I've always dreamed of being Elizabeth Bennett, and in this dress, I'm the closest I will ever come to dancing with Mr. Darcy in the halls of Netherfield Park.

Charlotte is working my hair into a complicated knot at the base of my neck when I hear George coming up the steps and entering my room. "We need to be on the road to town soon." He looks at me in my white wedding dress, offering no smile. His face holds his usual hard-to-read expression, but the sadness in his eyes gives away the true depth of his unhappiness.

"We'll be ready in a moment." Charlotte sticks a few more metal pins in my hair and steps back to check her work. It's a simple chignon, but my thick curls give it a little something extra. She reaches into the pocket of her apron and pulls out a long string of pearls. "These belong to you now."

Charlotte stands behind me, drapes the pearls around my neck, and fastens them below the bun at the back of my head. Her daughter would have known if these pearls had a special meaning to her. I don't. They're just one more item to play dress up with on the worst day of my life.

"They're beautiful. Thank you," I say, but the words don't sound like my own.

"You'll need to wear this over your dress while you're riding. We don't need Amat's men seeing you in this fancy dress today." Charlotte hangs a long deep-green cape over my shoulders and pulls the hood over my head. She reaches for my hand and leads me downstairs to where George is waiting in the entryway.

"The horses are ready." He motions out the window toward the three horses tied to the hitching post in front of the house.

I hoped to see Tapley's horse waiting for me, but my heart sinks when I only find shades of brown instead of Quinto's dark dappled gray. Tapley is nothing more than a ghost in the shadows along with everything else I still hold dear.

THE ROAD INTO TOWN is busy, but I keep my horse between Charlotte's and George's as we make our way to the Allcorts'. Their stone house sits near the center of San Antonio, a place where the family can always have one eye on their business interests. In the two days since I was last here, the number of Mexican soldiers has already doubled. Everyone seems to be going about their normal lives, but there's a hint of edginess in the air that I can't ignore.

George stops in front of Allcorts' two-story residence and dismounts quickly from his horse. He places the reins in another man's hands and moves to help Charlotte from her saddle as well. Robert appears in the doorway, a smug look on his face as he eyes me from the porch steps. He's dressed even more obnoxiously than the first time I saw him—a dark-gray silk vest over a crisp white shirt along with black pinstriped pants and shiny leather boots. His auburn hair is slicked back, and there's a faint hint of red-haired stubble on his face. For a last-minute wedding groom, he's impeccably turned out, although it doesn't make him any more attractive. He walks over to the left side of my horse and reaches for my hand in a gentlemanly manner. I know better than to fall for his sad attempt at decency. I can see right through him.

The moment my feet touch the ground, I'm ushered inside, leaving me not even a single second to rest from the ride. The house surprises me. In the home of a man wearing such outlandishly overdone attire, I should have expected overly elaborate furnishings, but I didn't. The whole interior seems stained in a deep-cherry lacquer. Everything is made of dark wood—walls, chairs, tables, floors—accentuated with too many jewel-toned fabrics and pillows. For a family living in the 1800s, their tastes are ridiculously expensive looking.

Robert leads me by the arm to a large room at the very center of their home. I'm sure the other me has been here before, but it's an experience I have no recollection of. The furniture has been pushed aside to allow for more space, and George stands quietly in the corner, sipping whiskey from a crystal glass. In front of a large wooden fireplace against the far wall is a robed man, with Robert's mother and Charlotte waiting nearby.

"I'm so glad you came to your senses, Aubrey." Robert pats my arm and hands me off to the women.

Charlotte undoes the clasp of the green cape and pulls it from my shoulders. My hair managed to stay in place during the ride here, but what's even more surprising is the fact that I managed to stay in the saddle with this dress on. Mrs. Allcort eyes me from head to toe and turns me around so she can inspect me further. As I spin back to face them, her smile catches me off guard.

"You truly look lovely, darling." She brushes her bony fingers across my cheek, and I'm relieved that she doesn't follow her compliment with a catty comment.

Robert clears his throat from behind me. "Shall we?" He holds out his arm for me to take, and I do so automatically. "Davy came all the way from the mission—I'm sure he'd like to return to the Alamo before he's missed."

Robert leads me to where the priest is waiting. We stand in the center of the room, with the priest in front of us and our family members behind us. I try to tune out the next ten minutes, forcing myself to breathe in and out as I listen to my life being handed over to this red-cheeked man beside me. By the time it's over, I've only said two words—a promise to a man I don't love and probably never will. I watch in slow motion as he brings his face close to mine and parts his wet lips. I try to swallow back the nauseated feeling that creeps up my throat as I feel his mouth press to mine, his lips lingering a bit too long as I stand frozen. Then it's over, and I suddenly find myself a married woman. I turn to look at George and Charlotte. Their faces are stiff with fake smiles, regret shining through their eyes.

"Let us celebrate as one family at our table." Mr. Allcort motions to the dining room at the front of the house.

As we take our seats around the table, I hear a commotion coming from the street directly outside the front door. The man who'd taken our horses from us is yelling at another person nearby, and then a gunshot breaks through the air, silencing him. The men in the room are quickly at their feet, scrambling to the front door as they leave the women sitting at the table. I know who's outside even before his enraged tone is audible: Colonel Amat.

"I'm here to speak—or whatever that nonsense is you people say," Amat calls from his spot on the street.

Robert and his father are frantically talking in front of the door as George loads gunpowder into the long barrel of a gun. I move to the window and peek into the street. Amat's sitting on top of his black horse, gun in hand, flanked by his soldiers. There's a man lying facedown on the road in front of him, and groups of people are observing from the safety of the buildings across the street.

"I will handle this," Robert stutters. His face is flushed red, and his hands shake as he opens the door. Robert's voice cracks through the air as he steps to the edge of the porch. "This is a private ceremony, Colonel."

"It's not private if my bride is inside your house without me as her escort." Amat nudges his horse a few steps forward, closing the distance between him and Robert.

"Seeing as she is now my wife, she no longer requires you as an escort," Robert replies with more confidence and pride than I expected.

At his words, Amat's face turns red, and his already dark eyes sink into a deathly shade of black. "Please, then, ask your new wife to come out here so I can congratulate her myself." His jaw is locked as he turns his gaze to the window, seeming to sense the audience hiding behind the sheer white curtain.

I move away from the window and press my back to the wall for a second as I try to decide what to do. Mrs. Allcort's eyes are wide, and her hands tremble as she holds onto her white handkerchief. I turn to Charlotte and George. Both of their expressions are solemn as they stare out the window. Then my feet are moving out the door before my brain catches up, and as I step into the daylight, I feel the eyes of the entire town on me.

"I'm so pleased you decided to step outside with your new husband. I would hate for only one of you to receive my congratulations," Amat snarls, pulling his shoulders back.

Robert turns his head to look at me, motioning for me to stand next to him on the top step. In Robert's moment of distraction, Amat's hand moves for his silver pistol at his side. I hear the gun click, and before I can make a sound, Amat pulls the trigger and sends a bullet straight into Robert's temple. I close my eyes, hoping to avoid the sight of what comes next, but that doesn't keep my ears from hearing the screams of women as Robert's skull shatters beneath the force of the bullet. Robert's lifeless body thuds to the floor by my feet. Warm sickly-scented blood sprays across the bodice of my dress, and my legs begin to teeter underneath me.

"You're still mine, Aubrey Harrison. Don't forget that. I'll be back for you soon," Amat yells just before he and his men gallop out of the town.

A pair of hands grabs my waist and pulls me back into the house. The door slams behind us. Even with my eyes still closed, I can sense the chaos of the room around me. Mrs. Allcort is screaming at the table, and Mr. Allcort is heaving somewhere at the back of the room.

"Aubrey, open your eyes!" George shakes me hard. I force my eyes open but feel them begin to roll into the back of my head. He grabs my head and forces my gaze to his. "You need to get to the livery stable, find your horse, and ride as fast as you can back to the house. You aren't safe here. Do you hear me?"

He leads me through some hallways and to a back door. "Ride, Aubrey. Don't look back. Find Tapley and leave San Antonio." He quickly wipes a trail of blood from my cheek, throws my cape over my shoulders, and pulls the hood over my head. George kisses my cheek without saying another word then pushes me out the door and into a back alleyway.

CHAPTER SIXTEEN

I can feel eyes on my back as I gallop down the road out of town. People scatter in all directions before the horse's hooves. I shake the hood from my head so the fabric doesn't muffle the sounds around me—I need to be able to hear if someone is following me, but I'm too afraid to look behind.

The farm is quiet as I turn the horse up the dirt road leading to the barn. I search for any sign of Tapley, but I don't see him. Hoofbeats pound faintly in the distance, and I turn to look over my shoulder, but the road from town is still empty.

I pull the horse to a stop, swing my legs over the saddle, and lead him into the barn. "Tapley," I yell into the empty space around me.

I tie the horse in the empty stall next to where Quinto usually waits. This morning, the hay is untouched and the gray gelding's saddle is missing from its rack on the wall. I check the corral outside the barn and find the mare and foal turned out but still no sign of Tapley or Quinto.

There's only one more place I can check before heading to the back pastures. I pause before turning the doorknob to his room. The place is completely dark. The fire appears to have died out hours ago, and there's a sweeping chill in the air. My coat is still hanging where I left it, and the cot is completely empty.

"There's not enough time for this. Come on, Tapley. Where are you?" I exhale, my warm breath puffing into the cold air around me.

A moment after the words leave my lips, I can hear the distinct sound of boots coming down in my direction. "Tapley," I whisper breathlessly, turning back to the doorway.

"I'm in here," I yell from the small room and take a step to the doorway. Before I can head back into the barn aisle, I run straight into a strong pair of arms and an even stronger chest.

"I can hear from your tone that you're eager to see me," a stranger's voice says before I place it. Amat.

The colonel's broad shoulders and tall frame are blocking my only means of escape. I try to take a step back, but I find his dark-olive hands wrapped around my arms as he grips me. His hands pull tighter as I struggle to free my arms.

"You're hurting me," I cry out, keeping my eyes away from his.

"Isn't this what you wanted? Pain? It's the only explanation for your actions today." He towers over me and takes a step into the room, pushing me back with him.

His musket is strapped across his back, but I can't find any sign of the silver pistol I saw him with earlier. I glance to either side of me, trying to find something I can use to defend myself, but unless I can break a leg off the chair by the fireplace, there's nothing. He grips my jaw and brings my face up to his, pressing his lips hard against mine as his other hand moves to the back of my head. Amat bites down on my bottom lip, and I can hear his sharp breaths growing heavier as he tastes my blood.

With his grasp lifted from my arms, I pull away from him and bring my palm hard across his left cheek. The impact does nothing to him—he doesn't move or flinch—but his eyes begin to turn the same deep black shade that crossed them right before he put a bullet in Robert's head.

This time, his hand is there to strike me just before he grabs my throat and pushes me hard onto the ground. I force my eyes to stay open. With his free hand, he pulls the musket from his back and sets it against the wall by the door before turning his attention back to me. My skin stings, and my eyes water as the back of my head cracks hard against the ground.

He's going to kill me. I try to pull air into my lungs so that I can scream, but his hand grips harder around my throat as his body pins me to the cowhide rug in front of the fireplace.

A sick smile breaks across his face as he stares down at me, watching me struggle to breathe. He smirks and squeezes my throat tighter, his nails digging into my skin. "Say something."

I can't reply. I can't even breathe, and my lungs burn more as each moment passes.

"Silence looks so much better on you, Aubrey." He leans down and kisses me another time, moving his hand from my throat to my chest as his fingers tear at the fabric of my dress. "Moving only makes it worse. You left me no choice but to ruin you for any other man. No one will want you after today."

I hear the fabric rip from one of my shoulders.

No, Aubrey, he's not going to kill you—it's going to be much worse. This dark part of history has been left out of our textbooks—the part where war brought with it not only death but rape and ruin. The dirty little secret my teachers hid was that the humanity that separates man from monster is a myth.

Amat reaches to undo his belt, his grunts breaking through the silence every few seconds. I try to bring my knee to his crotch, but he only pushes me down harder, biting the skin along my collarbone and groaning each time he does it. The bile rises in my stomach as I fight back tears and stare up at the empty doorway in front of me. I imagine footsteps running in my direction, but the only movement Amat makes is in the direction of my legs—his thighs burning against me.

I try to shut down, but before I close my eyes, I see Tapley staring down at me from the doorway. Tears pour down my cheeks the second my eyes meet his cold, angry stare. Tapley looks at the bayonet sheathed on Amat's right side and then at me. If he can manage to unsheathe the blade and stab Amat through the back, the blade will go through me. Instead, Tapley reaches for the blade of a long hunting knife attached to his boots. With a swift move, he drives the blade through the back of Amat's left shoulder. With his other hand, Tapley pulls Amat off of me. The colonel hits the ground next to me in a heap, cursing through his breath as he reaches for his trousers.

"How many people am I going to have to kill for this woman?" he screams, scrambling to his feet.

"Get out of here, Aubrey," Tapley yells, lurching at Amat. His weight hits the hunched-over colonel square in the chest, sending him straight into the wall next to the fireplace.

I try to steady my trembling legs long enough to move across the room, but the pain in the back of my head is making it hard for me to stay conscious. I reach to where my scalp is throbbing, and my fingers find wet, warm blood.

"Aubrey, you have to leave—now!" Tapley turns to look at me just as Amat's fist catches the side of his face. Amat has somehow managed to pull Tapley's knife from his shoulder and is now holding the blade in his hand as it drips a steady stream of crimson onto the ground. He lunges at Tapley, blade pointed right at his chest, but Tapley dodges the oncoming swing and crashes through the wooden chair in front of the fireplace as Amat's boot comes down hard on his back, pinning him to the floor. Tapley tries to move, but the weight of Amat keeps him on the floor.

The fury in Amat's eyes is dark and deadly as he crouches over Tapley and laughs. "You're mine." He spits blood onto the floor next to Tapley's face. "And then she's mine," he adds, pulling Tapley's head back by his hair and bringing the blade to his throat.

There's no way Tapley's going to miss the blade this time, and he looks over at me with regret. "I'm sorry," he mouths.

I look at the musket to my left. I've never shot a gun before, and I know I can't make a shot without the risk of hitting Tapley instead of Amat.

Bayonet. The thought finds its way into my mind at the perfect moment. I rush to Amat's side and unsheathe the long blade. His rage is focused on Tapley, and he doesn't react when my shaking fingers remove his weapon. With as much force as I can manage, I run the blade straight into his right side, the tip of the bayonet sliding smooth and deep beneath his last rib until it splinters his spine. He falls onto the floor next to Tapley, the hunting knife still in his hand, but this time, he doesn't get up. With Amat's weight no longer on him, Tapley pulls himself up and stumbles to my side. Amat tries to speak through bloody coughs as his eyes roll into the back of his head, but the only sound that escapes him is the gurgle of his own blood.

"I-I killed him—I killed someone," I stutter, staring at the blood on my hands.

Tapley reaches for the knife in Amat's still-twitching hand and brings the blade across the colonel's throat, quickly silencing him for the last time.

"No, Aubrey, *I* killed him. The blood is on my hands, not yours." He drops the knife on the floor and wraps my shaking body in his arms. "How badly did he hurt you?" He pulls the torn fabric back over my shoulder. The laces of the corset are the only thing protecting the skin of my breasts beneath it.

"You got here before he—" The rest of the sentences sticks in my throat. The reality of what almost happened to me sets my hair on end.

Tapley's jaw tightens, and the knuckles of his clenched fist turn a shade of white to match my skin.

"I came to find you," I try to explain through my sobs. "Amat killed Robert."

Tapley carries me to the edge of the cot and slowly sits me down next to him. "Tell me exactly what happened, Aubrey." He puts his hands on either side of my face and keeps my eyes locked on his.

"Amat came to the Allcorts' when he found out about the wedding. Amat shot Robert in the head right next to where I was standing." I glance down at the blood covering my dress. "George told me to ride back to the house and find you. He told us to leave together before Amat came back for me—but Amat followed me here, and I couldn't find you in time. I'm sorry, Tapley." I throw my arms around his neck and bury my head in his chest.

"Aubrey, don't be sorry. This isn't your fault," he whispers.

I can hear hoofbeats coming down the road, and both of our bodies suddenly go rigid.

"Can you ride?" Tapley asks.

"I don't know... my head..." I pull my gaze up to look at him, but I find him staring at me with wide eyes.

"We need to go—now!" He stands up, pulling me with him, then looks around the room frantically and heads toward Amat's body. Tapley pulls the end of the bayonet from Amat's side and straps it over my shoulders before he picks up the dagger by his feet.

Taking me by the hand, he silently pulls me into the barn aisle. Through the partially open barn door, we can see a group of Mexican soldiers riding up to the house where Amat's horse is tied. There must be at least eight of them, all with guns strapped to their backs. I keep looking for signs of movement in the house or smoke from the chimney, panicking that the soldiers are here for George and Charlotte.

"They're looking for him." Tapley nods to where Amat is lying facedown in front of the fireplace. He leads me out the barn doors closest to the corral, where Quinto is waiting. As soon as Tapley opens the corral gate, Quinto trots over to him. "I need you to hold onto me, Aubrey. Whatever you hear, don't let go." He stares into my eyes and places one of my hands on the pommel of the saddle.

"I won't." My other hand moves to the back of his neck, my fingers running through his hair. "I almost lost you," I whisper.

Tapley tilts my chin up to his face, his lips parting to meet mine, and kisses me softly. The familiar scent of him calms my nerves, and the taste of his lips is even better than I remember. "I told you last night that I would die for you a thousand times if it would give you your freedom." He presses his forehead to mine and runs his hand across my bruised cheek, where Amat's mark on me still rests.

"I just want you to live with me from this day forward. No more death, no more pain—just you and me." I kiss him again and turn to face the saddle as my fingers cling to the pommel.

"I shouldn't have let you go this morning, but I promise I won't ever let you go again." Tapley reaches for my leg and hoists me onto Quinto's back then pulls himself into the saddle in front of me. We stand motionless at the edge of the corral, the open gate and nothing but empty Texas countryside in front of us. "As soon as they walk into the house, we're going to ride as fast as we can out of here. Pull your hood over your head," he whispers.

I reach for the green hood lying against my back and lift it up. My struggle with Amat has pulled my hair free from its pins, and I try to tuck the long ends of my curls behind the safety of the hood.

Tapley pats Quinto's neck quietly, trying to keep the horse settled as we wait for the last Mexican soldier to enter the house. The horse's ears are pricked forward, and our eyes are locked on the group of blue-and-red-clad men standing on the porch.

"Don't let go," he says one last time. The words barely escape his lips as the front door closes. He gives Quinto the slightest nudge on his side, and the horse responds instantly, breaking into a full gallop as his stride lengthens, taking us in the direction of the thick cedar woods in the distance.

I hug Tapley's waist and lay my head against his shoulder, trying to keep the cold wind from burning my cheeks as we race away from the house. I can't wrap my mind around what has just happened, and I'm finding it harder to remember it the farther we get from the barn.

Maybe it's the pain in the back of my head that's making it hard to think straight, or maybe I'm just in shock, but either way, I close my eyes and try to keep my arms wrapped around Tapley as the sun begins setting around us. I'm not sure where we're going or how far we'll ride before we stop, but I know without a doubt that we can never go home.

CHAPTER SEVENTEEN

When the last bit of sunlight in the sky is finally gone, Tapley slows Quinto back to a walk.

The horse's neck is slick with sweat and foam, and his hot, rapid breaths push into the cold air. I'm not sure where we are or how long we've been riding, but I can hear water flowing close by. My head is aching, and the only way I'm staying warm is by clinging to Tapley's body in front of me. There's a thick layer of trees above our head, but I still feel as though I'm out in the open for everyone to see... to find.

"We're almost there." Tapley peeks over his shoulder at me.

Almost where?

He steers Quinto to the left through a narrow passageway in the thick brush. I can almost see the faint traces of a road on the ground below us, but the forest is so overgrown that any pathway that used to be here is long gone. We walk along the high banks of a river for a few minutes, the freezing water rushing downstream in the direction of town.

"Whoa, Quin," Tapley calls, and the tired animal finally comes to a stop.

There's a small house in front of us. The tall Texas grass reaches up to the height of the windows, and the front of the door is covered in thick green moss. Tapley stares at the house, not moving from the horse or saying a word. I have this itching feeling at the back of my mind that I should know this place, but I don't, and I'm afraid to ask where we are.

Tapley's chest expands slightly under my arms as he takes a deep breath, then he turns his shoulders and looks behind at me. "You're going to have to slide off first." He chuckles. "I'm still stuck between you and the saddle horn."

I rather like being this close to Tapley, but I feel bad for the horse for carrying us this far on his back. I try to slide down as gracefully as I can in this dress, which is now shredded and stained with blood. My feet quickly find the ground, and Tapley is almost immediately off the horse and standing by my side.

I don't notice the other building behind the house until I watch Tapley's eyes move to it. There's a remnant of what looks like a barn, but with the charred wood and caved-in roof, I can't exactly tell what it used to be. His face is hard to read except for the glistening hints of tears at the corners of his eyes, which he quickly wipes away. The soil is rocky below our feet, and the river makes a rushing sound. As I stare at the outer shell of the building behind the house, I wonder if it belonged to Tapley's family. Whatever tragedy he has been through must have started here. I reach for his hand as he stands quietly next to me.

He smiles down at me. "Let's get Quinto settled for the night and head inside before it gets too cold. There's a storm coming." He leaves it at that, but I'm not sure if it's the faint smell of rain in the air that he's talking about or the consequences of today's events, which are following closely behind us. With one hand in mine and the other holding Quinto's reins, he walks toward a small corral on the side of the house. "There's a well over there." He points a few yards away then bends over to pick up an empty wooden trough.

I leave him to untack his horse while I draw water from the stone well near the edge of the barn. The closer I get to the burnt wooden walls of the building, the more my hair stands on end. The grass has overrun the inside from where a short wall is no longer standing, but I can still imagine what it once looked like—the stalls filled with horses, the hay filling the loft on the second story. I can just make out the wire hoops of a covered wagon, along with a rusted metal plow off in the corner. Even with the majority of the barn burned to the ground, I can picture Tapley running through the aisle and up the stairs as a child, his laughter lingering in the stones as if he haunts this place.

The rope attached to the bucket in the well is old but still intact, and I haul it upward until I can reach down and grab the handle. With the weight of the water, it's heavier than I expected, but I grab it with both hands and carry it back in the direction of the corral.

"Do I need to go back for another?" I ask as I hand Tapley the bucket.

He dumps it into the trough by Quinto's hooves. "Let's get you inside and get a fire started. I can come back out and check on him in a while." He places his arm over my shoulder and leads me back toward the small house.

As we near the front, Tapley pauses. Then he pushes through the overgrown weeds and throws his shoulder into the wooden door, popping it open. The house is completely dark inside, and I smell the musty scent of rain and stagnant air as soon as I cross the threshold. I allow my eyes a moment of adjustment to the darkness, but Tapley seems to know the layout of the space by heart. He moves to a corner at the other side of the room, and I can hear him throw a few logs into a stone fireplace and the clicking of a flint before sparks emerge. After a few minutes of darkness, Tapley manages to get a small fire going.

The flames grow brighter by the second, and I can finally see the room around me clearly. What little furniture is still left in the house has been covered with thin white sheets, and there's a layer of dust resting on every surface. A steep staircase rises from the middle of the living room up to an attic on the second floor. A single empty book-shelf occupies space against the wall by the fireplace.

"I know it's not much, but it's the only place I could think of where no one would come looking for us. This is cursed ground in the eyes of the rest of the world—they'd be crazy to follow us here." He reaches for the white linen across an old wooden table and pulls it off.

"Here, let me." I take the fabric from his hands and quickly fold it.

He heads to an old wooden cabinet by the boarded-up front window and tugs open the locked door on the front. "Still locked—that's a promising sign." He reaches up to the top of the case, his fingers feeling along the edges and into the corner until he pulls out a small brass key. "I used to be too short to find the key to this cabinet, but by the time I was old enough to reach the top, I was old enough to drink what was inside it."

With a quick twist of the key, the doors pop open, and Tapley's hand reaches inside, returning with a glass bottle of whiskey. I turn to the mostly empty shelves in the small kitchen, scanning it for cups. Hidden at the back of a top shelf, I find a few small metal mugs, which I carry to the table.

Tapley hasn't waited for a cup, though, and by the time I make it back, he's already taking a long drink from the bottle. The bitter scent of whiskey fills the room as I pour it into the glasses. *You come a long way from this horrible taste during the next century*, I silently inform the liquid. After swirling it a few times in the mug, I toss it to the back of my throat. It burns the whole way down.

We sit in silence for a few minutes. Tapley drinks from the bottle as I sip from the metal cup. I don't know what to say to him about this place or about what happened today. His expression is hard to read, and I'm not sure whether it's entirely my fault or if he is focusing on memories that have nothing to do with me.

"Tapley, I can't even imagine how this place makes you feel... being back here after all this time." I walk over to him.

His head faces downward as he stares at the wooden chairs situated around the table. He places the bottle between his knees, his grip securely around it, as he watches the flames dancing in the stone fireplace. "That last morning... we were all sitting here together. My father, my mother, and my little sister, who was asleep in her cradle right there." He points to empty space in front of the fire. "My dad stayed home from the cattle drive because the new baby was due any day. He was sure it was going to be another girl, but I really wanted a brother." Tapley glances over at me, tears beginning to form in the corners of his hazel eyes.

"I should've stayed here. Your father and Tommy could've moved the herd across the river without me." He reaches for the bottle and takes a sip through broken breaths.

After all these years, he still blames himself for their deaths, and now he's forced to face his own ghosts underneath the roof of the place they still haunt. I stand quietly, trying not to disturb his grief as he fights to let it go. Resting one hand on his leg, I brush his tears away with the other. His eyes meet mine and stare into them as if searching for peace.

"Thank you for saving me today. Tapley, you are the reason Colonel Amat didn't succeed. You are the reason I'm standing here untouched right now. Alive. Even though you couldn't save your family, you were able to save someone else. That's not something a cursed person can do. Tapley, you are far from cursed." I kiss his forehead.

He pulls me into the space between his legs as he sits on the tabletop and wraps his arms around the small of my back. "Aubrey Harrison, don't you remember?" he asks, brushing my hair from where it's fallen across my face.

"Remember what?"

"You are the one who saved me." He rests his forehead against my collarbone and holds onto me as if he's afraid I'm going to disappear.

How is it possible to love someone this much? I would have died for him today without batting an eye or asking a single question. I wasn't going to let Amat take something from me that was never his to have. This might be a century in which rape, arranged marriages, and murder can all happen to the same person on the same day, but love can still prevail through the unforeseen evils that try to dim the brightness in our hearts. Had today been met with the worst of outcomes, Tapley and I would have still found our way to each other again. I'm beginning to believe that this feeling for him will follow me wherever I go. In darkness, pain, and death, love will guide me—it will be my flame, my *fire*.

"So what do we do now? Today I got married, became a widow, and killed an officer in the Mexican Army after he tried to rape me. It's been one hell of a day." I reach for the bottle and drink until my tongue goes numb.

"I don't know, Aubrey. I guess we leave this place, but I don't know how far we'll get. There's a man dead—a man whose death won't go unnoticed or unpunished. The moment we rode away was the moment we became wanted fugitives." He pushes his eyebrows together.

"So we'll take it one day at a time." I brush back his messy hair and try to smile at him.

Unfortunately, I can't ignore the anxious feeling beginning to run through my veins like icy water. This is 1836, and in these dangerous, wild times, people don't get away with killing someone by pleading self-defense. *If someone wants us dead, they'll hunt us down and kill us or pay someone who will.* I'm stuck in a land of bounty hunters and outlaws, and somehow along the way, I've become a fugitive.

"Yes, we'll take it day by day. But right now, we'll start with tonight." He finally smiles at me, his worry and sadness suddenly replaced with warmth. "We should probably get you out of that dress, though."

He tugs at the ripped sleeve as he stares at the stains of two different people's blood that soil the front. The wheels in my mind begin to spin out of control. I know what he is trying to say, but hearing him refer to getting me out of my dress sends a hot flush simmering beneath my cheeks.

"Aubrey, I didn't mean it like that." His cool fingers brush my blushing cheek.

"It's okay. I think I knew what you meant," I stammer, my heart racing as I struggle to rein it back under control. My voice must sound hurt as the words leave my mouth because a faint red tone surfaces in his skin.

"It's not that I don't want you out of that dress in that way, either... I just know it's been a hell of a day for both of us, and I don't want to do something... I don't want to scare you, Aubrey. After what Amat tried to do to you, I understand if you want to keep your distance." His hands move back down to his sides.

He's right. I should want to keep any man at arm's length after what I went through today. But Tapley isn't just any man.

"I'm okay," I whisper.

"You don't look okay." His fingers brush my shoulder and down along my collarbone. "You're covered in bruises. Bite marks." His jaw tightens.

I instantly feel dirty and not from the hours I spent on the back of a horse today. I'm covered in blood—wearing it on a white dress meant for my wedding day. There are marks on my body from a man who tried to assault and humiliate me. And on my hands are the stains of that same man's blood, a constant reminder of what had to be done to save the one person I can't live without. When I drove the end of that bayonet into Amat's side, I posted the words on my own Wanted poster and added Tapley's right beside mine.

I look at the torn fabric of my dress and am overcome with the urge to scrub away the stains. My fingers tug at the cloth, and I suddenly find myself crying as the dress feels like it's suffocating me, tightening around my waist with each breath I take.

"I have to get this off. I can't wear this." I reach for the buttons frantically.

"Aubrey—it's okay. Let me help you." Tapley places his hands over my arms, trying to calm me before I shred the dress to pieces. "Keep still." He stands and moves his hands to the long chain of buttons down my back. "Try to keep breathing."

I didn't realize I wasn't breathing. At his soothing words, I immediately exhale, pushing out the cramped air I've held tightly in my lungs. His fingers undo each button until the dress easily falls off my shoulders and onto the floor. Tapley pauses before his hands move to the strings of the corset, and I can feel his stare lingering on my chemise. He clears his throat then begins pulling each string until the corset loosens. I press my hands to my chest, keeping a layer still carefully covering me. By the time he's undone the final string, his hands are trembling the slightest bit, and I can hear his breathing growing shallow.

"You're shaking, love." I peek at him over my shoulder. His face is nearly as white as the sheets over the furniture.

"I've never had to undo a lady's dress before, and I definitely have never undone her undergarments." He takes his hands from my back and timidly turns to stare at the fireplace instead.

"So I didn't exactly have time to pack a change of clothes." I turn to face him, my arms still holding the corset to my chest.

"Right—sorry. I'll see what I can find." His eyes never turn to look at me. He walks to the steps leading upstairs and disappears into the darkness of the attic. I can hear him rummaging around upstairs for a few minutes before he finally returns with a baggy blue shirt. "It's too dark to find the clothes I'm looking for. This will work until there's enough light to dig around upstairs tomorrow." When he reaches the bottom of the steps, he hands me a faded-blue button-up shirt that's long enough to cover the essentials.

"Thank you," I say as he walks to the fireplace.

He turns his back, giving me privacy to change my clothes. I appreciate his gesture, but a small part of me wishes he would just glance over at me even the smallest fraction of a second. I don't want him to be afraid to touch me, to kiss me. He's all I have in this world. My left hand holds the unfamiliar, and my right hand holds him. Tapley balances my reality, and the more distance he puts between us, the more I feel like I'm slipping off the edge.

I drop the remainder of my dress to the floor and pull the shirt over my head. The fabric is soft, like old worn denim, and it smells like tanned leather and grass. I look down at my chemise and realize I'm stuck in an oversized shirt and puffy white cotton bloomers—not the most alluring outfit in the world. But even this feels better than the weight of that dress and the blood on the fabric, which serve as a reminder of today.

Tapley is crouched, poking at the charred logs of the fire. I walk over to him and rest my hand on his shoulder. His posture relaxes the moment I touch him, his tense shoulders dropping ever so slightly.

"I pulled the upstairs bed together for you. It's not much, but it'll be a safe, warm place for you to sleep tonight." He stands to face me, his shadow reflecting on the wall.

At even the smallest mention of the word *sleep*, I'm already yawning. Adrenaline has kept my exhaustion at bay the entire day. Tapley picks up the metal lantern he lit and begins the trek back up the stairs to the attic. I follow him carefully, trying to keep my balance going up the staircase without a banister. When I reach the top step, I have to slouch below the steeply sloped ceiling. There are old wooden chests lining the long wall down one side of the attic, and at the far end rests a bed underneath a small window.

Tapley stops a few feet from the bed, removes the white, half-melted candle from a lantern, and lights it. A second later, a warm, inviting glow surrounds us, the flame burning away at the blackness. As he returns one lantern to the foot of the bed, I catch him watching me, his dark eyes holding the light from the flames.

"I'll be just downstairs by the fire," he says, abruptly turning toward the stairs.

"Wait a second," I burst out.

Tapley halts, but he doesn't turn around—he just freezes as if he's waiting for something.

"Stay with me," I whisper, almost afraid for him to hear my voice.

The annoying feeling of the clock resting over my head is back again. I can feel one day about to end, and I'm now unsure about even making it through tomorrow. I'm living every second of each day as if it's an entire year of my life. Everything begins and ends before I can even make sense of it, and I just want time to freeze. I don't want to worry about tomorrow, or the next day—I want to worry about right now, and in this moment, I want to be with Tapley in every way humanly possible.

"Tapley, please stay." This time I beg, afraid that he's about to walk away.

His shoulders rise and fall rapidly as if his body is fighting with his mind over what he should do. He takes another step toward the stairway but then stops and spins around. "Aubrey, I don't know if I can just stay with you tonight. I'm afraid I'll push you further away from me, because I might—" He stops himself from saying more. "I'm afraid to have these feelings, but I'm even more afraid of not having them at all." He doesn't move, but I can feel the small space around us pulling together.

"Tapley, stay with me—I want you," I whisper, my hands trembling.

He takes a slow step forward, his eyes locked on mine, and then he takes another.

Stay with me.

He closes the distance between us, his hands wrapping around my waist and pulling me flush with his chest. His gaze burns through me, and the sensation of his eyes glancing over each inch of my bare skin is enough to set me on fire.

"I'm not afraid of you, Tapley. What I'm afraid of is not living every moment that I have with you—not loving you in each and every way possible." I tangle my fingers in his hair and kiss the base of his neck. At first, his breathing remains slow and controlled, but as my lips graze the hollow of his throat, he loses himself completely.

His body leans into mine, and his grasp around my waist grows tighter. "Aubrey, look at me."

At his whisper, I force my lips from his skin and bring my stare to his.

"You are my entire life—my existence. I will never hurt you. I'll never force you to do anything you aren't ready for." He runs his calloused fingers across my cheek and pushes them into my hair. The softest of shivers runs down my spine, and I can feel my cheeks flushing.

"I am ready to be with you—wholly, entirely, and in every way," I respond. *I'm ready to be your wife.*

I can feel Tapley's hunger for me as his face grows warm.

He nuzzles closer, resting his hot cheek against mine as he closes his eyes. I can sense him relax as his hands move up my sides gently. His touch is slow—never too urgent but just enough to make the longing seem impossibly unbearable. Tapley lifts his cheek from mine and covers the line of my jaw in kisses then moves down my neck to my collarbone. I try to quiet the moan lingering in my throat, but eventually, it escapes, and I give in to every emotion I'm feeling. I give in to him.

Tapley pushes me down onto the bed, and his lips find mine. I don't pull away from him or fear his touch as it moves below the baggy button-up shirt. His movements are no longer careful or premeditated. He doesn't struggle with himself or hesitate to touch me the way he wants. The feeling of him is undeniably beautiful, yet it's so unwaveringly strong that I'm overwhelmed with emotion. I reach for his shirt and tug it off his body, my fingers trailing along the curves of his muscles as he presses himself closer to me. He peels away my clothes with the same urgency then slows, gazing down for a long moment. His hands trail up my sides and across my chest as he brings his lips back to mine, and with each movement, our bodies pull closer together until there's nothing left between us. Tapley's lips stroke mine, the movement matching his body as he makes love to me underneath the pale moonlight shining through the small second-story window above our heads. Lips like his have never touched me this beautifully, this perfectly. His heart beats against my breasts, a feeling so moving that it nearly erases all my wounds.

With each brush of his fingertips and movement of his hands against my naked body, I feel myself coming undone—unraveling the guard I've had wound so tightly around my heart until the very moment my soul is bared to his. I take a deep breath of air into my lungs, and I silently pray that I'll never lose this man—that somehow I'll find him, no matter where I am in this world.

As his arms rest on either side of my head, I brush my fingers across his cheek. "I love you," I whisper as our stares connect. His face breaks into a smile, and I feel him melt at my words. Pulling my shoulders off the bed, I wrap my arms around his neck and bring his lips back to mine. I hold him tight inside my body and keep him captive to my kiss.

Emotions like these are so strong that they change you the moment they happen. I never knew I could be this way—this vulnerable and powerful at the same time. The feelings unnerve me, but I'm also willing to die for them. To love Tapley Holland is to live like it's my very first lifetime. From here on out, nothing else matters as much as him.

CHAPTER EIGHTEEN

Tapley's breathing matches his steady heartbeat, and I listen to its sweet sound as my head rests on his chest. We spent hours wrapped up in each other, trying not to give in to sleep until it finally overcame us both. As I lay curled up against Tapley's body, I dreamed of forever with him—a place away from the Alamo and even farther away from 1836. With the constant sound of minutes passing, I'll fall apart long before the storm of my choices hits.

We sleep well past sunrise, completely exhausted yet blissfully happy. It's almost surreal to wake up to him like this. He's so peaceful and contented that my heart feels fuller at the sight of him. I run my fingers down his chest just to make sure he's real, and he shivers at my touch.

"If you keep doing that, I'm going to keep you here all day." He looks down at me with only one eye open, an adorable grin pulling at the corners of his mouth.

"I had to make sure I wasn't dreaming." I scrunch my nose up as I peek back at him. He's even more beautiful with the sun shining through the small window above us than he was in candlelight last night.

Before I can even move, he shifts me onto his chest and brings his lips to mine. Even if I wanted to resist him, I couldn't. Just the taste of his mouth is enough to render me breathless all over again.

"Mmm." He pulls his face away from mine and lays his head back on the pillow.

"What?" I ask, slightly annoyed that he has stopped kissing me.

"I was just making sure you weren't the only one not dreaming." He smirks.

"Hey, that's my line." I cross my arms over his chest and rest my chin on top of them.

"You are something else, Aubrey Harrison. Last night…"

Before he can finish his sentence, I place a finger to his lips. "*Shh.* It doesn't need words. It happens to be perfect just the way we left it."

He kisses my finger then flips me onto my back. "We either get out of this bed and find some food, or we stay here and continue down this path, knowing there's a possibility we'll starve to death." His hand traces a line from the curve at the base of my neck down the center of my chest.

Tease. I almost say the word out loud, but I'm not sure he'd understand the term in its full twenty-first-century meaning.

As if in answer to his comment about starving, my stomach growls. "Is there even food in the house?" I sit up on the bed and wrap the faded quilt around my naked body.

"Of course not. We'll have to go hunting." His eyes shine with excitement as he reaches for his clothes, which lie in a pile on the floor.

"I'll need something else to wear, unless you're okay with me not wearing anything all day." I casually drop the quilt from my shoulders and look up at him. He stares at me for a few seconds, and I can almost see him struggling to keep himself from slipping right back into bed with me.

"You'll definitely need something to wear." Tapley brushes his fingers through his hair and turns to a large wooden chest against the far wall. He pulls up the lid and begins digging through piles of fabric until he finds what he's looking for. "These were my mother's. She was about your size."

He brings me a long gray floral dress with lacy sleeves. It's beautiful but simple, and I'm thankful to finally have a dress that doesn't require ten other layers of fabric. I pull on my chemise and step into the dress.

"Do you mind?" I turn my back to Tapley, hoping he'll assist with the buttons.

"I would rather not be buttoning you back into a dress, but I also don't want you to catch a cold." He kisses the back of each of my shoulders and quickly fastens the line of buttons.

There's a matching sash that runs right below my breast, and somehow, Tapley manages to tie it into a neat bow at my back. I peek over my shoulder to inspect his work then shoot him a smile.

"Thanks." I kiss his cheek, and color instantly rushes in beneath his skin.

"Let's go." He takes my hand and leads me back downstairs to the first floor.

Last night's fire has died down, but there's enough sunlight peeking through cracks in the boarded-up windows to light the room. Tapley doesn't linger in the house—in fact, he practically rushes me out the door and into the daylight. Quinto is waiting at the gate of the corral, and he nickers at us the moment we turn the corner.

"Wait here." Tapley leads Quinto to me then heads around the back side of the house.

"Hey, you." I stroke the gray gelding's face as he presses his nose into the space between my arm and my side.

Tapley returns a few minutes later with Quinto's bridle, a long bundle of rope, and a small rifle.

I point to the gun. "What are you going to do with that?"

"Hunt rabbits. It's a rabbit gun—what else would I do with it?" He laughs and quickly puts the bridle over Quinto's head.

Right... rabbit. There's a first time for everything, I guess.

I open the gate, and Tapley leads Quinto outside of the corral.

"I hope you don't mind riding bareback today. I think Quinto has earned a day without having to carry the weight of us and his saddle. Besides, I don't want to risk you being in the house alone—not when the Mexican Army is looking for you. At least out here, I can protect you." He smirks and lines the horse up with the side of the fence so I can easily climb up.

I manage to swing my leg over Quinto's back with little effort, and the fabric of the dress flows over my legs perfectly. *Now, this is the type of dress a woman should be wearing when she's forced to ride a horse.*

Tapley quickly takes his place behind me and puts his arms around my waist so he still has control over the reins. I feel odd being in front of him instead of riding behind him, but without the saddle to hold me in place, I'm thankful to have his body to lean against.

He steers Quinto along a small path that runs parallel to the river a steep drop below us. The brush grows in thick patches on either side, but with light in the sky above us, I can clearly see beyond the cedar treetops and into the rolling hills nearby. Quinto veers to the right and makes his way down a hill to a flat section of land close to the river. Bluebonnets have already begun to fill the countryside—a welcoming sign that winter is nearing an end and spring is finally here. Tapley backs Quinto up into a thick section of trees right outside of the field.

"What are we doing?" I ask.

"We're waiting," he whispers and points to the riverbank a short distance away. "Animals come here for water. If we're lucky, they'll show up before dark."

"And if we're not lucky?" I ask.

"Then it is going to be a very long night." He kisses the side of my neck, and I'm suddenly not so sure about what type of long night he's referring to.

We wait for what feels like an hour, Quinto standing perfectly still and neither of us saying a word. After a while, I hear a noise coming from behind us, and Tapley reaches for the gun strapped across his back. I glance back at him, and he gestures to his left with his chin. Following his gaze, I see something moving in the brush a hundred yards or so away. I can't quite tell what it is, but it's definitely bigger than a rabbit. A few minutes later, a lone doe appears at the edge of the field. She takes a quick look around her before crossing in the direction of the riverbank. I tense at the sight of her, but the deer doesn't seem as terrifyingly deadly as it did when I was stuck behind the wheel of a car.

Tapley tries to hand me the gun, but I look back at him with wide eyes.

"I can't shoot," I mouth and try not to breathe.

Without replying, he moves the gun to the soft space between my shoulder and my collarbone, then he guides my right hand to hold it in place. I move my left hand to the other side of the gun, not sure of where I should even be holding it, but Tapley places his left hand on top of mine as we steady the weapon together. His right hand reaches for the flintlock at the top of the rifle, and he slowly presses it down until it clicks.

"I'll aim it for you. Just hold it steady, and pull the trigger when I count to one," he whispers.

We watch as the doe bends down to take a drink from the river, and I try not to shake.

"Three... two..."

I hold my breath, waiting for the final number to leave Tapley's lips. I hear him cluck, and the deer instantly pulls her head up from the water and looks in our direction.

"One." Tapley holds my hands steady, and I close my eyes and pull the trigger. I expected the sound of the bullet blasting from the barrel to shatter my hearing, but I never thought I'd feel that powerful of a kickback from a weapon Tapley called a "rabbit gun." I exhale, and when I breathe in, my nose floods with the smell of gunpowder. The adrenaline from the shot numbs the pain fighting its way through my shoulder.

"Open your eyes, Aubrey." He peels my fingers off the gun before I pull my eyelids open. I can see the fallen deer at the edge of the field.

"Rabbit gun?" I'm practically yelling at him over the loud ringing in my ears.

He slides down from Quinto's back and looks up at me. "That's what my father told me when he gave it to me on my tenth birthday. I soon realized that he'd understated the caliber of the gun when I tried to shoot my first rabbit, but I kind of just kept the name for sentiment." He laughs and helps me down from the horse.

I glare at him and rub the sore spot next to my shoulder.

"Would you have pulled the trigger if you knew it was going to hurt that bad?" He takes my hand in his, and we make our way to where the deer is lying.

"Maybe—but a warning would've been nice." I throw him another look.

"There might soon come a time when you need to pull the trigger of a gun without me here to steady your hands. I just wanted to make sure you knew how to use one." He releases my hand and puts his arm over my shoulders, holding me next to him as we walk. Then he pauses, pulls off the bundled rope from over his chest, and attaches one end around the deer and the other around Quinto's neck. "Up you go." He glances at the horse's back.

I grab a handful of gray mane right before Tapley reaches for my leg and gently lifts me onto Quinto. This time, he doesn't take his place behind me. He pulls the reins from Quinto's neck and leads him back down the pathway toward the house as the deer drags a few feet behind us.

BY THE TIME WE NEAR the house, the sun has already begun to sink between the hills in the distance. Neither of us has eaten in more than twenty-four hours, and a warm dinner is quite possibly the best idea I've heard of all day. We round the last bend of the riverbank before the house comes into view.

Tapley freezes, his body growing rigid as he reaches for the gun strapped to his back.

"What is it?" I try to find what has his attention.

"There's smoke coming from the fireplace. Someone's inside the house. Stay here until I come get you." He loops the reins back over Quinto's head and places them in my hands.

He jogs to the front door and pauses before he enters the room. There's a horse waiting in the corral, but it's not one that I recognize. The minutes pass by too slowly, and I begin to worry when Tapley doesn't return right away. I haven't heard a shot ringing from inside the walls, but that doesn't mean anything. The person inside could have easily hurt him some other way. I can feel the drumming of my heart as my gaze darts between Tapley and the now occupied house. I'm not sure if I should remain hidden in the brush or follow him into the house.

Before I can second-guess myself, I slide down from Quinto's back and begin walking up the pathway to the front door. I obviously haven't thought this through very well because on the other end of the reins, securely locked in my grasp, is a horse that I completely forget about until Tapley pulls open the front door and stares at me with a confused look on his face.

"Aubrey...? What are you doing?"

"I was worried about you, so I was going to walk through the door and make sure you were okay..." My logic felt a lot more... well, logical, when the idea of saving him originally crossed my mind.

"Were you planning on using poor Quinto as your weapon of choice and then throwing the deer at them if that didn't work?" He unties the rope attached to the deer from around Quinto's neck and grabs the reins from my hand as a peculiar smile crosses his face.

"No. I just forgot to tie him up," I blurt, standing helplessly in front of the door.

Tapley laughs his way back to the corral as he takes off Quinto's bridle and lets the gray gelding loose with the other horse.

"I didn't forget about you, just so you know." He turns me back around and points me in the direction of the house. "I'm going to take care of this deer. Why don't you go meet our guest?" He looks inside the house, and I can see the silhouette of a man sitting in a chair near the fireplace. "It's all right. I'll be inside in a few minutes." He smiles reassuringly before picking up the rope to drag the deer around to the back of the house.

I pause before walking inside, nervousness spinning inside me as I look at the back of this nameless stranger. "Trust him, Aubrey," I mutter as I step inside and close the door behind me.

The figure by the fire turns to look over his shoulder, then he smiles at me as he gets to his feet and walks across the room to where I'm standing. He's tall, with a long face and dark hair that hangs below his ears. His skin is tanned and rough looking, but his clothes are nice, and his smile is almost childish as it matches the curious twinkle in his eye.

"Miss Harrison." He bows briefly. "My name is David Crockett, but you can call me Davy."

I smile and attempt my most graceful curtsy—to *Davy Crockett*.

"I hope you'll pardon my intrusion, but your father told me I would find you and Mr. Holland here."

This is not real life.

CHAPTER NINETEEN

I've always pictured him in a coonskin hat and a fringed suede jacket, but the man standing in front of me is relatively normal looking.

"Davy, I'm honored to meet you."

I smile at him warmly while quietly freaking out inside the safety of my own mind. He's one of those people who has been made a legend in the pages of the history books I've buried my nose in for three years. *If only Dr. Hubbell could be here now.*

"How is my father?" I ask, moving to the cabinet I watched Tapley pull the whiskey from last night.

"San Antonio has been lost to chaos in less than a day. I'm not going to lie, Miss Harrison—these are perilous times, and I suspect that even worse things are closing in on us as we speak. However, your father is doing well, as is your mother, all things considered. They came to me late yesterday evening after the news of Colonel Amat's death reached the town."

The mere mention of Amat nearly sends the bottle I'm holding to the floor. I immediately tense, trying not to remember what almost happened to me yesterday.

"Here, let me help you." Davy reaches for the bottle in my trembling hands and pours a single shot of whiskey into each metal cup.

Without hesitating, I pick up the glass and throw the sour liquid down my throat. "What happened in the barn with Colonel Amat... it didn't have to end that way, but I didn't have a choice."

"Tapley told me what happened in the barn. I know that you were only defending yourself. I'm not here to condemn you—I'm here to help you escape what's to come." He pours another shot into his glass and tosses it back. If history got one thing right, it's that Davy Crockett can probably drink an entire river dry.

Tapley comes back into the room a moment later, each of his hands carrying a freshly butchered section of deer meat. I have no idea what I'm supposed to do with it. I've never had to cook in a world without ovens or microwaves. The only thing I can think of is to use the flames from the fire.

Tapley must see my confusion as I stare at the meat on the table. "There's an iron skillet hanging on the wall over there." He points to the kitchen.

I walk a few steps across the room and pull it down from a hook on the wall. It's heavy but clean and big enough to cook a meal for all three people. Iron skillet in hand, I head back to the table, where Tapley and Davy are slicing the meat into small sections of backstrap.

"Good backstrap is hard to come by these days. Tapley, you must be a pretty straight shot to take this doe down and leave the best parts unspoiled." He drops a handful of deer meat into the skillet and reaches for another section.

"Actually, we have Aubrey to thank for dinner. She's the one who pulled the trigger." He smiles up at me proudly, not bothering to mention that I wasn't the one holding the gun steady enough to aim at the target.

Once the skillet is full, Tapley picks it up and sets it on top of the logs of the fire. I never would have imagined myself eating unseasoned meat from a deer I killed, let alone cooking it over the flames of a fire inside a small house along the San Antonio River. But then again, I would have never imagined that I would find myself traveling nearly two centuries back in time.

I fill my tin cup up one more time and take a seat on the faded sofa near the fireplace. Tapley follows close behind me with the bottle of whiskey, sitting next to me as we wait for Davy to join us. He paces in front of the fireplace for a few minutes, watching the meat cook as if he's trying to buy himself some time.

"May I?" He points to the whiskey bottle, and Tapley hands it to him just as Davy finally settles in a wooden chair across from us.

"It's all right, Davy. You can tell her," Tapley says.

Davy takes a drink from the bottle and clears his throat before his brown eyes fall on me. "Your parents are being watched, which is why they sent me to find you. Santa Anna has put a bounty on both of your heads—he wants you dead for what happened to Colonel Amat. The Mexican Army is gathering a few miles outside of town, and we've begun gathering our own forces to defend San Antonio. It's only a matter of time before they move to take it back, but we've sent for reinforcements, and we're waiting on their response." He takes another swig from the bottle and hands it back to Tapley, who quickly does the same. "Santa Anna is demanding that both of you be turned over to him along with the control of San Antonio. If we don't surrender you, they will find you themselves." He looks over at me then moves his stare to Tapley.

"So we'll leave as soon as possible. They can't all follow us forever, can they?" I ask.

Tapley reaches for my hand. "Aubrey, we won't make it out of San Antonio alive."

I turn my attention to Davy, whose eyes watch the flames of the fire.

"I don't understand... why are you even here, then? If there's no hope for us, why even risk coming all this way to find us?"

"Because you have another option, but it's an option that might not yield a different fate." His voice is quiet, hollow.

"What option?" I ask, but I already know what he's going to say.

He turns his attention back to me, and his lips are set in a tight line. "You can ride as fast as you can to the Alamo tomorrow, and while you're riding, you can pray that the fortress doesn't fall to those who want you dead." Davy stands up, wraps the hot handle of the skillet in a small pelt, pulls it from the fire, and rests it on the table. I sit down close to Tapley on a worn wooden bench, my mind consumed with thoughts of him, but he still feels so far away. The entire time since I've been living in 1836, I've known what's coming, but I never pictured that I'd be inside of those walls in a fight from which no one walks away. I either die at the hands of the Mexican Army, or I die among those trying to defend this town from its biggest enemy. No second or third backup plan exists to get us out of this.

"So we'll go to the Alamo." As the words leave my lips, I can't take them back—I can't change this fate I'm riding straight into. The only thing I can do, between now and the very last day the Alamo stands against Santa Anna, is live every second like it's my last.

"There's one more thing. You can't bring an unmarried young woman into the middle of a garrison's headquarters without risking her safety. To keep from having a scandal, we will be calling her Mrs. Holland. It's best not to let anyone know otherwise." He nods at both of us before excusing himself and going outside.

Mrs. Holland. I repeat the name in my mind, not to memorize the way it sounds but to memorize the way it makes me feel. I lean my head against Tapley's shoulder and pray for time to stop. I don't want to lose him, but I don't know how to save him, either. I just have to love him for as long as I can even if it will never be long enough.

IT'S A FEW HOURS PAST dark by the time Davy leaves. Tension is rising in San Antonio, and there's already a small group of people posted at the Alamo who depend on his return. Tapley walks outside with Davy to see him off, and I wait for him to return, but after a few minutes pass, I still find myself alone on the sofa. The crickets are singing in the night air, their chirping almost driving me mad as I struggle to think clearly. Part of me is screaming to take Tapley by the hand, get on Quinto's back, and ride as fast as we can out of town. We could make it farther in the dark, but we also have no idea where the Mexican troops are camped. Davy said that the city is surrounded by small groups of infantry. If we ride straight into one of them, we won't even make it to see the end of the Alamo.

My foot hasn't stopped tapping since I sat down—a nervous habit that somehow followed me back in time. I finally stand from the couch, unable to endure the empty room another second. I pull a quilt from the arm of the sofa and wrap it around my shoulders before heading outside into the chilled air. The moving water from the nearby river blends with the crickets in a steady flow of noise, and the huge Texas sky rests above me, a sea of stars spanning outward in every direction.

I turn to look at the corral and find Tapley leaning against the wooden gate. Other than the rise and fall of his shoulders as he takes slow breaths, he doesn't move at all. I walk quietly to his side, trying to soften the sound of my shoes against the dry grass. He's shivering, his face an even paler shade than the full moon above us. I take the blanket from my shoulders and place it over his, and he finally turns to look at me. Tapley reaches for me, pulling me in between his body and the gate. He tucks the edges of the quilt around my back so that it securely wraps both of us, but I can still feel him shaking. I rest my head on his shoulder as we stand together.

"What are you doing out here?" I ask him quietly.

He doesn't respond right away, but I can hear his heartbeat speed up.

"I just hope Davy is right about the Alamo. I have to keep you safe. This is the only thing that matters to me anymore," he whispers, his arms tightening around me. I can feel him clinging to me, his fingertips pressing against my skin and the heat of his breath brushing over me as it drowns out the chill.

How can I tell him that we'll never leave those stone walls? How can I tell him that everyone is going to die—Crockett, Travis, Bowie? We're destined to die, and I can't do anything about it. History is set, and I'm doomed to watch it play out.

"I know." My voice shakes. "Promise me that if something happens to me, you won't give up. Promise me that you won't stop fighting for your life even if I'm no longer there to live it with you." Maybe he gets away. I know there are no love stories that survive the Alamo, but maybe he survives alone. If Santa Anna wants him dead, Tapley will have to keep his survival a secret—one that future historians never even get wind of.

Tapley leans his head down to mine and kisses the top of my forehead. "I refuse to live if there's nothing for me to live for. Aubrey, you have given me a life when I lost everything. Even if it's not a long life, I would rather live a few short days with you by my side, as my *wife*, than endure endless days alone. I promise that when we make it out of the Alamo, I will marry you."

He doesn't realize how perfect yet how utterly heartbreaking his words are. I would rather die after just a fraction of my life loving Tapley Holland than veer down a safer road that leads me away from him. I'm now Aubrey Holland, who takes risks easily and even takes a chance at the impossible. I would die time after time just to be able to love Tapley for one hour, one week. In this reality, I've loved him for thirteen days, and the second we set foot inside the walls of the Alamo, I'll have thirteen more. I will take the impossible road—the dark, twisted, short road with only one ending.

"Come inside with me, Mrs. Holland."

I look up at him, and Tapley smiles, picks me up, and carries me back into the house.

CHAPTER TWENTY

We leave behind the small house by the river just before dawn, trying to make it back to town before anyone can recognize us. I've grown too accustomed to the sound of Quinto's hooves beating against the ground. The rumble shatters the still morning air, creating a welcome distraction, but all I hear during the brief moment between each galloping step is the sound of my heart breaking.

I cling to Tapley's back as we race underneath the low-hanging branches. He maneuvers Quinto around each sharp bend of the road without slowing the horse's pace as we try to outrun the quickly rising sun. There's a thin trail of smoke breaking through the air close by, and I think I can hear the thick accents of Mexican soldiers from somewhere in the brush a few hundred yards away. I keep my eyes straight ahead, afraid that if I look hard enough, I'll see them moving in our direction. Fortunately, as we push forward, the noise stays behind us.

The trees are growing thinner and the brush is worn down as the path widens near the edge of the forest. We're coming up to one of the main roads leading into town, but instead of staying straight, Tapley turns Quinto to the left, allowing the horse's speed to increase across a flat dry field. I can see the faint outline of San Antonio to our right, and all along the hilltops in the distance are chains of smoke marking where Santa Anna's camps surround the town. As the sun finally breaches the treetops, it casts a faint glow somewhere at the end of the empty field—a beacon shining over the Alamo as we near our destination.

Wooden barricades are placed at even distances outside the stone walls, and I can hear voices yelling as we head straight for the back gates. I wait for Tapley to slow Quinto's pace, but he keeps pushing the horse straight toward the closed gates. Right before I'm sure we're going to crash into them, the gates pull open.

I look behind us at the narrow space we just flew through, and the gates are already shut behind us. Tapley pulls Quinto to a skidding stop, and if my arms weren't securely holding his waist, I would surely be flying from the saddle and onto the dirt. Newton's laws of physics apparently still apply when you're in a saddle. I can feel the stares of at least fifty people weighing heavily on us both as we wait in the center of a large open yard surrounded by the outer walls.

"Tapley," a man yells from the top of a flat-roofed building in the corner closest to us.

With the sun shining right in our eyes, it's hard to recognize the man as he climbs down a wooden ladder to the ground below and jogs in our direction. "Mrs. Holland," the man says, and this time I recognize his voice.

"Davy," Tapley says, "I hope our presence doesn't cause any unrest." He looks around at the men staring at us.

"Not at all. We are all here, too, for the same reason—to defend San Antonio from Santa Anna. All these men know that they'll be fighting, and hopefully killing, the Mexican soldiers waiting right outside these walls. You two just happened to be the ones to draw enemy blood first. If anything, these men are disappointed that they didn't get to do the honors themselves." He laughs and reaches for my hand so he can help me down from the saddle.

Tapley slides off right behind me, pulling the reins off Quinto's sweaty neck.

Davy pats the gray gelding on the neck and motions for us to follow him. "Let's get this horse taken care of."

We walk down the center of the dirt yard and bring Quinto into a smaller square area where quite a few other horses are already resting. Tapley hands me the reins then loosens the cinch and pulls off the heavy leather saddle and blanket.

"You can turn him loose, Aubrey," he says over his shoulder as he carries his saddle to a wooden table a few yards away.

I undo the buckles on the bridle and slide the bit out of Quinto's mouth. He chews for a few seconds, probably glad to be rid of the bitter piece of metal. Then he turns and ambles to a large round bale of hay, where a few other horses are standing. He hasn't eaten anything but grass in the last few days, and I'm sure the unlimited supply of hay is a nice change. Tapley walks back over to where I'm standing and hands me the burlap bag with a few changes of clothes that was tied to the saddle.

"You two should come with me, and we'll try to get you settled someplace," Davy says. "I'll have you know that Mrs. Holland is the only woman inside these walls right now. It'll be best if you keep her close."

He throws Tapley a quick glance, and I can read between the lines what he's trying to be so discreet about. With a hundred men and only one woman, there's a distinct possibility that we will run into the Colonel Amat barn situation all over again. Without hesitation, Tapley picks up my hand and tightly fastens his fingers around mine. Of all the things to worry about inside these walls, the one that concerns me least is Tapley letting me out of sight.

Davy leads us away from the barnyard and into a long barrack-like building. There are cots pressed up against every free inch of space along the walls and blankets laid across the middle of the floor. We walk to the end of the hall, where a large set of double wooden doors rests. Davy knocks and immediately pushes open the door and enters the room.

It's a much larger room than the narrow barracks, and in the very center rests a wooden rectangular table with matching chairs evenly spaced around all four sides. Three men sit staring at us with tired eyes and furrowed brows.

The man at the head of the table has a thin face with long sideburns running along his jawline and a very defined, dimpled chin. He stands up and reaches for Tapley's hand. "You must be Tapley Holland. My name is Lieutenant Colonel William Barret Travis, but Travis will do just fine." He shakes Tapley's hand warmly then turns to me and bows. "Mrs. Holland, I presume?" He smiles at me.

Travis looks over at the round-faced man sitting directly to his right. "This is Jim Bowie, and next to him is Dr. Amos Pollard." The men rise to shake our hands then quietly sit back down.

Dropping the burlap bag onto the floor by my feet, I take a seat in one of the empty chairs and try my best to comprehend what exactly is happening to me right now. I'm in the same room, at the same table, as four of the people who helped bring Texas her independence. I know that all of these men die in just a few days, and I'm actually here to witness them as I breathe the same dusty air into my lungs that they do and hear their actual voices—the voices of legends. I look over at Tapley, and he seems much less starstruck, but then again, he hasn't read the same history books that I have. Tapley doesn't know the importance of these men to this fortress we've run away to.

"Is there any news from General Sam Houston?" Davy reaches for a metal pitcher near the center of the table and pours clear liquid into a tin cup. He slides the pitcher over to us, just as Bowie hands Tapley and me our own glasses.

The liquid alerts me to my thirst, but I'm cautious about taking a drink. Based on the way Davy drank last night, I could very easily take a giant swig, fully expecting water, and discover that it's moonshine. Just to be safe, I discreetly sniff the contents of the cup, waiting for the burning scent of alcohol to sting my nose. When I don't catch a trace of anything at all, I take a sip. As soon as the water touches my tongue, I gulp more of it down. Tapley is already pouring his second glass, and he fills my now-empty cup as well.

"I sent a letter to Gonzales early this morning. I expect to have news in a few days' time," Travis replies.

Jim Bowie finally weighs in, his speech slurred the slightest bit. "Another forty men arrived while you were gone last night. We have nearly a hundred 'n fifty men now." He begins coughing violently, lifting a white handkerchief to his face.

I worry as he struggles to breathe, but the rest of the men just look at him like they're used to the sound. I remember reading that Jim Bowie's health began rapidly declining in the days before the Alamo. As I see his face growing paler by the minute, I understand why Travis will take control of the garrison. I can't miss the passing glances between Dr. Pollard and Davy as they wait for Jim's coughing to cease. When he finally pulls the white cloth from his face, I can see traces of blood on the fabric. *Consumption! He's in the last stages of tuberculosis!*

"I saw at least double that camped out between here and the river. There's at least another five hundred or so men a few miles east. A hundred and fifty isn't enough, Jim." Davy's voice is hard.

"It might not be enough to win this fight, but it's enough to hold this mission until Sam sends backup," Travis says.

"How long do you think we can hold out before they try to breach the walls?" Davy asks.

"Seven... eight days maybe. That should buy us enough time." Bowie spins a knife on the tabletop as he speaks, letting the blade turn one direction a few times before stopping it and spinning it in the other direction.

You're wrong! All of you are wrong, I silently scream at them. *Eight days... you really think eight days is all you're going to need.* "What if it's longer?" I blurt.

I feel the eyes of five men suddenly focused on me, my question clearly catching them off guard.

Say something else, Aubrey.

"What I mean is… what if it takes General Houston longer than eight days to bring reinforcements?" I already know that no backup is coming, and a part of me wants to prepare them for the worst. I need them to think up an alternative plan that will last longer than eight days.

"If it comes to that, we will hold the Alamo for as long as possible," Travis answers with concern written across his face.

Tapley still sits quietly next to me, mindlessly tracing the edge of the metal cup with his finger. Looking across the table at Travis, he finally says, "What can I do to help you?"

"Well, word around the town is that you're one of the best horsemen we've got," Travis says. "We have nearly thirty horses inside the walls, and most of our manpower has been tasked with setting up trenches and stockades along the north wall. If you want to be of use and keep watch over Mrs. Holland, I could use you in the stable yard."

"There's a small room nearby. It's not much, but I figured it would give you two some privacy." Davy stands up from the table and heads back to the double doors as Tapley and I move to follow him. I nearly forget the bag at my feet, but as I trip over it, I'm quickly reminded that I'll be stuck in dirty clothes for nearly two weeks if I leave it behind.

The narrow halls of the Alamo are dimly lit with lanterns, and the walls are a few layers thick with stone. Davy leads us through a side passageway, which eventually opens up into a large room with a high ceiling, tall pillars, and a huge stone cross resting beneath the open windows on a far wall. I recognize the room instantly. I was inside these walls at least five times growing up. We're walking through the original old chapel that made up the Alamo mission. I can imagine the display cases filled with artifacts sitting against the walls as tourists peer inside them. One day, the original doors of the Alamo will be displayed where the stone cross now sits. I can see the past and future merging into one as I step upon stones I've walked on before.

Davy disappears down another dark hall, and we follow to where he's stopped outside a smaller wooden door. "When you're settled, meet me in the stable yard." He looks over at Tapley before he turns back down the short hallway and disappears around the corner.

Tapley pushes his shoulder into the heavy wooden door, and it opens with an eerie creak. The room is larger than I expected but no more than twelve feet by twelve feet. There's a small straw mattress lying on the floor, and at least a dozen unlit white candles rest on a ledge attached to one wall. Trails of hard white wax are melted onto the stone ledge, and the candles are burned down to varying heights. I'm surprised to find a few long matches dropped on the floor. I pick one up, strike it across the front of a stone, and bring the burning end to the charred candlewicks. I manage to get the last candle lit right before the flame reaches the end of the match and hits my fingertips. A warm glow fills the dark room, and even though it's still dreary, I'm thankful to have a little bit of light.

"How are you feeling?" Tapley wraps his arms around my waist as he stands behind me.

"I'm starting to feel better." I try to force a smile across my face, but as soon as my lips pull upward, a yawn breaks through instead.

"You should get some rest while I help Davy outside." He kisses the back of my neck and slides his hands down my hips.

"You should just stay here. We don't have to leave this room at all," I mumble, suddenly fully aware of my rapid breathing as Tapley moves his lips down the left side of my neck and across the top of my shoulder. "You're not supposed to let me out of your sight, remember?" I feel my eyes closing as I lean into him.

"Good thing there's a brace on this side of room, then. I'm fully confident that no one can break down the door while you're in here and I'm outside," he whispers then laughs. "I can't just lock myself in here with you all day while the rest of the men are pulling their weight to reinforce these walls. They offered us protection. The least I can do is help out where I'm needed." He kisses my neck one last time and releases his hands, which had drifted low enough down my stomach that my knees are weak and my head spinning.

"I love you," he says as he walks out the door and carefully shuts it behind him.

I pull the wooden brace securely across the doorframe and take a quick look around the room. The afternoon sun is now high in the sky, and I can see glimpses of light through small cracks in the stone above me. In a few hours, the sun will set, and the day will come to an end. I'll no longer have thirteen days left. Tomorrow I'll find myself with only twelve.

CHAPTER TWENTY-ONE

I've always been one to find a routine and stick to it, but everything changes so quickly inside these walls that I find myself doing different tasks each day—cleaning, cooking, feeding horses, and mending torn uniforms. Luckily, the main buildings that make up the inner walls of the Alamo aren't difficult for me to memorize. Narrow halls run into narrower ones, which then lead to corners or open into larger rooms. The only way I can get from one side to the other is by following the stone floors until I'm back where I began or by taking the shorter route across the stable area and through the large dirt yard. It's strange to imagine this structure as part of the original Spanish mission—a holy and revered place where people came to make peace with God, not to take the lives of their enemies. Travis and Bowie have turned the old mission into a fortress—a temporary stronghold where Texas will make her stand.

Nothing about the Alamo is big or daunting. Its stone walls are simple, easily breached. It's a place that was never meant to hold off an army of fifteen hundred men. I cross the abbey yard and walk beneath the heavy branches of the ancient oak tree at the center. Ten cannons are lined in a row at the far end of the dirt, and men are scrubbing the iron surfaces until the dark metal gleams in the sun. A few of them watch me as I walk past. I can feel their eyes on my back as I head away from them.

I remember Crockett and Travis's words to Tapley: "It'll be best if you keep her close." Not even a day after that warning, I find myself walking alone, but somehow, I'm confident that if I can take on Amat and walk away untouched, I will survive inside these walls.

Most of the men are either military-garrison members wearing faded-gray wool uniforms, or volunteers wearing clothes meant for anything from farming to hunting. As I stop to draw water from the well at the edge of the yard, I overhear a few of the men.

"I rode with Crockett from Tennessee a few weeks ago," a bearded man in his late thirties is saying to a gray-haired man leaning against the arches in front of the barracks.

"It must be an honor to have ridden by Crockett's side." The gray-haired man lets out a slow whistle. "He's built himself quite a reputation—even folks from my town in Ohio know his name."

Ohio and Tennessee. These men came all the way across the country to help defend the Alamo.

Tapley has told me that his family was originally from Ohio, so I make a mental note to ask him if he knows the gray-haired stranger. I've read about the defenders of the Alamo and how people from all over rallied to help Texas earn her freedom. There are even a few Scottish natives somewhere inside these walls, but reading about them doesn't do this reality much justice. These people surrounding me—the people whose blood will spill on this sacred ground—have come together for the sake of freedom, the idea this country was built on. The realization sends a chill down my spine, and I find my hands shaking as I pull the bucket to the top of the well.

Over the last few weeks, I've found it harder to recall what life was like before my accident. The memories I've made in 1836 overshadow anything from my past. As I listen to the men's stories, I remember meeting the Holland family on their journey to Texas from Ohio. It was the same time George and Charlotte headed south from Virginia. We met each other on the road, and the families ended up traveling together the rest of the journey to Texas. Tapley and I were only children, but I can picture him perfectly. This memory feels so real as if my mind is merging with the Aubrey of this life, and I'm becoming less of the Aubrey I once was.

Busy footsteps against stone floors bring my attention back to the garrison. A few smaller groups of men have arrived in the last two days, but even with an increase in soldiers, the number here is still small compared to Santa Anna's army. His men have already begun constructing a makeshift artillery battery on the west side of the river, and the camps have all moved within a mile of the fortress.

With just under two hundred men inside its walls, the Alamo has been turned into a stronghold almost overnight. Additional cannons are hiding just outside the walls behind reinforced wooden trenches. Artillery stations are spread throughout the wagonyard as men arrange barrels of gunpowder in stacks a few feet high.

I approach the stable yard and spot Tapley building wooden water troughs to accommodate the growing number of horses. At least ten more have been added to the herd, and the animals are restless with all the activity buzzing around them night and day. Tapley looks up at me just as I make it to his side, a smile crossing his face. There are dark circles under his eyes, and his skin has already taken on a slightly darker shade from working in the sun all day.

"Good morning." I crouch next to him and set the bucket of water down.

The Texas air is still chilly, and there are rumors that a cold front will hit sometime in the next few days, making it even worse. Tapley is sweating despite the cold air. I push away a few strands of hair from his forehead.

"Where have you been all day?" He puts down the rusted hammer he's holding, taking a seat on the straw-covered ground, out of breath.

"Travis asked me to patch a few of the men's uniforms, and I just finished a little bit ago." I sit next to him and pull out a crisp red apple from a pocket of the apron that covers the front of my dress. "I figured you worked through lunch again." I toss him the apple and watch as Quinto eyes it from nearby.

"I haven't seen much of Travis today." He looks over at me. "Davy mentioned that Bowie turned over control of the Alamo to Travis late last night."

"Bowie must be getting worse..." I force my expression to stay blank as I go through the time line in my mind. *If Travis just gained control of the garrison, then we must only be a few days away from this battle.*

"There's no word from Gonzales or General Houston, but Travis and Bowie are still confident that reinforcements will arrive in a few days' time." Tapley moves his attention to the horses nearby, their ears flicking forward and back. A worried look clouds his eyes for a single moment as he watches the herd grow restless, but then Quinto trots over to us with a bounce in his step. The rest and abundance of hay has cleared away any sign of the horse's exhaustion.

"Someone thinks I'm going to share." Tapley laughs and tosses a small rock in Quinto's direction, sending him trotting away with a swishing tail. "Not today, sir." He takes a bite of the apple and leans back on his elbows. "So good," he mumbles through another bite. Tapley looks over his shoulder at a group of men running down the center of the wagonyard then disappearing out of sight.

"What's that all about?" I close my eyes and tilt my face up toward the sun high above our heads, hoping the rumored cold front is exactly that—a rumor and nothing more.

"Who knows. They've been shooting at burlap targets on the far side of the wall all morning. I'm sure Travis is running drills or something. Davy mentioned that I should practice with him later in the day, but I don't want him to waste gunpowder for my sake."

"You should probably stick to deer and rabbits..." I laugh and throw a playful nudge into his shoulder.

I'm using sarcasm to hide my true meaning—I don't want him to practice shooting because I don't want him to fight. Maybe if he stays out of this war, we will walk away from it. *If he doesn't shoot at the enemy, he can't die—right?* But even as I try to convince myself, the little voice in my mind answers, *It doesn't work like that, Aubrey.*

"You are the great and mighty deer huntress… I'll leave that up to you." He throws one arm around my shoulder. I lean into him naturally, trying to remain as close as possible to his body at all times. As we stand together, the sound of gunfire rings from somewhere close by.

"And they're back at it again," he mutters after the sudden burst of gunfire. With his free hand, he tosses the apple core over to where Quinto has trotted off.

I keep my eyes closed, still enjoying the sunshine, until the gunshots suddenly change. At first, they still seemed like practice fire, but now the sound begins to come from outside the walls.

"Is that—" My eyes shoot open as I turn to Tapley.

"They're returning fire," he replies just as groups of men begin running in the direction of the southwest corner of the compound.

The horses begin panicking, the whites of their eyes showing as their pricked ears turn in the direction of the gunfire.

Tapley jumps to his feet and reaches for both of my hands, pulling me up beside him. "We need to get back inside," he says, barely audible over the yelling of the men.

"They're tryin' to occupy the jacales," a man calls as he rushes past us.

We push past them and head into the barracks. Tapley pushes me against the wall just before I get knocked over by a group of soldiers running to the wagonyard. Ten minutes ago, the inside of these walls was quiet, but now chaos has broken loose as Santa Anna's men move on the fortress for the first time.

As we turn the corner, Davy is jogging down the hallway toward us, and I see a coonskin hat on his head for the first time. Until now, I'd convinced myself that his signature hat was a strange, historical myth.

"Whatever you do, don't leave that room until I come and get you," he yells to us as he darts around the corner and disappears into the gunfire outside.

I grip Tapley's hand tighter, and for some reason, I find myself holding my breath.

It doesn't end today, Aubrey. It's still too early, I keep telling myself as Tapley leads me back toward the chapel.

The gunfire grows progressively louder, but I still hear the men yelling to each other, and the weight of their boots on the flat roof above us makes dust rain down upon our heads, christening our hair in ash-like powder. As we pass by the large stone cross at the far end of the chapel, I silently pray for each man. I pray they don't break, that they don't give in to fear as it weighs on their shoulders and clouds their minds.

Just get them through today. It's too early for them to lose hope.

We turn down the short hallway hidden on the back wall. The sound of our feet against the stone floor is the only noise in the empty chapel. Tapley pushes open the wooden door and immediately shuts it behind us, leaving us standing oddly silent inside the safety of the small room. I can smell the faint scent of burning cedar beginning to slip into the air. It reminds me of all the times I've sat on the tailgate of a truck that's backed up to the tall flames of a hill-country bonfire, but right now, the smell only means there are burning blockades somewhere nearby.

Over the last two days, I've grown fond of the small rays of sunlight that somehow find their way through any empty space in the room. Now the midafternoon sun is hidden behind a thick cloud of gun smoke, and the room is suddenly dark. I reach for a match and struggle to light the long row of candles with shaking hands. Tapley wraps his hand around mine to steady it, and a few seconds later, the candlelight is already filling the gray haze with a dim yellow glow.

He leads me to the straw mattress, and we both sit down, our backs resting against the wall as the soundtrack of war plays on repeat in the background. His arm guides my head to rest on his shoulder. I lean against him. Even as my reality begins to shatter, he's there to hold me together, wrapping me in his arms to keep me from falling apart completely.

"Just close your eyes, Aubrey. Don't get caught in the chaos surrounding us. It's still just you and me," he whispers through the sound of bullets cracking through the air.

Doing as he says, I close my eyes and try to take slow, steady breaths as my heart fights to race out of control. I try to send my mind back to last week—a time when we were dancing slowly and falling in love quickly. Dreaming feels like the safest place I can be while I live out my worst nightmare.

WEEKS SEEM TO HAVE passed since the beeping of a heart monitor haunted my dreams. In reality, I've only been trapped inside this sliver of time in 1836 for several weeks. Every time I blink, it feels as though I've started and finished an entire day before I can etch the details into my memory. These moments are suspended in the air for a few seconds and then are swept back up into the needy arms of the wind as they're torn away from me. I'm constantly trying to chase them down—to stop them long enough to fully tangle myself in emotions and past sensations. But I can't catch up to something that lacks permanence—time only moves forward, never back.

Tapley's fingers run through my hair as I lie in his lap amidst the constant serve and return of gunfire outside. The sound was terrifying at first, a sickening reminder of the nightmare I'm caught up in. But it never grew louder. Santa Anna's army didn't breach the walls of the Alamo though they exchanged fire with us late into the night.

I was afraid to close my eyes, but the feeling of Tapley's rhythmic motions finally soothed me into an unwelcome sleep.

Darkness overtakes my mind, and somewhere against the hum of war in the background, the quiet beeping begins to surface—slowly at first, almost so slowly that my heartbeat doesn't exist at all. I hear one beep and wait for another, but sometimes the sound doesn't come right away. I'm not sure how long I listen to the irregular beating of my own heart, but as I wait in the darkness, my mind begins to shift. Sharp pains interrupt the beeping, and the throbbing in my temple becomes so intense that I fear my brain is actually being compressed so tightly that it will surely burst. The feeling moves all the way down my spine—prickling, jabbing, constricting until I'm sure my bones are being bound together with barbed wire. My heart rate slows again, and it takes a full ten seconds for another to follow, then another, each beat slower than the last.

No, I scream into the darkness, and suddenly, the pain subsides. There's nothing but the deathly song of the heart monitor as it sends a warning that I'm almost gone.

Tapley's voice breaks through the darkness. "Aubrey, I'm not going to let you leave me."

He's here... Tapley knows I'm dying. Dead.

I try to pound on my own chest, but the familiar feeling of my limbs is gone.

I need to wake up. You can't die, Aubrey!

As the words flash through my mind, I'm suddenly conflicted. What if death means I'm stuck here? I don't even know if, or how, I'm still alive in my other life, but the sound of my heart monitor in the darkness always leaves a lingering of hope hanging over me.

"Breathe, Aubrey." My mouth forms the words as I try to pull air into my lungs.

Breathe.

The pain in my body returns all at once, and the beeping lurches forward so quickly that it races out of control. My head is throbbing, my legs weak and heavy, my ribs shattered and crushed as they scream with each shallow breath filling my lungs. Darkness begins to dim into a faint glow, and a few seconds later, the glow burns brighter, flipping to a shade of bright fluorescence as the intensity blinds me.

Tapley's voice is no longer there, but I can feel movement around the room and hear faint, frantic speech above me. I try to move my fingers, but they're too weak—too stiff. My eyelids begin to flutter open, but then I begin to panic.

If I open my eyes, where will I be? Will I be back in 2018, a world where Tapley isn't at the center of my life? I can't leave him to die alone—I can't just wake up not knowing the outcome of our future together. I can't give up on this life when embracing it caused us to be here—when loving Tapley will surely get him killed.

"No," I scream at myself and pull my eyelids closed.

Wake up, Aubrey, but don't you dare *wake up in that hospital bed. You will not leave him—not now.*

I slow my breathing, and the heart monitor responds. *Beep... beep... beep.*

There's one even, rhythmic pause between each beep as the noise fades back into the background and gunfire slowly resurfaces. For each heartbeat, I can hear a bullet—but this time, the sound of war isn't so daunting. It means I'm back in Tapley's arms. For now.

I pull my eyes open, and my gaze instantly finds what I desire most in this world: Tapley. He has finally fallen asleep. His head gently leans against the stone wall as his arms remain securely wrapped around me where I lie in his lap. His expression is soft, calm. It's as though he fears nothing at all, the horrors of his past blinding him to the looming tragedy of his future. I see no sorrow or regret as he sleeps—I see only satisfaction. Peace.

My eyes trace the lines of his jaw, the defined and perfect structure of his cheekbones. I'm too afraid of waking him to brush the fallen strands from across his forehead. His tousled hair is beautifully messy, and ironically, I think that's one of the things I love most about him. He's free, rugged, and a bit wild—things I've been missing in my life for far too long. Love should be natural and unpredictable, a feeling of such strength that it knocks the breath from your lungs and kick-starts your heart with such an intense electricity that it emits its own adrenaline. Loving Tapley is a rush that I will never be able to break away from, a feeling I never want to abandon—not even in death.

CHAPTER TWENTY-TWO

Footsteps echo lightly outside the door a few seconds before a quick knock interrupts the silence. Tapley's eyes open quickly, but I'm already moving to the door before he's awake enough to sit up. Standing at the door, Davy shoots me a tired smile then turns to look at Tapley, who's finally pulling himself stiffly off the mattress.

"Long night?" I look at Davy sympathetically, and I can see the pale-blue shadow of exhaustion underneath his eyes.

"The longest." He runs his fingers through his messy dark hair and leans against the doorframe. "You two better come with me. I think there's something you should see."

Tapley is up on his feet instantly, wrapping his hand around mine. "Mornin', Davy." He tries to hide a yawn that tugs at his mouth, but as soon as Davy spots it, his own yawn breaks across his face.

"Well, aren't we a lively bunch." He smirks and turns down the hallway. We follow closely behind.

Most of the activity around the compound has finally quieted down after the extended night of fire. Tired soldiers are asleep on every available flat surface in the hallway, and I carefully try to weave around them without stepping on anyone's extremities. We head out the west entrance to the barracks and into the large empty wagonyard. The air is still and stinks of gunpowder mixed with sweat. There's a dimly lit bonfire still smoldering with vague shades of orange and yellow against charred logs in the center of the yard.

A narrow stone staircase leads to one of the roofs of the main buildings, and Tapley lets go of my hand so we can follow single file to the top. A few men are standing at the far corner of the rooftop, their attention focused on the distance out to the east. Davy leads us to the stone ledge and brings his hand to his brow, trying to peer into the bright morning light as it breaks into the sky. At first it is hard for me to see anything, but as my eyes adjust to the brightness, I begin to make out movement on the road leading into town. A group of twenty or so men are leading a few head of cattle in the direction of the Alamo, and at the front of the group is a spotted horse that I instantly recognize.

"My father." I look up at Tapley with wide eyes.

"They are crazy for risking their own necks to supply us with food, but I can't say that I'm not glad to see them." Travis turns his attention over to where we stand a few feet away.

"Are they going to make it through the lines?" Tapley eyes the distance, where lines of smoke are rising from the heart of Santa Anna's campsites.

"They just might make it with a few extra hands." Davy sends Tapley a sly smile and motions to the stable yard nearby.

"Stay here with Travis." Tapley releases my hand and follows Crockett back down the steps, where they take off in the direction of their horses.

I don't like the idea of Tapley riding outside the safety of the walls, but I also don't like the idea of George risking his life to bring a few extra steers all the way out here. I cross my arms over my chest, and I find my foot tapping nervously against the stone roof.

"They'll be fine." Travis looks down at me. "Davy wouldn't risk riding outside of the walls if he thought it would cost him his life."

It's not his *life I'm worried about.*

I hear hoofs galloping through the wagonyard behind me, and the men guarding the main gate call for it to be opened. When the two riders break away from the Alamo walls, they head through the open terrain and right toward George and the other men. I remember the power of Quinto's gallop beneath me as we rode to the Alamo a few days ago, but I haven't realized the speed of the gray gelding until I watch him close the distance between the compound and the cattle in a few short minutes. Davy's dark-chestnut horse keeps Quinto's pace easily, and both skid to a stop right as they reach the group. I must have been holding my breath the entire time, and the air leaving my lungs when I finally exhale is louder than I expected.

"You all right, Mrs. Holland?" Travis raises his eyebrow as he watches me.

"I'll let you know when they all make it back here in one piece," I quickly reply, my eyes back on the group as they pick up their pace and start across the open field.

Travis chuckles and turns his attention back to the men. The large group is now circling around the cattle to keep them moving forward. Time moves too slowly as I stand silently on the rooftop. I try to keep my mind from heading down a tunnel of endless worrying, and I focus on the drumming of my heartbeat as it presses against my chest. For every beat, the cattle seem to move only a step closer, their stocky legs practically crawling across the dry landscape as their movements stir up a cloud of dust high into the air.

The Mexican Army must be able to see the dust cloud. They'll know something is moving in our direction.

I wait motionless next to Travis, my legs heavy, my body weak.

"Are you coming?" Travis's voice breaks through the tense air as he steps closer to the stairs.

I look back down at the group, which is now close enough that the taste of dusty air fills my mouth. Stepping back down the stone stairs, I listen to the rational voice in my mind: *Aubrey, just look away... they will be fine.* I pull my gaze away from Tapley and Quinto.

The moment I reach the bottom of the stairs, Travis jogs in the direction of the main gate. "Open both gates," he yells to the men standing post nearby.

They split into two groups, each taking a separate side of the wide wooden gates and pulling them open enough to let the cattle and horses through. My eyes find Tapley's at the back of the group, and then my attention turns to George. Just the sight of him brings tears to my eyes as memories of the last time I saw this man, who now feels like my father, flood my mind. I was never able to say goodbye to George or Charlotte, yet here they are. They drive the cattle into a corral right outside the stable yard, and the men immediately turn their horses back to the closed gates. For a second, I think George might leave without saying a word, but then he slides out of the saddle and walks over to me with a smile across his face.

"Aubrey!" he calls, and I run to him before I can even think.

"What are you doing here? Don't you know how close Santa Anna's men are?" I throw my arms around my father's neck as he hands Tapley the reins to his horse.

"The militia took most of the cattle we had left at the farm, but there was a small herd in one of the outer pastures they didn't get to. I would rather risk bringing them here than have them used by Santa Anna while the men inside these walls starve." He places his hands on my shoulders.

Tears brim at the edges of my eyes, but I refuse to cry. I swallow back the lump in my throat and force myself to take in a shallow breath.

"I'm sorry, Father—I'm so sorry all of this happened... to you... to *my* mother." The words pour out of my mouth in a scrambled, emotional mess. Tapley watches from a few feet away.

"Aubrey, don't you dare be sorry for what you did—not for a single second. You did what others in this town could not. You fought for yourself and for your loved ones because you had the courage to do so. You *still* have the courage, even now." He runs his finger across my cheek, wiping away an escaped tear. "You need to stay strong—for yourself and for Tapley. For everyone here." George pulls me into his arms one last time then takes a step back. Before I can reply, I feel Tapley's arm around my waist, pulling me close.

"George—I hope to see you soon." Tapley hands him back his horse.

"I will see you soon." George puts his foot in the wooden stirrup and pulls himself back onto his spotted horse.

I watch him take his place with the rest of the group of men as they wait for the gates to open so they can ride back to town. "Goodbye," I mutter, knowing full well that is truly the last time I'll ever see him.

THE RUMORS WERE TRUE. A cold front blows in the day after Santa Anna attempts to occupy the wooden hutches outside the southwest corner. Temperatures drop into the low thirties, showering the dry Texas land with a constant cover of rain. Luckily, the bad weather keeps the Mexican Army at bay for a few days, and overall, the fighting quiets down as we near the seventh day. We sit around the large wooden table with Travis, Bowie, Crockett, and Pollard almost every evening, but tonight, Jim Bowie's seat is empty.

"Is Mr. Bowie not feeling well?" I take a sip of strong wine from my metal cup. When you're stuck in a small space with almost two hundred men, water becomes rationed quickly, and wine is more easily available.

"He's not well at all. I'm afraid he won't be out of bed for at least a few more days," Dr. Pollard answers, his expression hardly giving away any more detail than his vague words.

"Our group is rotating onto the practice range this evening. You should both join us." Travis looks over to Tapley and me, and I nearly choke on my drink.

"You should probably save your gunpowder for someone who can actually hit something." I take another big sip of wine as I feel everyone's gaze resting on me.

"She can't be that bad of a shot, can she? Didn't you say Aubrey was the one to take down that deer we ate?" Davy asks with a smirk.

I can feel Tapley struggling for words, clearly uncomfortable with having to lie on my behalf. "Aubrey can handle a rifle. She just might need to spend some time getting a feel for it again." He glances over at me and turns his eyes away before he can catch my glare.

"Then we will make sure she has plenty of practice by the end of the day." Travis looks over at Davy and laughs.

I'm sure they're all thrilled to watch me make a fool out of myself. I sigh and throw back the rest of the bitter wine. I'm pretty sure that if there comes a time when I'll be forced to look an enemy in the eyes, hold and aim the gun, *and* pull the trigger without falling backward as it kicks into my shoulder, then we're all doomed, anyway.

"Great. Let's get this over with." I reach over for the pitcher of wine, but Tapley intercepts it and hands it to Davy.

"Probably a bad idea," he says. He has a point—drunken target practice is probably not the best route for me at the moment.

All the men stand up from the table and swing their rifles over their shoulders. Ever since Santa Anna's army returned fire a few days ago, Tapley has been carrying his rabbit gun with him everywhere. Trailing a few steps behind him as we walk, I stare at the gun, and my shoulder begins to throb as I remember how it felt to have the wind knocked out of me the moment I pulled the trigger.

Everyone either seems to be standing guard at their designated spots around the compound or sleeping. I try to keep my steps quiet as we walk past a room of men asleep in cots or blankets laid out on the floor. Travis turns through the doorway leading into the open wagonyard and keeps walking straight through it to where the burlap targets are set up near the back wall away from the chapel.

A small group of men are huddled around the barrels of gunpowder. All of them immediately come to attention as the Alamo's commanding officer walks past. Travis and Davy acknowledge their men and move to stand in front of their various targets at least twenty yards away.

Tapley takes a few minutes to load the gun then stands behind me and places the butt of the rifle against the same spot of soft skin to the left of my shoulder and right below my collarbone. I try to position my hands in the same way I did the other day, but this time, it feels much more awkward, almost like I have flapping chicken wings for arms.

"Relax, Aubrey. If you fire the gun when you're tense like this, you have a better chance of throwing out your shoulder." Tapley's breath is warm against my ear as he places his hands on my waist.

"Feeling your hands right there isn't exactly letting me focus on the weapon I'm holding," I mutter through gritted teeth.

He completely ignores my complaint and shifts one of my hips forward slightly in front of the other. "When you pull the trigger, put your weight on your forward leg, and when the gun pushes into you, use your other leg to brace against."

I hear Davy let out a low whistle, probably noticing the effect Tapley has on me.

"Ignore them," he whispers, keeping his hands firmly on my hip bones. "Look down the center of the barrel until you find the target, then try to keep the gun lined up perfectly with what your eye is focused on."

I follow his instructions, and at first, I feel myself going cross-eyed. I shut my eyes for a second, open them, and blink rapidly a few times before I look back down the barrel with my right eye. This time, the stuffed burlap bag hanging on the wall comes into focus, and I try to keep the gun from wobbling.

"Okay, I see it." Staying perfectly still, I force myself to take slow, shallow breaths so that my chest doesn't move the gun from its position.

Tapley moves one hand from my hip and pulls back the hammer at the top of the gun. "It's ready to fire when you are." He brings his hand back to me, steadying my legs. "Take a deep breath in, hold it for three seconds, and then release it," he says quietly. "When the air leaves your lungs, pull the trigger."

I take a breath, and he lets go of me. I count to three, exhale, and pull the trigger, careful not to let my right eye leave the target. I watch as the bullet hits the burlap sack. I don't fall backward or miss—I manage to actually hit what I'm aiming for and stay on my feet.

Crockett, Travis, and Pollard all slowly clap as they stare at me.

"Tapley, if you were an attractive woman and could teach someone to shoot like that, there might be some hope for the rest of these men to hit something with their guns." Davy laughs.

I look over at them and roll my eyes before turning to Tapley and smiling. He meets my stare with a smile of his own, and I can tell he's proud of me. I spend a few more minutes taking practice shots at the target before trading places with Tapley.

"You should watch this in case you need to reload quickly." He leads me over to makeshift wooden benches next to a section of broken wooden fencing that looks to have once been a corral.

"Now, this first step is the tricky part. Hand me the small metal flask on top of the post." He points left, and I hand him the container. "This is primer powder. Place it in the metal dish at the top of the gun, and then lock it like this." He pulls back the spring at the top of the gun until it clicks.

Next, he draws a tan pouch from a leather bag hanging on a nearby post. "This is the powder flask. You pour grains of shot down the muzzle until it settles. The piece of cloth rests between the shot powder and lead to make sure it's as tight as it can be in the barrel. Once the lead is in place, pack it tight with this metal ramrod here." He reaches for my fingers and places them on the metal tube at the base of the gun. "Remove the ramrod, and pack the barrel." He places the ramrod back in the holder.

"Is that it?" I ask, going through the steps in my mind. *Prime, click the spring, powder, cloth, iron shot, pack.*

"Almost. Before you can shoot, you need to pull back the cock behind the dish where you put the primer." He holds the gun with his left hand and cocks it with his right. "Now you are ready to fire." He walks the few yards back to the shooting line, aims the gun at the target, and pulls the trigger. "Your turn." He hands me the gun and gives me a crooked smirk.

We practice the routine of loading and reloading until the sky becomes too dark to see.

As we turn back toward the barracks, I hear a commotion coming from the main gate leading into the yard. Before I can ask what's going on, the men are already jogging in that direction. The gates are pulled open, allowing two riders to gallop inside. There's a man on a dark horse, and as I turn to look at the second rider, I'm surprised to find a woman with an infant wrapped to her chest.

"I'm here to see Commander James Bowie," the man says, quickly dismounting from his horse.

"Bowie is unwell, but my name is Lieutenant Colonel William Travis, and I'm now the commander of this garrison and its army."

"My name is Captain Almaron Dickinson, and this is my wife Susanna, and our daughter, Angelina. We were riding with Commander Fannin and the men he was bringing to you, but Santa Anna sent soldiers back to Goliad, and they were forced to stay and defend the city. I'm the only relief coming to you. I'm here to help defend the Alamo." He nods at each of us and then his attention turns to his wife and daughter.

"We'll take all the help we can get," Travis replies as he takes Captain Dickinson's horse.

I can't help but notice the disappointment in Travis's voice and the worry behind his pale eyes. He must be starting to realize that he'll make this stand to defend the Alamo with only his two hundred men, and there's no way around it.

CHAPTER TWENTY-THREE

I read about Susanna Dickinson years ago. All children and teenagers in this state have had a Texas history class or two in their lives. We were taught that there were only two survivors of the battle of the Alamo: Susanna and her daughter, Angelina. The moment she arrived inside these walls, everything in the garrison began to rapidly change. It felt as if the time line of the battle had just jumped forward. A part of me had been hanging on to a fragment of hope that Susanna would never show up—that Tapley and I would be the only two survivors. Our fate is now sealed.

One thing has changed since their arrival—the Alamo has endured prolonged cannon fire for hours late into the night. The outer walls are still holding, but there's no way we can work to repair the damage day after day without reinforcements.

Susanna and I grow close in a short amount of time. We work together to help pass out meals and repair clothes. A few men have already sustained injuries, and after Dr. Pollard tends to their wounds, we try to keep them as comfortable as possible.

With a metal pot full of soiled bandages, I head to the well near the center of the wagonyard to draw fresh water for boiling. Tapley begins pulling regular shifts with a group of volunteers under Davy's command, and I feel like I barely see him anymore.

By tugging on the long line of rope attached to the bucket, I lift it to the top of the well. The water supply is beginning to run low, and each pot used to wash clothes or bandages means less water for the men. Even if the walls could hold for a few more weeks, we'd run out of food and water long before then.

I pour as little water into the pot as possible, barely covering the pile of bloodied bandages, before I head back to the barracks. Susanna already has a fire going in the open courtyard nearest to where Dr. Pollard is keeping the wounded men. She quickly takes the bucket of water from my hands and hangs it over the flames.

"I think this is the last boiling we'll need for today." She straightens her back and looks over to where Angelina sleeps quietly in a cradle underneath the large oak tree.

"Have you seen Tapley?"

She nods in the direction of the meeting room where we eat every night. "There's a group of them in there right now."

Her husband has been close by Travis's side since his arrival, and so has Tapley. The differences between Captain Dickinson and Tapley are blatantly obvious—Tapley has no military experience at all—yet everyone treats him as if he's as highly regarded as any other important figure here. Since he's killed an enemy officer, he has apparently more than earned his keep.

"I helped Dr. Pollard tend to Bowie earlier," Susanna says, dropping her voice as she looks at me.

"He's still not improving, I take it?"

"Pollard doesn't know if he'll even make it till the weekend. He says his liver is failing, and soon, his heart will fail too." She pokes at the logs of the fire, causing the flames to jump upward.

Angelina begins to cry, and Susanna looks over at her with an exhausted expression. The baby has been restless since they arrived, and the constant movement and noise around the compound are making it nearly impossible for Susanna to quiet the child long enough to be able to sleep.

"I can watch over her. Just rest for a while." I smile and walk toward where the baby is stirring. She's only a few months old, but she already has a head covered in soft dark curls like her mother's and big brown eyes. "*Shh...*" I whisper, scooping her up into my arms.

I was never good with babies in my previous reality. In fact, I'm not even sure I ever held a child before Angelina. At first, the feeling of an infant in my arms was terrifying—I worried that I'd drop her or move her in a way that would crush her tiny little arms and legs—but the feeling has become more familiar, more instinctual.

My body rocks back and forth naturally, and after a few minutes, Angelina's cries eventually settle. As I turn to lay her back in the makeshift cradle, I find Tapley watching me from underneath the stone arches in front of the barracks. He's leaning back against the wall, and his arms are crossed in front of his chest. He almost looks like a ghost standing in the moonlight, but it's his eyes that catch my attention. They're sad as he watches me with Angelina, a hint of tears glistening in the corners. I tuck the blanket around the sleeping baby then quietly walk across the grass to where he's waiting for me.

"Are you tired?" I ask as he takes me in his arms.

"Yes, but having you here gives me something to hold onto. I fear it's going to be another long night," he whispers as he presses his face into my tangled curls.

"Please don't say you will be away from me tonight." I pull my head from his chest and look up at him.

"Aubrey, I will be with you tonight—I promise." He brings his hand to my cheek and brushes his thumb across my skin as I lean into his touch.

A bell begins to ring from somewhere inside the mission, and Tapley drops his hand from my face as he wraps his fingers around mine. "Come along." He tugs me in the direction of the wagonyard.

I look over my shoulder to see if Susanna is staying behind, and I find her walking next to her husband with Angelina in her arms.

"They're coming, too," Tapley says quietly as more and more people begin walking in the same direction.

I have a feeling that he knows something I don't, something that was discussed behind the meeting-room doors. When the Alamo's bell rings, everyone answers its call.

There's a crowd of people gathered at the main gate, and Tapley pushes his way closer to the front of the group. William Travis and David Bowie are standing on top of gunpowder barrels, their expressions solemn as they stare back into the two hundred faces looking up at them. They wait for the last few remaining men to take their places at the back of the group before they speak. Everyone is deathly silent.

Travis clears his throat and removes the rifle strapped to his back then holds it by his side. "Defenders of the Alamo, of Texas, in my hand, I hold a letter from General Sam Houston, informing us that reinforcements will not be coming to our aid. There are nearly two hundred of us inside these walls, and just outside, Santa Anna has brought fifteen hundred men to try to take this fortress from us. When they attack, we will likely not survive, but I will not surrender the Alamo without a fight, and if it's a fight they're after, we will give it to them." He jumps off the barrel, his gun still in his hand.

Looking out into the crowd, he unsheathes his battle sword with his free hand, brings the tip to the ground, and drags it across the sandy soil from one end of the main gate to the other. "I draw this line in the sand to give you a choice. If you wish to stay and defend the Alamo, you can remain on this side of the line, but if you're not willing to die for each other—for Texas—then you are free to cross the line and leave these walls."

Travis pulls his sword from the sand and straps it back over his shoulders. No one moves or breathes as the reality of his words sink in. Help is not coming, and the Alamo will surely fall if Santa Anna attacks. If they stay, they die, but if they leave, they lose Texas to Mexico forever.

Someone begins to stir from the back of the group, and all eyes fall upon one man as he walks toward the line separating all of us from the gate. He looks over at Travis and lays his rifle on the ground just as he steps over the line.

"Open the gates," Travis calls, and every single pair of eyes rests on the man who leaves, but not a single person moves to follow him.

I look up at Tapley, hoping to see him battling with this decision as much as I am, but his expression is set in a tense line as he holds tightly onto my hand. We're staying—I can see it in his eyes. He's determined to fight beside these men. He still believes that there's a chance we'll walk away from here with our freedom.

Would a life on the run really be so terrible, though?

Crockett steps down from his barrel and walks over to where Tapley and I quietly stand. "No one will think it wrong if you follow him out those gates." He looks at us with a serious face, his eyes soft and sad.

Tapley releases my hand and brings it to Davy's shoulder. "I have but one life—a life I will give to save Texas."

"Aubrey, you know the risk of staying here is just as great as the risk of walking out those gates. At least here, you can fight for freedom." Davy doesn't wait for my response. Instead, he turns his attention back to the other men, allowing Tapley and me a private moment.

My mouth is dry, and my palms are cold. I try to speak, but the words stick in my throat. I should leave. I should take Tapley by the hand and walk out those gates. But Davy is right—doing so would likely get us captured and killed.

"I'm staying with you, Tapley. Here," I choke out, and suddenly the weight on my body releases. When the words leave my mouth, the fear leaves with them. "I'm not leaving."

FOR THE FIRST TIME in several nights, there's silence. It's a haunting lack of noise—a calm before the treacherous storm. I don't sleep, wishing to be awake for as long as I am still alive.

Tapley stays with me just as he promised, his lips on mine and our bodies tangled together into the late hours of the night. There are no words to describe what loving him feels like, but it's as close to undying happiness as I'll ever get. To be able to love him for a short time has become the reason for my existence, my sole purpose that keeps me moving forward when the walls are closing in on me.

I lie on his chest. His breathing is steady and soft as he rests. It's too cold to be naked together underneath the thin layer of blankets, and I don't want to risk being caught without clothes by any unwelcome guests the closer we move to dawn, either. I keep my eyes on his face beneath the dim glow of candlelight, studying every detail of it and trying to engrave the image of him forever in my mind. Just looking at him and feeling his body next to mine is enough to break my heart a thousand times over.

After Travis's speech last night, I wrote Tapley a letter, which has been hidden under the corner of the mattress. I sit up quietly, trying not to wake him as I fish out the piece of parchment and hold it in my hand for a few seconds.

I'll never understand why I woke up in 1836 or why I'll die in 1836, but if the only reason I'm here is to love Tapley, then I understand my fate. It's a cruel reality, but maybe it's the reality I'm destined for—the twisted happily ever after that is my life's own rewriting of the tragedy of Romeo and his Juliet.

I gently open the front pocket of his shirt, tuck the letter inside, and move my face up to Tapley's, kissing him softly on the lips as he sleeps. "I love you," I whisper as a tear falls from my eyes onto his cheek—my silent last goodbye.

I look up to the small hole in the roof, through which a faint hint of light is beginning to shine as dawn approaches. A loud knock at the door startles Tapley awake. Another knock follows, and this time, he places his finger to his lips, making sure I stay quiet as he stands up and heads to the door.

Tapley pulls open the door just enough to see who is waiting on the other side. "Captain Dickinson?" he whispers and opens the door the remainder of the way.

Susanna has Angelina wrapped in her arms as she stands next to her husband in the doorway.

"We're needed at the north end of the wall," Dickinson says, ushering his wife and daughter into the room with me.

Tapley reaches for his rifle then brings his eyes to mine. "Stay here, and don't open the door for anyone," he says, almost begging, as he turns back to the open door.

Before I can say anything, he's gone. I stare dumbly at the door for a few minutes, not sure what to do or what just happened. I let Tapley walk out of this room, knowing that the walls are about to be overrun with Mexican soldiers. My breath is trapped in my lungs as I try to exhale, but I can't breathe. Susanna is watching me begin to melt down.

"I have to go after him—" With trembling fingers, I reach for my shoes.

Just as I'm about to stand, I hear a cannon break through the quiet dawn, followed by the very first gunshot. Angelina begins to scream. I stare at Susanna with wide eyes.

"Aubrey, you can't just go out there..." she pleads, but her voice is so far off in the distance that it's barely audible above the sound of war.

"Lock the door behind me, and don't open it," I yell, and I break out across the threshold and race down the narrow stone hallways.

The chapel is still quiet, but I can hear the chaos that's already swarming through the yards outside. As I turn the corner toward the stable, I see a flash of red and blue coming toward me. I press myself against the dark opening of a nearby doorway, holding my breath, as three Mexican soldiers run past me. Someone opens fire at them from across the stable yard, striking the man closest to me in the back of the head. The two remaining men run in different directions, yelling at each other in Spanish.

I force my eyes to the dying man near my hiding spot and the thick pool of crimson blood covering the stone floor underneath his body. Before I can think twice, I reach for his gun and take it in my hands. *Reload. You need to reload the gun.* "Prime, click the spring, powder, cloth, iron shot, pack." I whisper the steps over and over again until the gun is reloaded.

Most of the gunfire is coming from the wagonyard. I peer around the corner just to make sure I'm not running right into enemy fire. Cannon fire hits the wall at the far end of the stable yard, and the horses run out, scattering.

"If you don't move now, this place will be swarming with a thousand men," I mutter then take a deep breath and run as fast as I can through the smoky air.

I need to make it to the north wall, where I hope Captain Dickinson and Tapley are still alive. I stop just before the path opens into the large yard at the back of the compound. At least sixty men are frantically firing at the Mexican soldiers breaching the outer walls. My feet quickly cover ground before I can think about it, and I try to weave around the chaos. There are already dozens of bodies covering the ground. I force myself not to look down at them as I close the distance between the men and me.

I see Tapley aiming his rifle at the wall as he tries to pick off each person who climbs over. He pauses and reaches for the pouch of gunpowder at his side. I'm less than a hundred yards away from him. There's an unmanned section of the wall, and out of the corner of my eye, I catch movement coming over the top. Captain Dickinson turns his aim toward the men, but before he can pull the trigger, one of them shoots him in the chest. Tapley looks over to where Almaron lies on the ground, and I watch in slow motion as the same gunman points the rifle at him.

My hands are shaking, but I manage to pull the heavy gun to my shoulder and cock it just as Tapley had taught me. I take a deep breath, but there's no time to count to three. I release the air from my lungs in a warm gasp and pull the trigger. At the sound of the gun, Tapley turns to look in my direction, his eyes widening when he realizes I shot the man who was about to kill him.

I stand frozen, unable to move my legs from where they're solidly braced against the ground. Tapley runs to me, but it feels like slow motion as men around me fall and others send bullets flying through the air toward the wall. He grabs my hand and pulls me out of the way just as someone fires in my direction. We sprint to the other side of the wall, where there's a small overhang at the front of a now crumbling building.

"What are you doing here?" he yells over the noise, his hands coming to my face as he pulls my trembling gaze to his. His thumb traces my chin, and his eyes are sad and tormented as he studies my face.

"I couldn't just stay inside that room and wait for you to never come back. You didn't even say goodbye. You didn't even say I love you," I spit out at him as angry tears roll down my cheeks.

I watch as his strength falters, his courage crumbling as he realizes why I'm out here—why I'm standing across from him with a gun at my side. A gun I just used to save his life.

"I'm sorry, Aubrey. I didn't think it was going to be like this. I just thought that maybe a small group was nearing the walls, but when we got here, there were already Mexican soldiers in the yard."

"I need to hear you say it," I say bluntly, wrapping one hand around the back of his neck.

He looks at me, confused for a second, but then he understands exactly what I need. "I love you, Aubrey." He smiles at me, his eyes suddenly bright. As I look into them, I can see the reflection of sparks flying from the guns around us as they shoot a canopy of bullets into the air. The image is beautiful—like fireworks on the Fourth of July—as the light bounces in his irises. But this war. Tragedy. Nothing about this should be beautiful. Nothing.

My mind moves backward in time to the morning in the barn that I finally told Tapley that I loved him. "Say it again."

I look into his hazel eyes, and I suddenly see everything so clearly—my past, my future, and my terrifying present. The person I was a few weeks ago is completely gone, but I have never felt more myself—more alive—than I do right now. This is where I'm supposed to be. I have never been surer of anything in my life—this nightmare around me is my destiny.

"I love you," he says.

As I look at Tapley's face, bullets buzz past us, filling the air with screams and violence as the sun breaches the walls of the Alamo on the thirteenth day of the siege. I don't deserve a love like this—a love so complete and full that his face consumes my thoughts. Tapley Holland is the reason I'm alive, and he's the one thing I can't live without even though I know I'm about to lose him forever. He's given me more than I can dream of, and he brings me to my knees.

"One more time." I lift my free hand to his face and run my fingers along his cheek. I can feel the tears pouring from my eyes as I watch him, as I lose him.

Just stop. Time, please stop. I'm begging you. Don't end.

A few yards behind him, a shade of red approaches from around the corner, and before Tapley can speak, I hear a bullet break through the air, rippling the space around us. Tapley lets out a sharp breath as it hits him in the back.

His body sinks forward into my arms, but he doesn't scream in pain or cry out for help. He only brings his head up to my ear and whispers, "I love you," one final time before his legs crumble, the light in his eyes suddenly erased like the wick of a candle being snuffed out.

The blood from his back soaks into my skin as my hands lock around his body. My body begins to heave as I struggle to keep him standing, but no matter how hard I try, I feel us falling to the ground. I never let go of him, not for a single second. I lay his body in my lap as I sit against the cold hard dirt. I run my fingers through his soaked hair, keeping my eyes focused on his as they flutter open and closed a few more times before settling into a peaceful stare.

"And I love you, Tapley Holland." My last words to him are broken by sobs as I hear footsteps nearing me.

I close my eyes, knowing full well what's coming, but I'm not afraid. I wrap my fingers around Tapley's still hand and wait for the bullet, but when it finally comes for me, I find myself feeling no pain at all. There's only darkness and the sound of beeping growing louder.

CHAPTER TWENTY-FOUR

At first there is nothing, but the longer I linger in the darkness, the more I feel the screaming pain in my chest. Everything remains dark for what feels like an eternity. I'm stuck inside my own mind, my thoughts fighting with the pain for my attention. I feel myself falling in and out of consciousness, and I force myself to remember what just happened, hoping that if the wheels in my mind keep turning, my body won't give up.

A gunshot rings through the pitch-black darkness of my mind, and then everything fades quickly as if my body is being torn away while my mind is left behind in solitude. My memories are lost. Someone's face flashes through my thoughts for a single second before disappearing forever. I try to call out to that person, but a moment later, the urge is gone, and there's nothing—no sound, no heat, nor cold, no pain. Nothing.

And then the familiar beeping noise breaks the silence from miles and miles away. *I must be dreaming.* The beeping slowly changes—its normal steady beat turns sporadic, racing out of control and growing louder and louder until it pierces the darkness like a blaring storm siren. Then as quickly as the noise came, it changes, pulling into one continuous note. The beeping flatlines. *I've flatlined.*

"Aubrey?" a voice calls in the distance. "Aubrey, don't leave—don't give in. Fight it."

I recognize the man's voice, but his presence confuses me. *Tapley?*

I'm abruptly and violently thrown back into consciousness, the background blowing up as people are yelling and screaming, their hysteria drowned beneath their choking tears. A woman's voice gives instructions to others, and their shadows flash across the darkness of my eyelids as they quickly move around me.

"CPR. Now!" she yells.

The blackness is interrupted in a fierce blast of warm air. I can feel each pound of pressure pushing on my chest as they try to bring me back.

"Again," the voice commands, and the pressure begins again.

There's another burst of warm air, and this time, my entire body responds—as if I've taken a blow from a hammer straight to my heart. The room grows quiet, and the constant beeping returns. I can feel the sensation of my fingers and toes. Then the weightlessness of the rest of my body diminishes, and I'm suddenly aware of my own skin.

My eyes shoot open. I'm staring up at a whitewashed ceiling and a blinding bright light.

"Aubrey," the woman's voice calls out. "Can you hear me?" A blurred face pushes into my line of sight.

"Yes," I croak against a dry and brittle throat.

"Welcome back." The woman above me smiles and turns to look at a monitor to my left.

Welcome back? From where?

Then the memory of the accident comes flooding back in a blast of screeching tires and shattered glass. My stomach turns over and over. Knots of nausea form as I feel my body flying through the air time after time with the flipping movement of my vehicle.

The bile rises in my stomach, burning my throat as I fight against it. "I think I'm going to be sick." I look at the doctor as tears form in the corners of my eyes.

A nurse in pale-blue scrubs instantly appears with a sterile plastic bag. I can't fight my stomach a moment longer. I close my eyes as I struggle to take breaths between gags.

"I'm giving you some medicine to calm your stomach." The nurse's cold hands touch mine as she forces something into the IV connected to my hand.

I count to ten, waiting for another wave of sickness as my stomach tightens and loosens, but when it doesn't come, I slowly open my eyes. The nurses are pulling back the window curtains, and a member of the nursing staff pushes the crash cart back into the hallway.

I reach to my chest, where the electricity from the paddles still lingers. I'm warm and freezing cold all at the same time, and my palms are sweaty. There's a taste of stagnant copper in my mouth and an itch at the back of my throat that I can't scratch. I carefully move my hand, but the tape keeping the IV strapped in place pulls my skin uncomfortably. *I guess I'll lie still, then.*

A moment later, the room floods with people. My parents, who look oddly familiar and unfamiliar all at once, are smiling through tear-stained cheeks as they take their places on either side of my hospital bed. I smile meekly back at them, but suddenly, I feel my eyes growing heavy as sleep swoops in to take over.

Before my eyes shut, I catch a subtle movement from a third person standing quietly at the back of the room. His face is pale with dark, tired circles shading the skin below his eyes—his deep-hazel eyes. I know those eyes. For some reason, they're the most familiar thing in the bland white room around me.

"Lee." My words are mumbled and quiet, confused, but I can see a beautiful smile cross his face as he watches me say his name before my eyelids pull shut.

A FEW HOURS LATER, I finally wake up to a dimly lit and quiet room. There are vases full of colorful flowers filling every inch of table space beside my bed and beneath the television. The walls around my bed are plastered with Get Well cards and old pictures of my closest friends and me.

Wow. They really went overboard with the decorations. I giggle then try to sit up for a closer look. My movement wakes a person I hadn't noticed fast asleep in an uncomfortable-looking hospital chair in the corner across from my bed.

"Hi, Mom." My voice sounds oddly unfamiliar as it breaks through the beeping of my heart monitor.

She visibly fights back tears as she rushes to the side of my bed. "Oh, honey! I thought we'd lost you earlier."

My memories of everything that happened since the accident are almost completely nonexistent. I remember hitting my head through the empty opening of the car window. I remember taking shallow, hard breaths as my entire body felt torn from the inside out—but then there was nothing but darkness. Minutes and seconds blended together into days and weeks full of lost time. I remember nothing since the moment my head found asphalt on the way home from Chilifest.

"What happened?" I ask.

My mother brings her hand up to my face, brushing the hair away from my eyes. "You were in a terrible accident on your way home from Chilifest. We're so lucky someone saw your car flip off the road." She stops, barely able to choke out the words. "Or else it might have been too late..."

"Who found me?"

"One of your classmates. Lee Holland."

"Lee found me?" I can feel myself blushing, the heat racing to my cheeks as the beeping of my heart monitor quickens.

"He was driving behind you when he saw you hit that deer and turn off the road. If he hadn't been there, the paramedics wouldn't have gotten to you in time."

"He was here earlier. I saw him right after I woke up." I quickly scan the room, hoping he's in the same place.

My mother smiles at me, studying my face curiously as I look around the room. "He's hardly left this room for weeks." She motions to the chair in the corner.

I stare at the hideous teal, peach, and yellow cushions, and I can almost picture him sitting there—almost hear him speaking to me as if his voice was the only thing I recognized in the darkness. I remember the words he said right before the doctors rushed into the room. He seemed so familiar with me, almost like he knew I could hear his voice—that I was listening for his voice.

"Where is he now?" The question leaves my mouth with an unexpected urgency, a strange need that I'm not expecting.

"He went home to sleep for a few hours, but I'm sure he'll be back in the morning, sweetheart." She squeezes my hand and grabs one of the twenty plush stuffed animals lining the windowsill.

"Everyone went a little crazy with all of this." I motion to the room around me.

"You have a lot of people that care about you, Aubs." She hands me a stuffed black dog with an obnoxious red bow around its neck. "This one's from Porter."

Ugh, Porter. It feels like a century since I've thought about Porter, but suddenly, the bitterness of our fight centers itself back in my mind—the fight that caused me to leave Chilifest in the first place. *I know I'll have to deal with him eventually, but not right now.* I'm planning on putting that off for as long as possible.

"Uh, not this one."

I hand the black dog back to her and eye the remaining lineup of plush animals. At the end of the row, my eyes come across a stuffed gray horse with a pale white mane and tail and small light-gray dapples. Something about the color of its coat and the soft brown of its eyes holds my attention.

"That one." I point at the horse then wrap it in my arms the moment my mom hands it to me.

A cell phone rings, and she reaches into the depths of her purse and fishes it out. "She just woke up," she says to the person on the other end of the line. I try to listen to what else she says, but I'm already dozing off again, beginning to dream of a strange place I don't quite recognize.

I can feel a person standing next to me, their fingers wrapping around mine as the sound of a rushing river comes from somewhere nearby. I turn my head, and I feel myself melt when I see Lee smiling down at me. I don't move an inch as I study the subtle differences about him—the way his hair curls around his ears, the tan glow radiating off his skin as if he possesses his own sun. I feel content, like I could stand here for hours or even years with his hand in my hand. The place is still, peaceful, familiar.

<h1 style="text-align:center">CHAPTER TWENTY-FIVE</h1>

College Station, Texas
October 2018

After a week of being awake in the hospital, I'm stir-crazy. I've been losing my mind watching Harry Potter movies with Paige and my parents in between meals of terrible hospital food and morphine-induced naps.

Lee has been in and out a few times during the week. He always sits in his corner chair, and he never comes to see me alone. For someone who hardly left my hospital room while I was in a coma, he sure keeps his distance now that I'm awake. The first day he visited, it was strange to see him walk into the room as if he'd been there a thousand times. He smiles at me, asks me how I'm feeling each day, then goes quiet as if he's waiting for me to say something, not even forcing small talk just to escape silence. He seems completely okay with silence, and he wears it well. By the time he leaves for the day, I miss his silence—I miss *him*, too. It's a feeling I can't quite wrap my mind around.

I've caught him watching me on a few different occasions, our eyes always connecting for a few seconds before he tears his away. It's hard to explain what those few seconds do to me, and all I know is that it's like time stops and the world spins slower for a solitary moment, leaving me breathless with a racing heart and shaking hands. Most of the time, the increased beating of the heart monitor forces his eyes away from mine, and I wish I could pull the plastic clip off my finger to give my heart some privacy.

I've waited six days for today to finally arrive. Today, I'm finally escaping the white walls of my hospital jail and heading back to the sweet familiarity of my apartment and college town. My dad arrives with the car at exactly two o'clock in the afternoon, and my mom and Paige wheel me out the automatic doors at the front of the hospital and into the bright March morning. I try to tell the nurses that I'm fully capable of walking out of this hospital on two legs, but the fact that I was stuck lying on my back in a hospital bed for nearly a month has left them skeptical.

The moment I spot the car, my hands begin to sweat, and an intense feeling of dread sweeps over my entire body. I start to hyperventilate, memories of the accident filling my mind. Paige reaches her hand down to my shoulder and squeezes it reassuringly.

"It'll be okay, Aubs," she whispers, pulling me slowly to my feet and walking me to the car door.

I stare at the back seat for a few seconds, and I can feel everyone's eyes watching me as I fight my inner battle.

Paige slides into the back seat and pats the empty seat next to her. "Come on, slowpoke. We have hours of Netflix to catch up on." She smiles as she fastens her seat belt.

I take a deep breath, slide in next to her, buckle up, and exhale.

MY FIRST DAY BACK AT school after being in a coma for almost a month is worse than the first day of freshman year. When I was eighteen and scrambling around a college campus for the first time, upper classmen would throw dirty looks at me that said, *Get out of my way, or you die,* or *Take my seat in this classroom, and I'll let all the air out of your bike tires.* It's not even ten in the morning, and this day is already much, much worse. Instead of glares and middle fingers, I'm getting looks of pity as I walk through my old history building and on to my first class of the day.

It's an understatement to say that my car accident made the local news. It made every newspaper and news channel, and to top it all off, I'm sure it was trending on Twitter for at least an hour. Everyone on campus now knows my face and my name. My ability to remain invisible on a campus with over fifty thousand students ended that night after Chilifest.

Fortunately, Dr. Hubbell's classroom is empty as I make my way to what used to be my usual seat in the back of the room. But not long after I take my Texas history textbook from my bag, another student enters the classroom. At first he walks right past me, but something about my body being in a seat that was previously empty earns me a stare. The guy turns around to gawk at me—really, truly *gawk*—with his mouth open.

"Good to see you're okay," the guy stammers. I have never seen him before, but he seems to know who I am.

You mean, you're glad I'm not dead, I think as he takes his seat a few rows in front of me.

The awkward stares and comments continue for the next few minutes, and I suddenly regret not wearing a jacket with a hood I can pull over my head and hide beneath—although, I'm not sure a hood can even save me from all of this.

"You okay?" Lee asks. Until I heard his voice, I was unaware that he'd taken a chair four seats down from me.

"Not really..." If I could cry, I would. I miss being invisible. I miss the feeling of being able to walk across campus with no one noticing that I'm not okay. But if anyone could know the truth of what I'm feeling right now, I'm okay with it being Lee.

I look over at him, sucking in a deep breath of air as I fight the tears constricting my chest. His eyes seem to peer right into me, as if he sees my fear. Picking up his books, he moves over and takes the empty chair next to me. I find myself instantly leaning against him as if it's the most natural reflex in the world. My head fits perfectly on his shoulder. He moves to put his arm around me, a feeling that almost takes the emotional weight off my shoulders and replaces it with him.

Dr. Hubbell walks into the room, and the class instantly goes silent as they wait for his usual instruction at the beginning of class. His pudgy face turns to look up at where I'm sitting, and he smiles at me. He clears his throat and straightens his maroon tie so it lies flat against his white button-up shirt. "I want to take a moment to welcome back a member of our class whom we've greatly missed over the last few weeks. Welcome back, Ms. Harrison." As soon as he finishes his sentence, the entire class turns around to look at me.

I can feel my cheeks burning as I force myself to smile at the room full of faces.

Am I supposed to make a speech or something? My mind races as I try to think of what to do.

"She's glad to be back with us," Lee says, projecting his voice through the room.

Dr. Hubbell immediately calls the class back to attention. "Turn in your texts to chapter thirteen." He walks over to the dry-erase board at the front of the classroom and writes in all capital letters in bright-red marker:

FEBRUARY 23, 1836.

The familiarity of the date itches annoyingly in the back of my mind as I flip to chapter thirteen. *Maybe it's one of my friends' birthdays.* The thought disappears as quickly as it came, and my heart nearly stops when I read the title at the center of the page.

"The Fall of the Alamo." I hear Dr. Hubbell's voice reading the title, but my mind has taken off in a world of its own.

Flashes of color begin dancing in front of my eyes, and I almost jump out of my chair when the sound of gunshots erupts in all directions around me. I force my eyes open not even realizing they were closed. The classroom is still—not a single person moving—as Dr. Hubbell reads from the text.

"Did you hear something?" I whisper to Lee.

He looks away from his notes, his hazel eyes meeting mine. Until now, I haven't noticed the flecks of bluish gray in his eyes, a color so subtle that it's only visible under the right light. The fluorescent bulbs hanging on the ceiling above us must be bringing out that color.

Lee doesn't say a word—he only looks down at my empty piece of notebook paper and mouths, "Notes."

He must not have heard anything. The truth is, if gunshots had gone off anywhere near the history building, I don't think my classmates would be calmly sitting in their seats.

Just breathe, Aubrey. I try to do exactly that, pushing air in and out of my lungs and hoping that somehow the simple act of breathing will make things clearer. It doesn't work. Thoughts of the Alamo are now circling in slow motion through my mind in pictures that are too vivid and real.

FOUR CLASSES AND NINE hours later, I'm finally headed to the one place where I can shut my door, put on a pair of sweats, and hide away from the rest of the world: within the walls of my own apartment. *Home.*

Ever since I came home from the hospital, Paige has done a good job of giving me my space. She's spent most of her free time with Matt, and I'm glad that she finally seems to have found someone to make her happy.

I shut my bedroom door behind me, and instead of flipping the switch to my ceiling-fan light, I turn on the small bedside lamp. After pulling my favorite Texas A&M hoodie over my head and trading my jeans for a pair of baggy basketball shorts, I slide under the covers and reach for my laptop.

There's plenty of homework for me to catch up on, but for some reason, I can't stop thinking about today's history class. Something about the Alamo struck a chord, and it has annoyingly placed itself at the top of my priority list. I open an Internet browser, type "Battle of the Alamo" into the search bar, and wait for the millions of hits to flood through. Then I scan the text below each link, hoping to come across something I don't already know.

Living in Texas my entire life has given me the basic knowledge of the siege of the Alamo, but what I'm looking for is much different. I want detailed descriptions of that day—a person's actual point of view. *What did they smell, feel, taste in the air as the war swirled around them in an angry fury?*

I keep having these pictures flash through my mind as if I'm watching the scenes play out with the detail of real time. I'm walking—or am I running? I hear gunshots, cannon fire, and stones from the walls being blown to pieces as people scream in the distance. I can almost draw the entire layout of the Alamo without consulting a map. I'm relying on memories that feel like they've been formed from years of studying the same things over and over again—memories that have no way of being my own.

There's a loud knock at my bedroom door. For a second, it gets lost inside the sound of gunfire reeling on repeat in my mind. The knock breaks through again, only this time, it's loud enough to bring me back to reality.

"Hey, Aubs. You alive in there?" Paige's voice rings from the other side of the door.

"Yeah. You can come in," I yell back and close my laptop.

She opens the door, and I can see the troubled look on her face before she even speaks.

"What's wrong?" I blurt, pulling myself out of bed.

"I've tried to tell him that you just need space, but... he's here, and he says he's not leaving until you talk to him." She frowns and motions to the living room.

There's no need for me to even ask her who's waiting outside because there's only one person I've been avoiding like the plague. *Porter.*

"I'll just go on downstairs and check on my laundry." She hurries out the door as if she doesn't want to be within ten miles of the conversation I'm about to have with Porter.

I gather my hair into a sloppy bun on top of my head and check myself over quickly in the mirror. *Let's get this over with.* Knots are forming in my stomach as I walk through my open bedroom door and into the living room.

Porter looks terrible. There are bluish circles under his red eyes, and his hunched shoulders make him look like a train wreck. He stands and wraps his arms around me in a hug that's abnormally tight.

"You've been avoiding me for days, Aubrey, and I couldn't take it anymore—I had to see you," he whispers, his lips grazing the side of my face as he holds me.

Normally, I would have loved to see him this torn up after one of our fights. Porter Collins doesn't often say, "I'm sorry," and when he does, he doesn't sound sincere. Today, I don't even need him to say the words for it to be real—he is truly sorry—but something in the deepest parts of my heart is telling me that this time, it won't be enough. I pull away from him and take a seat on the couch behind me.

Porter quickly sits next to me. "I'm so sorry for what I did at Chilifest—"

I don't let him finish. "I know you are, Porter. I don't blame you for what happened to me." I'm lying, because a part of me does blame him, but that part is going to keep quiet right now.

"I thought you died that night, and when I woke the next morning, I realized that you might not be there by the end of the day. In the last few weeks, I've realized so much about our relationship that I want to make up to you. I haven't been a good boyfriend, and I haven't put you first, but I promise you that I'm going to change that." He reaches for my hand and weaves his fingers around mine.

I pause, thinking hard about my next words and knowing that this conversation is going to end one of two ways: either I forgive him and start back into a life of mediocrity with him by my side, or I stop it now—I can change my path in the hope that there's something better for me out there, knowing full well that Porter might have been as good as it got.

I take a long breath and steady my mind so that I can think straight and speak straight. "Porter, I forgive you, and I believe that starting today, you would do everything possible to make things up to me and put me first. But I don't think that's what I want." My voice is steadier than it sounded in my own mind, and I slowly unwrap my fingers from Porter's.

"What do you mean?" he asks.

"By almost dying, I realized a few things on my own, too. I don't want to live in the shadow of someone who will never be happy with the way that I am now. You shouldn't have to change yourself to make me feel like I'm your priority, just the same way that I shouldn't have to change myself to become your priority. I love you, Porter, but I'm not good for you." I watch as the tears begin forming in his eyes, and I can tell he knows that I'm right.

He only stays for a few short minutes, and the rest of our conversation consists of him making sure I'm okay and asking if I'll be okay a week from now. I answer him honestly—I owe him at least that after being with him for three years. I tell him that today I'm okay, but I don't know about next week or the week after that. The only thing I know how to do is make it through one day at a time without falling apart.

After he leaves, I return to the comfort of my bed and allow the tears to flow, breaking down the barrier I'd locked them behind. I'm afraid to shut my eyes—afraid that sleep will only bring back the nightmares of the accident—but after exhausting all of my strength from crying, I can't fight sleep any longer. Instead of a dark two-lane highway and four screeching tires, I find myself dreaming about a foggy Texas dawn and the calm before the storm of war somewhere inside the old stone walls of the Alamo.

CHAPTER TWENTY-SIX

Paige's navy-blue Honda is waiting in the empty parking lot outside. She shoots me an excited smile below a pair of black sunglasses. "You can definitely pull off that dress better than I can."

I buckle my seat belt across my chest. Paige loaned me one of her longer maroon sundresses for today's game. The car accident did a number on more than just my head—my once-flawless long legs are now scarred in places I'm not ready to let the rest of the world see. The majority of the school knows my face, but the damage I'm hiding underneath my clothes is my own burden.

"Thanks," I reply with a forced smile. "If I make it through this car ride in one piece, I might be able to strut my stuff in this dress."

"It will be okay, Aubs. There aren't any random deer running through campus, especially not on game day." She sends me a sympathetic glance before slowly backing out of the parking spot.

"Maybe not deer, but definitely horrible drivers," I mutter as I try to hide my clenched hands.

College football games at Texas A&M University literally shut the entire campus down for the day. Students live and bleed maroon and white, the women bringing out their best game dresses and heels to stand from kickoff until the final whistle and the men wearing maroon polo shirts and white ball caps. Game days used to be a novelty to me. I'd stand in the blinding Texas sun all day with thousands of other students packed into the stands as we yelled at the referees and cheered at the tops of our lungs as a single voice when the Aggies had the ball. Now the joy of game day is masked by the dull pain still present in my legs and the fear that anytime someone glances in my direction, they will be talking about my accident or my scars. Instead of feeling like another cheering fan in a stadium of one hundred thousand, I feel a spotlight over my head when all I want to be is invisible.

"So, are you ready for Fightin' Texas Aggie football?" she yells over the country music coming from her speakers.

"I think so. It's going to be different this season. I've never gone stag to a game."

"What? You aren't going stag. You'll be with me... and Matt. Besides, he got us first-deck tickets. You should be excited!"

"I am! I just don't want to invade your date time with Matt." I glance at her, but she's too busy merging into traffic to listen. Paige and Matt have been dating seriously for almost a month now, and she's taken on her new role of a *corps girlfriend* with flying colors. Matt and Lee are both in ROTC company K-1.

Even the thought of driving the short distance to campus was almost enough to keep me hiding in the apartment all day. Paige has been amazing, driving me to the places outside of the walking distance from our apartment—never pushing me to drive before I'm ready. I don't know if I'll be ready to sit behind the wheel anytime soon. Or ever.

A job in a place with safe public transportation is becoming a definite must-have on my after-graduation list. My dreams of graduate school have been put on hold. I think some time away from College Station after graduation could give me a breath of fresh Porter-free air.

"We have to stop at the quad for step off. I borrowed someone's parking garage pass to snag us a spot at UCG." Paige smiles at me.

I try to smile back at her, but between my death grip on the door handle and the tight seat belt, I'm finding it hard to take a breath.

"Hey, Aubs... I'm really glad you came out today." She reaches over and squeezes my arm, taking her eyes off the wheel for a split second.

"Car!" I yell at her, and she immediately slams on the brakes to avoid the truck veering into her lane.

"It's not even kickoff, and there are already drunk idiots driving." She lays on her horn and mutters an angry mess of cuss words. Paige watches my body tense as I try to fight back tears. "We're almost to the garage—just hold on. I'll have you out of the car in a second." She quickly turns into the line of cars waiting to get into the parking garage.

I count to thirty silently and try to focus on anything other than the car ride. "It's nearly impossible to get a spot in the garage on game day," I say, trying to distract myself. "Who did you sweet-talk into letting you borrow their parking pass?"

"Oh, Matt just asked one of his freshman cadets to trade me passes for the weekend." She giggles.

"Asked?" I raise my eyebrow at her. Seniors don't *ask* freshmen to do anything. It's more of a *tell and do* arrangement.

I swing open the door before she can even put the car in park. The smell of fresh air instantly calms my nerves. We still have a few minutes to make it to the corps' step off before the road leading to Kyle Field fills with the tan uniforms of squadrons and companies walking in formation to the game. Paige is wearing her favorite white strapless dress with maroon heels and a matching maroon bow. The look is completely wrong for a football game, but she matches the thousands of other girls strutting in heels across campus. Before the accident, Paige would never have let me leave the house in a pair of simple brown sandals, but fortunately, today she doesn't mention them. At least I've managed to fix my hair in loose curls down my back and forced myself to put on makeup.

It's only been a week since I broke things off with Porter, but Paige is already constantly on the lookout for Mr. New Boyfriend on my behalf. I can't blame her for trying to ease my transition into singlehood. I did the same for her when Dillon was no longer in her life.

The quad is already packed full of people watching as the cadets gather in their formations and prepare for step off. Paige takes me by the hand and leads me to where K-1 is standing on one of the long sidewalks leading between the corps' dorms. She quickly finds Matt and lays an obnoxiously big kiss on his face before he takes his place with the rest of his company. I find myself scanning the unfamiliar faces around me, looking for Lee in his tan uniform and polished knee-high senior boots.

"He's standing with the Cav." Paige points to the evenly spaced line of cadets making a wall on either side of the cannon in the center of the quad. I can feel her watching me curiously as my gaze falls on Lee.

He's only a few yards away, making sure no one crosses in front of the cannon's line of fire. I wave at him dumbly, not sure what else I should do. His hands remain behind his back, but a beautiful smile crosses his face, and he mouths a silent hello to me. Against the other cadets' bland tan getup, the cavalry are dressed in their midnights—dark-green uniforms with bright-yellow cords and campaign cover. He looks good in dark green—more than good, actually.

I didn't know he was a member of Parsons Mounted Cavalry, but I guess I've never really asked about his life outside of class. He's been so attentive to me lately, and I haven't even taken the time to get to know him. For some reason, I feel like I already know him—like I've known him for as long as I can remember. Maybe it's the fact that he spent weeks with me at the hospital that makes him so familiar. I make a mental note to ask him about Parsons in class on Monday.

For a single second, the entire quad grows deathly quiet. All cadets are standing still, their eyes facing forward as if they're waiting for something. I bring my gaze back to Lee, and out of the corner of my eye, I see movement behind him just before the air around us is broken in an earthshattering blast of smoke and cannon fire.

I try to shut my eyes as the shock of the sound makes its way through my entire body, but before I can do that, the space around me changes. The smoke from the cannon grows thicker as it covers the ground. I look over at Paige, but she's no longer standing next to me—in fact, no one is next to me at all. People are running in all directions, panicked looks across their faces as some of them scream. I try to move my legs, but I can't feel them—I can't feel anything. My sense of hearing and smell, though, are working overtime. Broken stone walls surround me on all sides, and as I look to the ground, I find nothing but dirt and the scattered bodies of bloodied men. A scream breaks from my chest, and I close my eyes, hoping to wake up and find redbrick dormitories and concrete sidewalks.

I pull my eyes open, and just like that, I'm back to the busy quad with the Aggie band pushing down the sidewalk in front of me as the individual formations of cadets fall in line behind them. My gaze finds Lee, whose hazel eyes are wide as he stares at me. He looks around him to see if anyone's watching, breaks from his place by the cannon, and runs to my side.

"Aubrey, what's wrong?" The words are out before he even makes it to me.

"The cannon—I must have closed my eyes and panicked or something because everything was different."

"What was different?"

I can see Paige trying to get my attention from a few feet away, but I ignore her. I can't tell him that I closed my eyes and suddenly found myself in the middle of a war with the number of dead people by my feet growing by the second. "I don't know. I must have posttraumatic stress or something." I don't realize how bad I'm shaking and shivering until Lee grabs my hands to steady them.

He studies my face for a second, his hazel eyes burning like embers, pulling me out of the darkness. "Even if you think you're going crazy, you can always talk to me—don't ever forget that." He glances behind him as someone calls his name in the distance. "I have to go, but you are okay, Aubrey. You will be okay." He pauses then jogs off into the crowd of beige with the steady sound of boots against the concrete.

Before I can turn around, a hand grabs my shoulder. "What are you doing? We're going to miss the march in," Paige whines, tugging me to the sidewalk.

"The cannon just startled me—sorry." I try to hide the lingering panic in my voice, but she's already focused on catching up to Matt's company near the front of the line.

We make it to the far side of Kyle Field in record time and stand at the entrance closest to the jumbo-sized screen behind the home goal posts. She smiles at Matt just as he walks onto the field. I turn my attention to the screen in front of us, watching the live feed of the march as Matt turns away from our line of sight. Parsons Mounted Cavalry is making its way around the track, its dark-bay horses walking in two synchronized rows.

I find Lee riding at the front of the group a few yards behind the large mule-led wagon escorting the cavalry around the football field. I've seen the wagon at every home football game for the last three years of college, and I never once started crying at the sight of it, but this time, I feel the tears falling down my cheeks. As I reach up to wipe one away, the image of Lee comes across the screen, but this time, his horse is no longer dark bay, and his green uniform has been replaced with a faded and dirty blue button-up.

"What the...?" The words leave my mouth in between gasps of air. I stand on the tips of my toes trying to peer over the crowd of people as the cavalry heads down the farthest side of the field. I find a clear line of view to where Lee is still riding in the same place, but he's back in green, and his gray horse has returned to its dark color.

I'm losing my mind.

I close my eyes and try to calm the restless beating of my heart, but as my eyelids press tightly closed, I begin to see light breaking through them. The sound of hooves beating against the ground drums in my ears, growing louder, drowning out the roar of the stadium around me. As the sounds grow louder, the light behind my eyes evolves into a foggy early morning, the sunlight barely breaking through the thick trees around me—around us. I'm on the back of a horse as it races across the empty dirt below, and my arms are wrapped around the person in front of me. He looks over his shoulder to the right, and the horse responds to his movement and begins turning. Even in the dim light, I can see the person's face clearly, and my cold breath sticks in my chest when I recognize Lee. His hair is longer, and his skin is tanned.

The horse breaks through the trees, and I can feel Lee push the horse faster as we cross into wide-open ground. I can see a building off in the distance, a small stone-walled fortress. *The Alamo.*

As we near the building, a voice breaks through the air. "Look, Aubrey—I can see Matt on the screen," Paige yells.

Paige... why would Paige be here?

The moment the thought crosses my mind, my eyelids shoot back open to the scene of Kyle Field. I watch as the screen shows Matt leading K-1 down the field, but my mind is no longer at this football game as I stand next to Paige. I find myself far away in a place that's so familiar that I can picture almost every detail of it.

"Eighteen thirty-six," I mutter.

"Did you say something?" Paige yells.

"I said it's one thirty-six," I lie, but at least the time on the scoreboard backs me up—there are twenty-four minutes until kickoff.

But somehow, I find myself lost in 1836. My fingers are wrapped around my cell phone. Without thinking, I slide my finger to unlock it, find Lee's name in my contacts list, and open up a new text message.

Text to Lee Holland: *Would you be able to drive me somewhere?*

I press Send and relock my home screen. With the game about to start, I don't expect to get a text back from him for a few hours, but I at least wanted to send it before I forgot. I should ask Paige to drive me, but for some reason, I don't. I'm not sure what I'm looking for or what I'll find when I get there, and for some reason, I want Lee with me. Maybe it's because he doesn't ever force me to talk about things—my feelings especially. If he sat by my hospital bed while I was in a coma, I feel sure that he can endure a few hours of silence in a car with me.

Who are you kidding, Aubrey? He'll probably say no anyways.

With the corps march in coming to an end, Paige and I enter the stadium and start in the direction of our section on first deck. Typically, only the dates of the cadets can sit in the corps section, so I'm guessing Paige acquired my ticket the same way she acquired her parking pass. The section is quickly starting to fill up with cadets, and I hear Matt call our names from somewhere inside the mass of people wearing identical uniforms. I follow closely behind Paige as she weaves us to our seats.

"Hey, Aubs." Matt gives me a quick hug before turning all his attention to his date.

"Hi—" I start to say back but stop as soon as I realize he's not paying attention. *And the afternoon as a third wheel officially starts now.*

Luckily, there's an empty seat next to me, and the little bit of extra space makes trying to breathe while surrounded by sweaty cadets a little less terrible. I don't know how they can endure the Texas heat in stiff polyester uniforms. I would most certainly not be able to stand for three hours like that.

Aggie fans have their hands in the air, waving their white 12th Man towels as they wait for kickoff. I completely forgot my silly little white towel today, but now that I think of it, I've never brought my

12th Man towel to one of the games. I don't actually know if I have a 12th Man towel. Even though all students remain standing during football games, I feel someone pushing through our tightly packed row toward me. I hold my breath, hoping they don't stop at the empty space next to me.

"Is this spot taken?" I hear Lee ask.

I look up at him. His usual perfect smile is framed by dimples.

"Not unless the person who pulled this seat decides to show up." I smile back and step closer to Paige so that I'm not taking up both spots.

"Well, it's a good thing that I happen to have this, then." He pulls a ticket from his pocket and waves it at me.

"I thought the Cav doesn't usually sit in the corps' section," I try to yell over the crowd just as kickoff begins.

"Well, I heard you needed a ticket to the game, and it just so happened that I needed a date," he yells back at me.

Paige looks over at Lee, waves, and not so subtly nudges me closer to him.

So that's how Paige managed to get my ticket.

"I'm sorry that Paige talked you into pulling me a ticket. I'm not the most fun person these days." I frown, feeling bad. He could have invited someone he actually wanted to spend the rest of the game with.

"Paige didn't convince me to do anything—it was my idea." He winks at me and turns his attention to the field.

His idea? If he pulled my ticket, that means I'm his date... and there are certain Aggie traditions for those who go to football games as dates. I start to panic, but not from a looming sense of dread. I'm panicking because I'm Lee Holland's date—a guy I never would have expected myself to be feeling anxious butterflies over as he stands next to me.

Paige leans over and whispers, "I knew you wouldn't come to the game if you found out it was a date. Promise you won't hate me forever?"

I turn to look at her and run straight into her best doe-eyed pouty face. She bats her long eyelashes at me.

"I'm not mad." I smirk.

I'm actually not mad at all. I move closer to Lee, trying to see over the taller cadet in front of me.

"So where are we going?" he asks.

For a few minutes, I'd forgotten about the text message. Now I'm surprised he's already seen it.

"San Antonio, if you're okay with driving that far." I look over at him, almost afraid to see his expression. He's studying me with a strange look on his face, almost like he's relieved.

"Interesting choice," he replies, keeping his eyes intently locked on mine. "We'll go tomorrow."

Tomorrow? That's less than twelve hours away. He wants to drive me to San Antonio tomorrow?

I try to say something back to him, but he's already turned his attention to the field as the Aggies snag an interception. The entire stadium erupts in cheers.

CHAPTER TWENTY-SEVEN

Lee was waiting outside my apartment with his old blue Bronco just after six in the morning. It's a three-hour drive from College Station to downtown San Antonio, a drive I've made too many times to count, but today feels different. I'm not even sure why we're going there or what I'm even looking for. The only thing I'm positive about is that the knots in my stomach aren't going to quit pulling tighter until I act on this gut feeling that's been consuming my mind for a few days—I need to go to the Alamo.

Lee has the windows cracked and the music turned up as it flows through a busted speaker. I focus on the songs just to keep myself from tapping my foot anxiously against the floorboard. He doesn't look over at me or try to force mindless conversation to pass the time. He just drives silently and leaves me to my thoughts.

Spending the football game with him yesterday was the most fun I'd had in months. There was no pressure for me to be or act a certain way—I was able to be myself, and by the end of the day, I felt like I was escaping from under the gray cloud of the accident that's been with me since the day I woke up in the hospital.

While Matt and Paige shared a kiss each time the Aggies scored, Lee and I kept our eyes glued to the field. I could feel electricity in the air between us, and as the last few minutes ticked down on the scoreboard, I secretly wished for one last touchdown or field goal—one last chance for him to steal a kiss from my lips. I found myself longing for his lips on mine. The way he was taking things so slowly was unfamiliar. It was like he was holding this handful of cards until he found the perfect moment to play them.

When he dropped me off at the end of the night, I almost asked him to come inside—to stay with me for a little while longer. But in the back of my mind, I knew that he would turn me down. As I shut the door to my apartment, I realized that Lee was nothing like Porter, and it was the one thing about him that I felt drawn to the most. Sleep didn't come easily. I found my mind spinning between Lee and my strange visions of him. All of my thoughts have been on him—my entire mind has been on him, and I've just been trying to connect the pieces of this puzzle, hoping that when I do, it will all make sense.

By the time Lee pulls his Bronco down the Commerce Street exit toward the Alamo, the streets are already busy with tourists.

"Keep your eye out for a parking garage." He flips his blinker on and moves into the right-hand lane.

"There." I point to a four-story garage a block away.

It's still early enough in the day that the garage isn't completely full, and Lee easily finds a spot on the second floor. He puts his car in park and looks over at me. "Now what?"

That's the big question, isn't it? I really have no idea what to do now that we're here, but I decide that the only place we have to start is Alamo Plaza.

"I'll lead the way." I pop open the car door and stretch my legs to the cement ground. Three hours isn't a long drive, but for some reason, there's an ache lingering deep in my bones.

I take a deep breath, steal a quick glance at Lee, and head in the direction of the stairs leading to the ground floor. He walks quietly beside me as we weave around people on the sidewalk. I grew up in the small town of Bulverde, just outside city limits, so San Antonio is the first big city I learned how to navigate. My feet seem to know the streets by heart as they lead me toward Alamo Plaza without asking my mind for directions.

The towering branches of the ancient oak trees at the center of the plaza have already begun to lose their leaves as the chill of fall grows colder every night. I stop the moment my eyes find the bell-shaped curves running along the top of the Alamo's historical stone front. This view is not new to me—I've seen the building more times than I can remember—but I've never felt it move me like this before. High-rise buildings, cars, and tourists have modernized its soil, yet it sits almost untouched. It's a relic so monumental that an entire city grew into the space around it and left the Alamo at its very center like a beating heart—like the life force of this place.

Once again, my feet move, unable to resist the pull my heart feels from this building. We take our place in the small line of people waiting to go inside, and my eyes begin tracing every single stone, every crack of the building. The ends of my fingers tingle, and the hairs on my arms stand on end. I long to touch the stones—to feel the rough texture of the walls.

"Aubrey, are we going inside or staying outside?" Lee asks, pulling me out of the strange trance I found myself in.

We're somehow standing at the front of the line, the large wooden doors leading into the Alamo towering a few feet above our heads. My hands begin to tremble, and my heart jolts beneath my skin.

I reach for the door and pull it open. Lee waits for me to step inside the large open corridor, then he quietly follows right behind me. The air feels cold, and the sudden heaviness of my body makes it hard for my legs to move forward. A large metal chandelier hangs over our heads as we stand at the center of what used to be the Alamo chapel. This room was the heart of the mission, with barracks, stone walls, and empty convent yards around it. People are peering into the glass cases filled with old relics on either side of the room, but displayed against the back wall of the chapel are the Alamo's original wood doors. Everyone else in the room almost disappears into the background as I walk to the doors. My shoes hit the stone floor, and each step I take echoes in the air around me.

I stop just in front of the velvet-covered ropes in front of the doors and stare up at them. The thick dark wood is damaged with nicks from bullets, and the edges are weathered and rough. I bring my eyes to the displays in front of me with names of the fallen Alamo defenders embossed onto metal plates and scan the names, looking for something familiar. I move from one display to the next and then to another before I come across the words that nearly stop my heart.

Written in bronze is a name, a name that's so familiar, yet it's not quite right:

Tapley Holland.

I can feel Lee watching me, but I can't bring my eyes to meet his.

It's just a coincidence, Aubrey, I tell myself over and over again, but the name begins to haunt me.

I turn away from the doors, trying to catch my breath. There's an exit leading to the convent yards to my left, and I nearly run out the door, hoping to find some fresh air. I came here looking for answers, but suddenly, I find myself terrified of what I might find inside these walls.

Lee has yet to say a word, but he continues to walk next to me on the sidewalk running from the chapel to the old barracks. There's a large oak tree sitting at the center of the yard, and in front of it sits an old iron cannon on display. I brush my fingers across its surface, the sensation of cold metal almost turning to scalding heat at my touch. Lee continues down the sidewalk as I pause at the ancient tree's curved branches, which skim the ground by my feet. He ducks underneath a narrow doorway into the barracks and disappears. The moment he's no longer by my side, my heartbeat quickens, and like a magnet to metal, I find myself moving in his direction. I jog down the sidewalk and cross under the threshold and into a long hall lined with more glass display cases.

There's a tour guide with a group in front of us, but I find Lee standing in front of a small case in the corner. His stare is focused downward on the contents of the display, his expression lost. I follow his gaze to a faded piece of parchment sitting between an old leather book and the rusted long blade of a hunting knife with a cracked wooden handle. As my eyes begin reading the stained paper, I recite the words by heart—words I have never seen before until this very second.

March 5, 1836

My Dearest Tapley,

Tomorrow is the thirteenth day since the siege began. I know this might sound strange, but I know what tomorrow brings, and it's nothing but heartbreak and pain. Before I close my eyes tonight, I want you to know how much I love you, how much these last few weeks have meant to me. You have changed my entire world, and for the first time, I've learned to live and to love without fear. I'm not afraid of tomorrow, and I don't want you to feel fear, either. Whatever happens, know that I don't have a single regret. There is only one thing I would change if I were given the chance to live this life all over again. I would choose to love you sooner. If I had an eternity, I would choose you every day for the rest of forever. But if a day ever comes that you needed to remind me of my choice, promise me that you won't stop reminding me—you won't stop waiting for me. Stay with me always.

Aubrey R. Harrison

I choke on my own name as I read it out loud—a name that's written in my handwriting. I close my eyes and let the tears fall, knowing that I've found what I was searching for.

"I need you to see what's in this envelope. When you are ready, meet me outside," Lee says.

I turn to look over at him, but he's no longer standing next to me. Lying against the top of the glass case is an envelope with my name written across the front. I reach for it with shaking hands and pull out a folded piece of paper. My heart stops when I find the image of myself staring back at me in subtle strokes of charcoal—the details of my face, my hair, and my clothes expressed perfectly. There's a date written in the bottom right-hand corner of the paper: *February 21, 1836.*

"Tapley," I whisper, and as soon as the word leaves my lips, I find myself so overwhelmed with emotions that I can hardly stand. Memories engulf me—*my* memories. The envelope falls from my hands, and as it hits the ground, I can see something hiding inside that I missed. I reach for it off the ground and find a photo of a couple in their late fifties standing in front of the Alamo, surrounded by a very different San Antonio. The city is futuristic and sleek, rising high into the air around an unchanged historic landmark—the three-hundred-year-old heartbeat still rooted firmly on the same Texas soil.

"This isn't possible," I mutter as I stare at the faces.

I turn to the open door behind me that leads back into the convent yard, and I find Tapley sitting quietly on a stone bench in a secluded corner. He's watching me, waiting for me to move. I force myself to walk toward him. My body feels weightless though the sound of my feet keeps me grounded.

"Where did you get this?" I pull the picture to my chest.

"You should sit down, Aubrey." He glances at the empty space next to him.

I practically collapse onto the bench, my head spinning so far out of control that I can't keep myself standing. "I remember—*everything*," I whisper and meet my stare with his. As I look into his eyes, I see everything differently. From the day I woke up in the hospital, his face has been the most familiar thing to me, but now that I actually see him, I see the 1836 Tapley, the one I'm in love with.

"I have to get back there! I have to stop you from dying." I move my hand to my mouth as my panicked breathing finally peaks.

"You can't go back. We can't." He moves my hand from my face and takes it into his.

"But you'll die, Tapley. If I don't go back, you will die."

"Aubrey, we both died." His expression falters, and his eyes grow misty.

"Then, how did you get this picture? This is us, but not here... not now," I say, placing the picture into his hands—a picture of us alive, together.

He doesn't answer my question; instead, he asks me a different one. "Do you remember how you got back here—how you left in 1836?"

"I heard your voice calling my name, and when I opened my eyes, I was in the hospital."

"When I died, I opened my eyes to this life," he says, pointing to the picture. He turns it over and hands it back to me.

I read the date written on the back: *March 15, 2138.*

"I opened my eyes to our life in the future." His words hang in the air, sending an icy chill up my spine.

"But why did I wake back up in 2018? Why didn't I wake up in the same place as you?"

"Because you were still alive in 2018. You returned to your first lifetime. *This* lifetime." He watches as the wheels begin turning in my mind—the gears clicking together as the time line falls into place.

I can't speak. There's not a single word I can say as I try to wrap my mind around everything.

"When we met in 1836, it was my first lifetime, but it was your second. After your accident, you woke up in 1836 while your body stayed alive in 2018. But when you died here, at the Alamo, the link was broken. You woke back up to your original life like nothing ever happened. When I died on March 6, 1836, I woke up in a new life completely, but I woke up to a life with you. *Our* life in the future."

He tries to smile at me, but there's still a hint of sadness in his eyes. I can feel my question fighting its way out, but somewhere deep inside me, I think I already know the answer.

"If your second life was in 2138, how are you here right now?"

He pauses for a few moments as if trying to choose his words carefully. "The only way you can wake up in a different lifetime is if you die during your last one," he says, and I can feel my heart shatter.

"So I have to lose you all over again in the future?" That annoying timer is back again, and I can feel it slowly ticking away at the seconds.

"How long have you been here, waiting for me to remember all of this?" I wipe a tear from my cheek.

"The day you introduced yourself to me in Dr. Hubbell's class marked my third year in this time period."

My eyes grow wide at the reality of his words. For three years, he had been in a reality where I had yet to choose him. He has watched me each day, waiting for the moment when I finally fall in love with him—the moment I choose the road that leads to Tapley.

"You've just been waiting for me to remember?" I struggle to get the words out.

Tapley rises to his feet and kneels on the ground in front of me. He takes my hands in his, and his hazel stare meets mine with such an extraordinary power that I feel it coursing through every vein in my body. I remember everything about him... every touch of his hand and brush of his lips, the night we first danced in the livery stable, and the night he made love to me for the first time.

"Aubrey, I knew we would be together, but that's something I wanted you to realize on your own. You asked me to wait for you in that letter—to stay with you until you remembered your choice. I died with that letter in my pocket—the pages are stained with my blood. The second I opened my eyes, I found you lying next to me three hundred years in the future. I don't know if this is heaven or if we're somehow cursed to a hell where death repeats itself over and over again. All I know is that I'm to keep finding you, no matter what it costs me." He takes a deep breath, a smile breaking across his face—the familiar Tapley smile that melts my heart.

"I'm here to make you another promise. I will wait for you to choose me until the day I die, and if I open my eyes to another life, I will still be waiting for you. I love you, and there's not a single force or power in this universe that will keep me from loving you today, tomorrow, or yesterday." He stands up and pulls me into his arms underneath the same ancient oak that witnessed the tragic end of one love story only to see the beginning of another.

"I love you, Tapley Holland." And just like that, the timer above my head stops as we stand on the ground where everything first began, ended, and finally begins again. He presses his lips to mine for the first time in what feels like forever—in our strange and twisted reality, it's been a few short days separated by centuries.

The Alamo is cursed ground below our feet, yet right now, it's hallowed as love blooms on soil once fed by the blood of our own sacrifices. Even if our history is doomed to repeat itself for eternity, we will stand and fight against it until the day finally comes where our pasts no longer mark our futures.

Acknowledgements

I could not have written this story without the support and encouragement of my family.

Patrick, thank you for inspiring the feelings behind every page, and the countless versions you've read, even while deployed.

Tapley James, even though you came into our world after this story was finished, you are still very much a part of everything this book represents.

A very big thank you to my agent, Jessica, who has been a champion for this story from the very beginning.

I could not have written this story without my experiences as a student at Texas A&M University. Thank you to the students, traditions, and history of such an incredible school. You changed my life in the best of ways.

About the Author

Rebecca Elise graduated from Texas A&M University with a BA in Science. She also has a MA in Children's Literature and is working on an additional MA in Early Childhood Education. When she's not writing romance, Rebecca is working on developing non-fiction projects and curriculum for early childhood programs.

Rebecca is also a Literary Agent with Golden Wheat Literary. Outside of the publishing industry, you can find Rebecca at the barn with her horses, chasing around her very busy toddler, and dodging whatever curveball the Army throws at her family. Rebecca currently lives in Oklahoma with her military husband, rowdy son, and their zoo of animals.

Read more at https://www.rebeccaangusbooks.com/.

About the Publisher

Dear Reader,

We hope you enjoyed this book. Please consider leaving a review on your favorite book site.

Visit https://RedAdeptPublishing.com to see our entire catalogue.

Don't forget to subscribe to our monthly newsletter to be notified of future releases and special sales.